"You'll not forget this first-person narrator. . . .
The architecture of the storytelling is faultless." —JOHN IRVING

THE WILD

INSIDE

a novel

JAMEY BRADBURY

HARPER LUXE

For my parents, Kit and Jim Bradbury

1

I have always had a knack for knowing the minds of dogs. Dad says it's on account of the way I come into the world, born in the open doorway of our kennel, with twenty-two pairs of canine eyes watching and the barks and howls of our dogs the first thing I ever heard.

Back then, there wasn't no clinic in the village, so the community health aide come out to our place once a month. When Mom was partway through carrying me, the aide told her to stay in bed and not tire herself out. Mom minded that advice right up till the night I was born. First of March, so cold the ends of her hair froze. She went outside and crossed the dog yard, got as far as the kennel's doorway when a pain come over her. She crouched down, holding her belly, and hollered for my dad. I slid right out. I was in this world before she knew it, with barely any help from her. She said it was the only thing easy about me.

Why was you in the kennel? I asked her one time.

She shrugged. Said, I suppose I missed the dogs.

I come out big and heavy and always hungry. Mom told me there's some women have trouble getting their babies to take the breast, and I have seen it in some pups, how they will ignore what instinct tells them and refuse to nurse, and then you have to strip the milk from the mother and feed the pup by hand. But not me. I clamped down first thing and didn't want to let go. Mom had never seen a baby like me, she said I was *voracious*. She fed me till she thought she'd run dry, and then she kept on feeding me.

There's pictures in the family photo book, all four of us working together in the yard or gathered round a dog sled before the start of a race. Scott and me both with Mom's dark hair, Dad's brown eyes. I learned in school that blood has a memory. It carries information that makes you who you are. That's how my brother and me ended up with so much in common, we both carried inside us the things our parents' blood remembered. Sharing what's in the blood, that's as close as you can be to another person.

That's probably why I run into so much trouble when

me and Scott started school. I didn't share nothing with the other kids. Before, we done school at home. Mom was our teacher, she give us problems to solve, numbers going down the page in a column and meant to be plussed or minused. When I was little, if I done my work right, I got a star. Ten stars meant I could go outside. I'd get my stars done fast so I could spend most of the day out in the dog yard or running through the woods, or wrestling and chasing Scott, usually just playing but sometimes roughhousing, and Mom would holler at us to stop.

Our place was the best place. It was my granddad who built it, before my dad was born. He found a patch of Alaska he liked, then cleared a ten-acre circle in the trees and in one half built our house and in the other half built the kennel, a long building with a workshop at one end and plenty of room for gear and sleds. In between the house and the kennel, we had forty doghouses. Then trees all around and a trailhead at the back of the yard, the trail cut through the woods three miles to Ptarmigan Lake, then another thirty miles or so before you crossed the river, then beyond that, just more trees, then mountains, then tundra.

I spent as much time as I could in the woods. To look at me, you might of thought, But you are only seventeen, and a girl, you have got no business being off in the wild by yourself where a bear could maul you or a moose trample you. But the fact is, if they put me and anyone else in the wilderness and left us there, you just see which one of us come out a week later, unharmed and even thriving. I rode the back of a sled practically ever since I could stand, and by the time I was ten I could take small teams down the trail on overnight runs, sometimes even for a few days, off on my own with only my dogs for company. I run the Junior Iditarod soon as I was able, and when I was sixteen I competed in my first professional races. I had already logged enough mileage to qualify for the Iditarod, soon as I was eighteen I could enter. I even managed to win back my entry fee when I finished the Gin Gin 200 women's race in the top five. To be honest, I didn't care much about the money. I only wanted to be on my sled, outside, as much as I could.

Which is how come I didn't care for the way Dad pitched his keys at me come Friday afternoon and said, Pick up your brother from school, would you, Trace?

I snatched the keys out of the air with one hand and tossed them right back. They landed in the grass next to the snowblower he was tinkering with.

Can't you do it?

Sure, Dad said. And you can stay here and fix this machine for Eleanor Andrews. Get it done fast, though, since she's supposed to send her nephew to pick it up in an hour.

Would if I could, I muttered, clawing through the grass to find the keys.

Here, he said and fished a piece of paper from his pocket. Put this up at the village store while you're in town.

It was an ad, meant for the corkboard posted by the front door at the only store in town. Folks pinned their signs on the board, some of them said FOR SALE—ATV TIRES or FREE FIREWOOD, YOU CUT.

Dad's sign was made out in his slanty handwriting, all the letters leaned backwards like they was standing against a strong wind. *Room for Rent. Small Room back of House, private, Clean. Woodstove. No Water or electric. You are Welcome to use kitchen and bath in House. Located Mile 112. No Vagrants.* Then Dad's name and our phone number wrote along the bottom.

What room? I asked. Our house was good-sized, me and Scott each had our own bedrooms. I wasn't about to move in with him so some stranger could pay to sleep where I belonged.

The shed wasn't always a shed, Dad told me. When your granddad built it, he meant it to be a proper cabin.

Besides the house and the kennel and the forty doghouses that took up the space between, we had two

other buildings on our property. One was the woodshed, which was more like a roof with three walls, we
stacked all our firewood inside. The other was a real
shed, it had a good roof and a woodstove, and even a little window cut into one wall. It had become a catch-all
sort of place, we put anything we didn't need regular
there, the mower with the broken blade, sawhorses,
fishing poles, greasy parts for the other truck that was
up on blocks.

It'll clean out real nice, Dad was saying.

And some stranger's supposed to live there? I said.

We need the money.

But if I'm going to be around to help out— I started
and he cut me off.

Because you've been such a help since you got
kicked out?

That wasn't fair. I had done what I could to make up
for the trouble I had caused at school. All week while
Dad had drove Scott into town and left me behind, I
made sure to clear the table of breakfast dishes before
I sat down to do my schoolwork, because it turns out
that when you get suspended, they still expect you to
do your lessons. And maybe I didn't finish half the
work that got sent home to me, but that was because
I needed to hunt. Where else was Dad supposed to get
pelts to sell or trade? A nice marten fur, stretched and

tanned, could bring in fifty dollars or more, and that wasn't nothing.

Playing in the woods doesn't count as helping, Dad said like he could read my mind. Now could you please do as I ask without giving me twenty reasons why you shouldn't have to?

I slid behind the wheel of the truck and waited for the engine to decide to turn over. The dogs barked after me as I inched down the driveway, mad that they wasn't going for a ride. I looked one way up the highway, then the other, then back again, two or three times before I pulled onto the road. It wasn't that I wanted to make trouble for Dad, and I wanted to help, really help. But not like this. I didn't care to drive, even before what happened. And I never liked going into town, especially when it meant going to school. If Dad wanted my help, I didn't see why I couldn't stay on our property and do real work, like making sure the dogs was trained proper, shoveling the dog yard, leading our younger dogs on walks so I could take note which ones minded good and which ones seemed like potential lead dogs.

But the day I got kicked out of school for fighting, Dad had told me, *No dogs.* I wasn't to run them or play with them or even feed them, which really just meant more work for him. He was awful mad about what I done to that girl in my class, and it was the worst punishment I reckon he could come up with, other than telling me I couldn't hunt.

I worked to become a good musher, but I have always been natural at hunting. I liked to do it and I liked to read about it, we had plenty of books round the house on the subject. My favorites was: *A Knife and Your Wits: Minimalist Survival* by Joe Wilcox, and *What's Good to Eat: Edible Wild Plants* by Nancy and Bill Philomen, and *Traps and Trapping* by Alec Cook, and best of all, *How I Am Undone* by Peter Kleinhaus, which is not a guidebook but a regular book, but I still learned a lot about survival from it. Peter Kleinhaus is this guy who come to Alaska from the lower forty-eight and tried to live outdoors for one whole winter, and the only shelter he had was whatever he built himself, and the only food he ate was whatever he killed or scavenged. He lost an earlobe and two toes to frostbite but other than that he come out okay in the end.

I have always liked the Kleinhaus book best because there's parts where he stops teaching you things and just writes what he was thinking, and I tell you what. There are books out there that when you read them, you wonder how some stranger could know exactly what's in your own mind. There's a part where Kleinhaus has been outdoors for about three months, and it has been snowing a blizzard for almost four days straight. He is stuck on a ledge on the side of a mountain, no fuel for his fire. So he wakes up in the middle of the fourth night and finds the snow has finally stopped. The sky is clear, with all the stars like metal filings shook out across a black cloth, and the cloth is so wide it never ends but goes on and on so you feel you could be swallowed up by the sky, and you almost want to be swallowed up, just to be part of something so big. And even though he is cold and has no fire, he just sits and stares up into the sky. He writes, *Under this vastness I forget myself. My humanity slips away and I am no longer recognizably me, but one more animal under an ancient, heedless sky.* First time I read that, I had to shut the book and go outside. It made my head spin.

Driving made my head spin, too, but not in the same way. Trees whisked past and the sky unrolled overhead, gray with the promise of snow that hadn't yet been delivered. I was cruising well under the speed limit, but the truck's studded tires whined something awful on the pavement, and I eased up on the gas as I come round a curve in the road and tried not to look at the shoulder.

My mom died the month before I turned sixteen. It was a car accident. She wasn't driving but walking alongside the road. All the places we got to walk on our property, but she decides to take a walk on the shoulder of the highway.

The road that goes past our place is mostly a straight shot with good visibility. But there's one spot where the road curves sharp and runs downhill, and if you are coming round too fast you might not see whatever's on the shoulder till it's too late. The guy driving the truck said he only looked away for a second. I didn't even see her, is what he told the village safety officer, he only heard his car hit what he first thought was a big dog or maybe a moose calf.

The impact threw my mom into a tree. I suppose that is what killed her. If you trap a squirrel and it ain't dead when you find it and you are not yet strong enough to snap its neck with your hands, you can knock it hard against a tree and do the job that way. What I wonder is what went through her head as she sailed into the air. Was it like how you hear, how time stretches out and you have what seems like hours to think about your life or watch how the snowflakes fall around you like stars drifting down and settling on the ground and the night gets brighter when everything is clean and white? If she thought of anything, I hope it was that.

What I also wonder is what she was doing out, middle of the night, walking along the road. It is not a pleasant place to walk. When a car whizzes by, it spits up rocks and snow and dirt, pummels you with the wind that kicks up in its wake. I can't see the draw of a place like that. But there she was, on the road, alone in the dark, till a pair of headlights lit her up.

Scott wasn't there when I pulled up to the school, I waited and watched the other kids stream into the schoolyard, the ones who lived farther away loaded onto the bus, which is how me and Scott used to get to school till I got us kicked off the bus, too. According to the principal, I had been trouble since day one.

Finally I got out of the truck and brushed past the groups of older kids who was horsing around, talking and laughing before they got on their four-wheelers to head home. And there was Beth Worley, a splint on her nose and a bandage covering the stitches she'd got earlier that week. I was surprised she was already back in school, the way she cried when they carried her off to the clinic, you'd of thought she was dying. She glared at me, and her friends fell quiet as I walked by, then started their whispering when they thought I was far enough away. But I have always had better hearing than most.

I found Scott kneeling outside his classroom, his books scattered all round. Wasn't till I got close enough to help him scoop them into his backpack that I seen he had a nice bruise blossoming at the corner of his mouth.

Who done that? I asked.

He shook his head. Doesn't matter. Let's go.

You know I'm the one who's supposed to get in fights, don't you? I told him as we left the building.

You're a trial, Tracy Sue Petrikoff, he said and sounded exactly like Dad had sounded back in September when he got a call from the school saying I'd kneed some kid in the groin after he threw a ball straight at my head in gym class.

I reached out and socked Scott in the shoulder, not hard enough to hurt, just playing.

Shut your hole, I said.

He pushed me back.

Shut yours.

Watch out, Scotty! some kid called from across the schoolyard. She'll bite your face off!

Then laughter from a group of kids that wasn't even in my grade. Word spreads fast when you got too many people in one place, all of them running their mouths.

Go to hell, Scott hollered back.

Hey, I said. Ain't that kid your friend?

Scott shrugged. Yeah, but he's also kind of a jerk. And you're my sister.

I ruffled his hair, the way I knew he hated. He smacked my hand.

We swung by the village store like Dad asked and I made Scott run in and put up the sign. Then I steered us back toward home, me growing more at ease the farther we got from the gas station and the roadhouse where folks was lined up at the counter, practically shoulder to shoulder, like them little fish in a can. The inside of the truck smelled like grease and wet fur, it made me think of all the times all four of us would cram into the cab and ride into the village to stock up on supplies, and sometimes, before we headed back, we would eat at the roadhouse. That's when men would come over to our table to shake Dad's hand or buy him a drink. The entire state knew the name of Bill Petrikoff Junior. Seemed like a whole other life back then, like something I must of read in a book. After Mom died, things changed fast.

It was like this game me and Scott used to play, Before and After. Mom would give us two pictures that at first looked alike, but if you studied them closer you'd see there was tiny differences. A man wearing a cowboy hat in one picture, but in the other he would have a baseball cap on his head. A red shoe would be blue. A bird flying in the sky would be vanished altogether. You was supposed to catch the differences.

For us, everything was dogs in the Before picture. A yard full of them, and Dad repairing a sled, and Mom standing over the fire, cooking a pot of green fish and beef tallow to pour over kibble. Making bags for food drops, sewing booties for the dogs' feet. Enough money to pay for extra hands to help us prepare for each race, right up till the big one. When the Iditarod come round and Dad's team was in the chute, Mom would handle one of the big wheel dogs, that is a dog who is harnessed directly in front of the sled. The horn would sound, and all the handlers let go of the dogs, and Mom would turn and give Dad a quick kiss before he slid past her. Then she'd hurry over to me and Scott on the sidelines, and Dad would look back and wave to us, wave till he crested the first small hill then disappeared.

After the race, we would meet Dad at the small landing strip where the plane he chartered brung him and our dogs back to us from Nome. We'd load up the truck and head home, Mom on one end of the bench seat and Dad on the other, and me and Scott in the middle, like a sandwich where our parents was the bread. Cold outside but always warm in the truck. Flakes of snow lit up by the beam of the headlights.

That was Before. After was Dad standing with his hands on his hips when I parked the truck in our driveway, looking like a little kid's drawing of himself, just a collection of skinny lines. All the padding gone from his bones, and his eyes big and dark, like they was sinking into his head. He frowned while he waited for us to get out of the truck.

Hey, son, he said and give Scott a smile that didn't reach his eyes. Go on in and get after your homework, you hear?

Yes, sir.

You, Dad said and I stopped short, my stomach dropping at the tone of his voice. You are grounded. And I don't just mean no dogs. I mean no leaving the yard, no hunting, no running the dogs. Not for a good long while.

My stomach dropped.

What?

The school called while you were gone. You got yourself expelled. I told you—

No.

Excuse me?

No, I said. This is bullshit. I'm the one who's been training, up till you told me I had to stop. I'm the one who cares for the dogs most of the time. This is the last year I'm eligible for the Junior. The *first* year I'm eligible for the Iditarod!

He shook his head. You're not going to be racing this

year, Trace. Even if you was still in school, we can't afford the entry fees.

The sun throwing shadows of the trees across our yard, long columns of dark soaking into the brown grass. Our dogs had started wondering what we was up to. They sat on their haunches and cocked their heads at us. A couple nosed their bowls. I imagined Dad out there, his hands gentle on each one, checking their paws or massaging their legs after a long run. I couldn't remember the last time he'd got on a sled.

The thought made me grit my teeth and clench my fists, made me want to hit something. I felt the way I'd felt the day I broke Beth's nose, rage building inside me like a fire rolling through a forest, consuming every tree and blade of grass.

The madder I got, the quieter Dad seemed. He give a sigh like he was deflating.

Your mom was better at this, he said.

Better at what?

This, he said. Doing what's good for you. Knowing what you need. It was easier when you were little. You just wanted to be outside all the time, following me around.

I wanted to tell him it wasn't true. Mom was good at lots of stuff, and there was a time we would spend hours together, just talking. But there was plenty of things she didn't tell me. Sometimes she would be on the edge of something, like standing on the bank of a creek, deciding whether or not to cross. Instead of putting her foot in the water, she would turn round, walk away from whatever it was she wanted to say to me.

But I didn't say anything. It was rare for Dad to bring Mom up, rarer still for us to talk about how she used to be, or what she would of done. I half-expected her to wander outside right then, poke her head out the front door and ask, You two telling secrets out here? I caught myself actually waiting for her. It feels dumb to say how disappointed I was when I didn't see her. Like just talking about her could conjure her up.

That's still what I want, I told Dad. Just to be outside. To race.

You're not the only one doing something you don't want to.

He was so quiet, it seemed mean to shout at him. But I couldn't help myself.

You could do what you want! Instead of wasting time fixing other people's shit, building stupid tables and shelves to sell—

How do you think I pay for food, Tracy? How do you think I keep the lights on?

You're a musher! My voice hit him almost like a fist. It hurt me to see him hurt, but I couldn't stop. Part of me didn't even care. You're supposed to be a musher! *That's* your job! I'm the only one who raced at all last year—

His face dropped. I did stop then.

He cleared his throat. When he spoke, his voice was calm.

I've said my piece, Tracy. I'd appreciate it if you'd go on inside now. You can get dinner ready tonight, too.

It was worse than if he had yelled back. A chill rolled through the yard. He give me a wide berth as he headed to the dog yard. Soon as they seen him, the dogs hopped to their feet, barking because they knew it was suppertime.

I watched till he disappeared into the kennel, then punched the truck. My knuckles come away scraped and hurting but I punched it again. Then I launched into a run, I blew past the house, across the circle of our yard. To the woods. The cool, solid ground under my feet. Dad would be steaming when I come back. But I had to do something.

There is satisfaction in running fast. When you run you are going one place but you are also leaving another place behind. A feeling comes over you like a blanket. It wraps itself round your mind and quiets your thoughts so you can stop listening to the voices in your head and focus on the rustle of brush or the chattering of a squirrel in the treetops. I run as fast as I can for as long as I can. My mind travels somewhere else, and I become only breath and bone and muscle. The feeling is serene and focused, powerful and energized, all at the same time.

This is how I shake off anger and worry like a dog shakes water off her coat. This is how I empty myself out to fill myself up again.

After a while, I veered off the trail and plunged deeper into the woods. All the leaves whispering in the wind. Fall is brief in Alaska, like Peter Kleinhaus wrote, *the leaves browning and turning and tumbling to the ground in the space of one day.* But it is a good time to put out traps or go hunting. There's places you can find where moose have rubbed the trunk of a tree raw with their antlers and if you put your hand there the wood is soft as a cheek.

I felt how soft it was and asked my mother, What about a moose?

Even after she was gone, I would find her in the woods sometimes. Barely there, a cobweb I could put my hand through. I could conjure up the memory of her voice, thin as a scrim of ice on a puddle.

A moose is too big, she said. What would you do with it?

I shrugged. But the thought of taking something big as a grown moose made my insides flutter.

You shouldn't ever take more than you need.

When she was alive, she had showed me a place where voles made little runways through the grass, with their droppings here and there and tracks all round, you know them by the two middle toes that point forward and the two smaller toes on either side. There was a time when we would walk into the woods, hand in hand, till she let me go and told me *monkshead* or *fiddlehead* or *cloudberries*, and I would run up the trail and find what she'd asked for, and then she would explain which one is good to eat and which one will make you sick or even die.

But she never had to tell me how, in the mornings, squirrels begin to move about and look for food, and this movement is like a signal, soon after they stir, other animals start moving through the woods, too. In the evening a squirrel will return to its tree and if you know which one it calls home you can fashion a funnel, like so, use a log or some debris that you lay on the path the squirrel will take, and at the end of that funnel there will be a snare which you have made and set about two or three inches off the ground. Then you hide yourself in the brush and make your breathing shallow. You watch till you see movement in the leaves on the ground nearby. The squirrel will stop and sit on its haunches, its black eyes searching, and this is when you must be most still. Then it darts into the funnel and when it comes out the other end, it is caught.

Its body is still warm. This is how you want it.

There's two ways to really know another creature's mind, and neither of them involves talking, which is just a distraction. One way to know a person is to live and work with them side by side. You are quiet as you each go about your chores and get to know how the other one moves, how his body shifts and changes, how a thought flickers over his face and tells you more than words could. That's how it was with me and Dad, before. We would get out a sled and lay the rigging on the snow and choose a team of dogs to put on the gangline, all without ever exchanging a word.

The other way of knowing is a kind of watching and listening that happens deep in your head. It's as close as you can be to another animal. You empty your own self out and there's room for something else, you drink it in, and then you know.

I used my knife on the squirrel. There is a place in the neck you can cut and let the blood drain out so the body will go limp in your hands.

After, I come back to myself. What I found was the same burning anger I'd tried to shed by running into the woods in the first place. I thought of Dad, walking toward the kennel, his back thin under his coat, his shoulders slumped. The calm, disappointed way he'd spoke to me. A tiredness rose over me, strong as the anger. My mother had warned me time and again about staying in control of myself, but days like this one, it took too much effort. My muscles thrummed under my skin, my legs eager to take me back to the trail, deeper into the woods, where there was plenty other critters to hunt.

I turned, then staggered as something barreled into me, a shoulder hitting me in the face, stars exploding across my vision. I blinked them away. Pushed at the man the shoulder was attached to, a big bear of a guy, barrel-chested and grizzled with days-old stubble, tall as a tree and blotting out the rest of the woods. He lunged after me, his full weight bearing down on me. I caught him, tried to shove him away. Dug into my pocket for my knife. His fingers gripped, pulled my hair, his voice rasping, *Wait*— Then my knife in my hand.

I flew sideways, airborne for a brief second. Stars again, this time they was followed by a black wall that separated me from the woods and the man and the shout that echoed through the trees.

When I come to, my head ached something fierce, my temple tender where it had met the knob of a gnarled root sticking out of the ground. It was full dark, moonlight leaking onto the ground between tree limbs overhead. Still, I have always had better sight at night than in the harsh light of day, and I could make out where the stranger's feet had trampled the grass leading from the trail to this clearing. I could also see the broken stalks of devil's club where he must of pushed his way out of the clearing, on his way to who knows where after he knocked me out.

My heart yammered like a riled squirrel, all the hairs on my neck prickled, and I held my breath, listening for him, certain he was only yards away, wearing the inky evening like a cloak. I hadn't set traps in this part of the woods, but I felt I had stumbled into one of my own snares, tied to one spot while I waited for the stranger to show himself. After a long spell where every birdcall and twig snap sent me jumping out of my skin, I finally stood up. The trees danced in a circle round me, I put my hand out to touch one and they all stopped, the dizzy spell passed. I spotted my knife on the ground, stained with dried blood. I must of dropped it when the stranger pushed me aside. Hadn't I cleaned it before I put it in my pocket, after I drained the squirrel? It wasn't like me to put my knife away dirty, doing so would dull the blade. Unless I'd used it a second time. I folded the blade and stuck it in my pocket. There wasn't nothing to do now but go on home.

The light was on in the kennel when I got back, so I walked between the rows of doghouses and put my hand out for Peanut and Hazel to lick. Stopped to give Flash a good scratch on the belly. The rest of them, just fourteen racers left, pawed at me and wagged their tails as I passed.

Dad stood at his table saw in the workshop end of the kennel, he was making a shelf for a lady in the village who'd offered to pay him. He was likely mad. I was risking making him madder by rummaging round on the shelves where we kept our gear and paying him no mind. But the truth was, his anger and our fight was the least of my worries. I still felt jumpy, certain any second a figure would come barreling at me out of nowhere. I kept thinking I should of heard the stranger sneaking up on me, but the squirrel I'd caught had warmed me and filled my thoughts, and the part of myself that should of been alert was preoccupied with the fight I'd had with Dad.

The shelves was a tangle of lines and harnesses, sleeping bags and tents, canisters of heating fuel, extra tent stakes, an old bag of dry food for the barn cat we used to have. I found what I wanted, a whetstone. I put a bit of oil on it then sat on a stool near the door and took out my knife, rubbed the blade clean on my pant-leg, drew it down the stone. It made a scraping sound I could feel more than hear.

When the saw died, Dad said, Did you go deaf ear-lier, or are you trying to piss me off?

My hands went still. My knuckles was scraped and raw from hitting the truck.

I had to check my traps, I said.

I had laid them here and there in our woods, most near enough our property I could get to them on foot. Some of what I caught was too small to bring home, but some made for good eating, and the rest had fur Dad could sell or trade in the village.

Any luck? he asked over his shoulder.

Not this time, I told him because tanning a squirrel hide is more trouble than it is worth, and anyhow, I had dropped the squirrel when the stranger come at me.

I flipped the knife to work its other side. The saw whirred again, Dad run another board through the blade. When he finished cutting, he switched the ma-chine off. Wiped his hands on the front of his shirt, bits of sawdust fell to the floor. He sighed and paused in the doorway of the kennel. The automatic lamp Dad had rigged in the dog yard cast a circle of light that made the rest of the yard seem even darker. The dogs was all settled for the evening, most of them curled nose to tail, some of them paddling their feet in their sleep, dreaming of running.

It had been more than a year since Dad had got suspended from racing. Before Mom died, I would of bet my life such a thing wouldn't never happen. But the night she was hit by that truck, it triggered an avalanche. I have read that if you are caught in an avalanche, the best you can do is swim against the snow to try and keep yourself buoyed. We hadn't swum hard enough, though. We were still struggling to get back to the surface.

Don't be too long, Dad said over his shoulder. It's about time to turn in.

He walked through the puddle of light cast by the lamp, then disappeared when he stepped into the darkness. Leaving me on my own in the kennel, surrounded by all our gear, the half dozen sleds at the back of the room, all waiting for someone to stand on their runners. A yard full of empty doghouses. A handful of dogs who didn't just want to run but needed to.

That need was in me, too. I ached to get on a sled. I felt the trail tugging at me, every acre of land behind the house yearning for me to roam its familiar hills and hollows. Any other evening, I might of stole away for a few more minutes, long enough to satisfy the craving in me.

But underneath that pang was my heart, stuttering, and my skin, prickling. A pair of eyes, a hunched shadow, hidden by the night and waiting. Thoughts of the stranger made my breath stop, and it wasn't a feeling I enjoyed. I wouldn't feel settled, I realized, till I knew he wasn't no longer a threat.

2

I was a lot like you when I was your age, Mom told me. She sat on the edge of my bed, tried to brush the hair from my face. I ducked away from her hand, still angry.

She sighed.

I might have been even younger than you were when I started running round in the woods, she went on. Chasing my big brothers, stalking animals. I never learned to trap like you have. But I would stay out for hours, come home covered in mud. I was a wild thing.

I studied her through the curtain of my tangled hair. She was clean and pink from a hot shower, wrapped in her fuzzy white robe. The glasses she wore to do close work like sewing perched on her nose. Her fingernails clipped short, her hair wet but combed.

You wasn't, I said.

She smiled.

Believe it or not.

How come you never go in our woods, then? I asked.

People change, she said. Your grandma and granddad brought us up in the bush. You know where McCarthy is, right? I grew up near there. We had endless woods to roam in. You could be gone for weeks, not see another soul. You could peel away from your brothers, wander off, get lost. Plenty of people did—get lost, I mean. Or in trouble, or hurt. Not everybody negotiates the wilderness as well as you do, Tracy.

You got lost? I asked.

No, I never did. I always knew where I was, even when I was far from home. But there was a boy who—he got lost. People searched for him for days. I even went looking for him.

Did you find him?

You never know who you might run into in the woods, she said instead of answering.

She touched my cheek.

Have you ever come across anyone when you've been hunting?

Not all the woods was our property, if you went far enough you'd find yourself on national park land. I knew that much from the geography lessons Mom give me. Summers, especially, I would cross paths with hikers carrying big packs and canisters of bear spray. Usually I would hear them coming and climb a tree, hide till they'd moved along.

I told her as much.

That's fine, she said. But if you're ever hunting and you run into someone—come home. Just turn around and run on home.

Besides the hikers, we would get a stranger or two every year, a wanderer who spilled out from the woods into our yard or who was hitchhiking their way to Fairbanks or Anchorage. They come to our door looking for work, and sometimes Dad would tell them, My front walk needs shoveling, or Wouldn't mind someone raking them leaves away from my barn. Afterward, Mom would wrap up some food for them to take away, and Dad would hand them a bit of cash. I asked once why they didn't mind sharing even when money was a little tight or we had ate leftover stew three nights in a row. Dad said, Because it's the right thing to do. Mom added, Because sometimes if you tell someone you don't have anything for them, they look around at your house and your land, and later they come back and take what you didn't give them.

I wasn't so angry no more, I was interested in Mom's story about growing up wild. I sat up on the bed, my

stomach grumbling, and said, What about the lost boy?
Did he ever get found?

Tracy, did you hear what I said?

Run home if I see a stranger.

Right.

Because you can't trust them?

That's right, Mom said. Don't stop to talk to them
or see if they need help. Even if they're hurt. Come get
me or your dad, and we'll take care of it. Understand?

I nodded.

Run if I see a stranger, I said. Because they might be
dangerous.

Good girl, she said.

The morning after I met the stranger in the woods, I
woke with her voice in my ears. I dressed and washed
my face with threads of that memory clinging to me.
My head was sore where I'd fell against the root that
knocked me out the day before, a purple bruise veined
with blue, but my hair hid it, and I went ahead and put
my hat on for good measure.

In the kitchen, our two retired dogs, Homer and
Canyon, lay by the woodstove. Each day, we give one
racing dog a turn to be the house dog, today it was Old
Susitna. She was the dog who led Dad to both his Iditarod wins, but she was coming up on retirement soon.

She got up to greet me, nosed my hand to see if I had treats. I give each dog a good scratch.

Dad stood at the sink, sipping his coffee. He had let me sleep through breakfast, and he'd already took Scott to school and come back again. The eggs and slices of bologna he had fried up that morning was still on the stove, cold. I folded the bologna in half and ate it in two bites.

Dad drained his mug.

Sleep all right?

I shrugged.

Hope so, he said. Going to need plenty of energy to get through that list of chores.

I skimmed the scrap of paper he'd left on the table and seen that he had found plenty to keep me busy and not just away from the dogs but inside the house most of the day. Vacuuming, dusting, mopping the kitchen floor, the only thing on the list that got me out of the house was number one, *Clean out the Shed.*

It wasn't the chores I minded. I knew it was a trade, that you have to work for what you get. That seemed fair to me. What wasn't fair was the nature of that list. It was another punishment, except it was one he snuck up on me. It would be dinnertime before I finished every chore on that list, and then he would tell me to do my schoolwork, and when I finished that, he would remind me I wasn't to go into the woods, not as long as I was grounded. He thought taking the outdoors from me was the same as taking Scott's comic books or his old camera from him, but it wasn't. My stomach clenched and I breathed deep, tried to push a lid down on the panic rising inside me.

Better get started, Dad said.

I followed him outside, meaning to get the shed done first. The sky was low, full of solid clouds, white and heavy. Everything still. Days like that usually smell flat, clean. There is electricity in the air, your skin tingles with it and you know soon snow will blanket everything. Underneath, you can still catch the fuzzy scent of fall, like wet leaves and rotted wood, things decaying and going back to the dirt. It's an outdoors smell, a seasons-changing smell. A scent that don't have nothing to do with people.

The day smelled wrong.

I seen him before Dad did. Before the dogs even got wind of him. Just where the trailhead spills into the yard, the stranger come stumbling out of the trees.

Then the dogs was barking, and Dad looked up to see the man stagger, fall. Dad dropped the axe he was holding. I watched him run to the heap of person. I was rooted where I stood. Thinking of the memory I'd woke with that morning. Mom asking, Have you ever come across anyone when you've been hunting?

Instead of what happened the day before, I remembered the time I come across a moose calf. The steel cable snare had been set too high, it caught the calf instead of the smaller critter it was meant for. I do not use snares unless I am waiting and watching, but there used to be a man who set traps so close to our property you could call it trespassing. The calf must of felt the cable round its neck and panicked, pulled at the cable, which only made it tighter, till the young moose was strangled. That's when I come across it.

Tracy!

Dad's voice jolted me.

Tracy, bring me a towel!

The stranger, motionless on the ground.

Move!

I tore myself from where I stood, run into the house. Then sprinted across the yard, it seemed to grow wider the longer I run, my legs wouldn't move fast enough, till suddenly I was there, kneeling beside the stranger. The ground under him already red. The wound a puncture, a hole in the gut that opened and let the blood out.

Help me get him up, Dad said, and he pressed the towel against the wound. We need to get him to the clinic.

I leaned over the stranger. He had a set of old scars running across his face from eye to cheek, like claw marks, pink and puckered. I tried to recall the face that come at me in the woods the day before, whether I remembered scars, or the size of the hands that had grabbed at me. Were they the same size as this man's hands, now gloved in his own blood? But when I searched my memory, I only seen a blur of green and brown, then the stars that had filled my vision. Then nothing.

I put my arm round him and made ready to help lift him when his eyes fluttered open. They locked on me, then got wide. He tried to speak, but all that come out was a wheeze.

It's okay, Dad said. Stay calm. We're going to get you some help.

The man clutched at Dad's shirt. I staggered under his weight. He was taller than Dad and solid. We drug him like a felled tree across the yard and into the truck.

I'll call you when I get to the clinic, Dad said.

Dad—

Shut the door.

He whipped the truck round, the tires spitting gravel. A cloud of dust left in his wake.

Quiet as a vacuum after so much commotion. The dust settling. My breath ragged, like I had just run a mile fast as I was able. The sky so white it hurt to look at it. Over in the dog yard, Marcey circled then settled in front of her house. Flash give a whine.

I tried to think, and tried not to think.

When I come upon that calf, I'd wondered how long it had been there, hanging by its neck. Not long enough to go cold or grow stiff, there was new snow all round but none on its body. I held my breath and waited. Watched for its flank to rise. A moose calf is big, they have real sharp hooves, and if it was alive I didn't want to get too close, it might spook and clomp me.

I waited till I was certain. Then I used my knife.

But when I drew back from the slit I had made and the blood was spilling out, I heard the calf bleat. A sound so small I might of imagined it. Its eyes rolled, landed right on me.

And then it was dead, and it was dark outside, so much time had passed and I couldn't account for any of it, except that I was still in the woods, running. I never give a second thought to that calf till I stood in the driveway with a layer of dust on my skin, thinking about my own knife, sheathed in the blood I'd cleaned off later on my pantleg, and about the stranger who'd stumbled into our yard, bleeding from a wound not deep enough to kill him.

When Scott was still inside Mom's belly she would tell me, Put your hand here, and I would feel him kick. I pictured him like a sleek river otter, swimming with the current of her blood. Dad told me one time she wasn't supposed to have another baby after it went so rough with me. The health aide warned her she would be sick and have to stay in bed till he was born, but Mom was fine. In fact, it was the only time I remember her skin looking warm and brown from the sun, she was fat and healthy all that summer, happier than I'd ever seen her. Planting her vegetables and weeding the raised garden beds right up till Scott come along. He was born in the clinic like regular babies, a skinny, long-legged thing. He smelled funny and looked like a hairless opossum. When he was small, I watched her bite his fingernails, one by one, and spit them out.

She said, Come away from there, Trace.

She didn't like me standing over his bed.

Sit down, she told me. She lifted Scott from the crib then lowered him into my arms. Support the head, she said.

He was heavier than he looked. I was always pestering her to let me hold him. Now he was so close I could see the blue veins at his temples, just under the surface of his skin. He stuck his fist in his mouth and sucked on it.

Good, Mom said. You need to be gentle with him. Understood?

It was an accident, I told her.

You bit his finger till it bled.

He had screamed when I done that.

Be Gentle with the Baby wasn't the only rule Mom give me when I was little. Rule Number One for being outdoors was Never Lose Sight of the House. After Scott was born, I could play in the yard and even go into the woods but not so far that I couldn't still see some part of the house or the kennel or the dog yard. If I call you, Mom said, and you don't come running, I'll know you're too far from home.

I was almost five, too small to trap or hunt, but I could run all day and never get tired. I wanted to be outside from sunup to sundown, even when winter come along and the days got short, the dark didn't scare me and the cold never bothered me much. From far enough away, the windows of the house was just squares of light, when you slipped behind a tree the glare from the squares went away, the woods grew darker and you could see better. What was once just shapes and shadows sharpened to become a rock or a snarl of roots at the base of a tree.

Before I learned to read books, I learned to read the woods. I crouched against a tree trunk and learned why squirrels come down to the ground even though they could travel limb to limb. I learned that a chipmunk will make the entrance hole to its tunnel under a rock or a fallen tree so there is no mound of dirt to attract its natural predators.

At first I was content to sit and watch, it was like television. Except the chipmunk show and the squirrel show was better than anything on TV. You watch critters like them long enough, you learn their habits and, one day, when you are six or seven and you have found a large stone, you pick a tree near the entrance hole and do not move even when you hear your mom hollering your name. You sit, barely breathing, pretty soon all the sound drains away, except the sound of claws scratching against dirt, and then it pokes its head out but still you do not move, you wait till it darts across the ground right in front of you, and then you bring the heavy stone down.

That first time, I missed, I did not brain the chipmunk the way I intended but crushed its leg and when I picked it up to finish the job, it wriggled and bit me. I howled and dropped it, then stomped it with my foot. The blood come then, trickled from its mouth and nose.

After that, I wasn't content to learn just by watching.

Rule Number Two was Be Home for Dinner. I heard Mom hollering then, she must of been shouting and calling a long while. When I come running into the yard, I could see through the kitchen window dinner was on the table.

Sorry, I said to Mom.

What have you got all over you?

I showed her my hands.

Is that blood?

I brought my hand to my mouth, the blood was dry on my skin but I could still taste it.

Tracy.

She grabbed my hand away.

Go inside and wash up.

I done what she said. That night, she give me Rule Number Three, which was Never Come Home with Dirty Hands.

Dad's list of chores was waiting but the woods grasped at me, till finally I give in and started to run. But I did not let it become the kind of running that give my mind a place to hide. Instead, I moved through the trees and every stride was a memory of the day before. I sprinted up the trail and thought of the tree with its soft, raw spot where I'd put my hand. I leaped over a fallen log. The squirrel in its funnel. Left the trail, weaved between bushes, splashed through the shallow creek. I turned round, and the stranger grabbed me. Then I'd took my knife out—

But after that, all I found was a wall, the one that had fell on me when my head struck the root. Next thing I could recall was coming off the trail yesterday, my belly warm. Then I was in the kennel, cleaning blood from the blade of my knife.

I reached the small clearing in the woods where I'd hunted the squirrel. Even if you wasn't good at tracking you would of noticed the matted grass where two people had stood. The prints left by my own bare feet was easy to spot, they was small and you could make out all five toes. Beyond the clearing, the other set of tracks had to be the stranger's, the feet that had made them was bigger than mine and had worn a pair of boots with fairly new tread. The blades of grass red where he'd stood, where he must of fallen. Little spots of blood leading back to the trail like the kind a moose will leave if you shoot and wound it and have to follow it through the trees till it collapses. I do not like guns, they are too loud and there is no art to them, but I have been hunting with my dad and am a decent shot.

I could see how the man must of staggered away from me, his path back to the trail marked by broken branches, a trampled patch of devil's club. A bit of blue thread, snagged from his shirt by a prickly stalk. He'd stopped and put his hand out to steady himself against a tree, there was the brownish shape of a handprint, blood long dried, on the trunk of a paper birch. I touched the outline of the hand on the tree, but my fingers come away clean.

The snow started then, the hesitant small flakes of the first snow of the season. They fell fast and thick, and soon the green and brown of the woods was blotted out by white. I begun to shiver. Not from cold, but from how my mind contracted, the thoughts in my head tighter as one possibility after another fell away and I got closer and closer to what every clue told me.

I had run into folks in the woods before, hikers and hunters, people just passing through. No matter who I come upon, though, they was always louder than me. I would hear their voices, brush rustling, sticks snapping underfoot, and I would shimmy up a tree or lay in a patch of tall weeds and wait till they passed. Always thinking of what Mom had told me, that if I come upon someone lost or hurt, I should run home. But the hikers wasn't lost and the wanderers didn't seem hurt, and no one I ever crossed paths with seemed specially dangerous. I didn't see the point in running home for no reason when I could hide long enough to be alone again, then carry on with my hunt.

Tiny flakes landed on my skin and melted, stuck to my clothes. I left the clearing, pushed through brush on my way back to the trail. The snow drifted down heavier, everything clean and white. Except for a scream of red as I reached the trail—a backpack half-hid by a leafless bush. Hid, or dropped by someone who didn't have the strength to keep carrying it?

I kneeled and opened it, then pulled my hand away quick, as if it had snapped at me. The money inside was loose. I dug out a handful of bills, ones, tens, twenties. There was maybe a little over three thousand dollars, all told.

Holy shit.

Other stuff inside, too. Matches, a rolled-up tarp tied with a thin rope. A plastic bottle half full of water. A thin, worn-out sleeping bag that wouldn't be much warmth once the weather got colder. Some socks, a pair of gloves.

At the bottom of the pack there was a dog-eared paperback I recognized. I could of recited parts of it by heart, including the first lines: *Like most of my bad ideas, it started with desire. I desired a different life, a chance to know who I could be. I desired the solitude required to hear one's inner voice. And so I came to Alaska.*

The stranger must of loved the Kleinhaus book as much as I done if he bothered to bear the unnecessary weight of it as he walked through the woods. I should of felt even worse, knowing me and him had something in common, we might of got along if we had met under different circumstances. But a hardness rose up in me.

I dropped the book back inside the pack. Went to shove it back under the bush where I'd found it, then hesitated. If the stranger didn't bleed to death in Dad's truck or at the clinic, odds was he would come back. The book, the money—you don't leave what belongs to you behind, specially something so valuable.

Then again, he'd come into the yard bleeding an awful lot. And even though a few thousand dollars seemed like a fortune to me, I had seen how little time it took for Dad to blow through that much money, and he wasn't a frivolous person. He'd won the Copper Basin 300 right before Mom died, and come home with about that much in his pocket, but once there was a funeral to pay for and no more money from sponsors or from Mom training other people's dogs, a few thousand bucks dried up fast. For a grown-up, specially one that had nearly got killed in these woods, was the money in the pack a sum worth coming back for?

It was true, what Dad said about the entry fees for the races I wanted to run. I wanted to trick myself into believing that somehow we could afford to pay almost twelve hundred dollars for the Iditarod alone. But I wasn't about to give up my chance to run the Junior, at least. Problem was, I didn't have no money of my own to enter.

Till now.

I shouldered the pack and started running again. I couldn't say how long I'd been gone and I needed to beat Dad home if I didn't want him to see what I'd found.

When I got back, his truck was still gone. I shoved the pack under my bed, then come down to the kitchen and stoked the fire in the woodstove. Let the retired dogs out to do their business. Looked at my list of chores. There wasn't time to properly start number one, *Clean out the Shed*, so I moved on to numbers two and three, *Sweep the Kitchen* and *Wipe Down the countertops*. My ears straining for the sound of the truck in the drive as I worked.

I was on number four, *Do the Dishes*, when he got back. His truck rolled up the driveway alone, no VSO following behind, and no passenger riding along with Dad. I let go of the breath I didn't even know I'd been holding. Dad climbed out, his face grim. My legs went watery. I gripped the edge of the countertop, and hated myself for the hope that welled up in me.

Dad stomped his boots clean of snow in the mudroom, then went over to the coffeepot, it was cold but he poured himself a cup anyway and sipped it, black. He didn't say nothing, just leaned against the counter, drinking. Watching me rinse a handful of forks and butter knives. My throat so dry it clicked when I swallowed.

He's all right, he said finally.

I put the silverware down so he couldn't see how my hands begun to tremble.

You talked to him? I managed to ask.

Dad shook his head.

I talked at him plenty. To keep him awake on the drive. But it was the nurse who told me he ought to be okay. I stuck around and filled out his paperwork best I could. Had to go through the man's wallet just to find out his name. Tom Hatch. He ain't from around here.

So he ain't dead? My voice cracked.

He lost a lot of blood, Dad said then laughed, it sounded like a bark. He said, You should see the truck, blood everywhere. Trace, you always keep your knife on you, don't you?

The plate shattered when I dropped it, so many shards against the floor. My heart thundering in my chest.

I didn't mean to. The words come out choked, my throat like a pinhole. It just happened, I said.

It's okay. Dad was out of his chair and kneeling on the floor, picking up the bigger chunks of plate. Don't cut yourself, he said. Get the broom so I can sweep up the rest.

When I handed him the broom, he could see how my hands was shaking. I felt it inside me, too, like an earthquake happening in my guts.

Hey, Dad said. Hey, it's okay. He pulled me to him and wrapped his arms round me, stroked my back. The tremors inside me slowly went away, and soon all I felt was the solidness of him. I tried to think when was the last time he'd held me like this. Remembered him swinging me off my feet after the first time I run the dogs on my own. His arm a comfort round me after I had to scratch my second Junior Iditarod on account of dropping too many dogs. His hand on my shoulder as we walked to the truck after Mom's funeral. Always solid, always there, no matter what happened or what I done.

A thousand words behind my lips, like dogs in the starting chute. All of them desperate to tumble out, to make it all plain.

You got your knife on you now? he asked.

I always had it. I drew it from my pocket and offered

it to him. I hoped he would keep it, not get rid of it even though I supposed it was proof of some sort. Once Dad told the VSO what I had done, I probably wouldn't see that knife again.

Dad nodded but didn't take the knife. He started to sweep up the bits of broken plate.

Good, he said. I know you think of these woods as your backyard. You know them so well, you think nothing bad can happen out there. You forget just anyone could wander through.

He dumped the shards into the trash, leaned the broom against the counter. Put his hat on.

Them chores ought to keep you too busy to do much running round the next few days, but when you go back into the woods, I want you to keep your knife on you. And if you see anything out there, you tell me, hear?

I turned the knife over in my hand. You want me to keep it?

He zipped his coat. You never can tell who's going to come roaming through the woods, he said. Don't go looking for trouble. But if you see someone— He shook his head. It's just better you have a way to protect yourself.

Not minutes before, I'd had so many things to say to him I couldn't choose one. Now I didn't have a single word.

What's wrong, kiddo? he asked. Is it the plate? It's not a loss. Your mom always hated them plates, anyway. He tried to squeeze my shoulder, but I shied away. Pocketed my knife.

It's been a rough morning, huh? he said. You get after those chores, maybe we'll take a walk later. Sound all right?

I didn't bother answering.

Good girl, he said.

Then he was out the door. I watched him through the window, seen him pause halfway between the house and the dog yard. It was still snowing, lighter now, and the clouds so low the mountains beyond the trees had vanished.

I went on drying the dishes, the whole time aware of the weight of the knife in my pocket. All the relief and worry I had felt before drained away and got replaced by a buzzing inside me, I could hear it growing louder and louder, like a swarm of bees in my head. I stared at the plate in my hand. Used to be, I could tell him anything. Bring him a problem, he would tell me how to solve it. There wasn't no secrets between us. Then I had one thing I couldn't tell him. The problem with having one secret is that it turns into two pretty quick. Then three, then so many it seems like anytime you open your mouth you are in danger of spilling everything.

I wiped the last plate dry.

Good girl. That's what he'd called me.

I threw the plate at the floor.

Long as I followed Mom's rules, I could stay outside all day if I wanted. I run and wrestled with the dogs, watched chipmunks jump branch to branch and voles make their burrows in the grass. When Scott got big enough, I showed him how to climb the big tree in front of the house. We made swords from switches and chased each other round the yard till Mom hollered us in to dinner. Then I'd eat everything in front of me, seemed like I was always hungry. Dad would say, She's a growing girl. Except I never seemed to grow much. I was always small for my age, muscular enough and wide across but never very tall. Scott would push his food round and whine about having to eat this or that, and Dad would say, Look at your sister, she doesn't complain.

Scott stuck his tongue out at me. Mom cut his meat for him, and watched us, silent.

I was seven when I got real serious about trapping and shelter building. Dad showed me how to make a basic snare, how to build a lean-to that would give you enough cover if a storm come up unexpectedly. I dug myself a snow pit round the base of a white spruce behind the kennel, packed the walls real good and laid down branches on the floor of the pit, and when Dad come to see my work, he said, Good job, Trace. Then showed me how to lay more branches over the top of the shelter to keep the heat in.

The more time I spent outdoors, the harder it got to come in. Mom stood at the back stoop and hollered my name over and over, till I finally come out the woods, rubbing my hands against my shirt and leaving smears of blood.

Clean up, she told me but then grabbed my arm before I could walk past her. What's this?

She dug into my pocket and pulled out the rock I had found near the creek. I had chipped away at it with a second, harder rock to make an edge, I hoped to get it sharp enough to cut through fur and skin since my own teeth could not break through a critter's tough hide.

Inside, she said. Don't come back late again.

I held out my hand, but she didn't give the rock back.

I should of been smarter and stuck by her rules. But when you are creeping toward the first lynx you have ever seen near your property, you move so slowly you don't seem to be moving at all, it takes nearly half a minute to place your foot completely on the ground so that the weight of it does not snap a twig and send the animal running. A thing like that can't be done quick. In the end it didn't matter, I got close enough to smell its breath, musty and spicy and cloying, but then I lost my balance and had to put my hand out, and the sound of me stumbling spooked it. The lynx darted away, and the sun was long past set, and my dinner was cold.

Mom told me I wasn't to leave the yard for the next three days.

I had learned pretty quick that a couple days without going into the woods put me out of sorts. It wasn't just my head that suffered, neither. If I went too long without hunting, my belly ached something awful and my muscles went all trembly. I felt weak and woozy while I tried to do the schoolwork Mom put in front of me, the numbers floating on the paper and switching places.

So by the third day, my stomach was like a hollow pit, nothing I ate would fill me up, and I shivered even as I sat close as I could get to the fire in the den. Scott on his belly nearby, coloring in his book.

You want to do this page? he asked.

Leave me alone, I said.

He frowned. You sick?

I didn't bother answering. He only went outside if we was playing or helping with the dogs, and he'd never caught an animal on his own. He got cold quick when we played together in the snow, even though he was bundled in three layers or more. And he could stay inside for days on end, sounding out the words in his picture books and coloring all afternoon. He never seemed to get sick the way I done. It was hard to believe sometimes we was even related. Except for the way he could annoy me, only a brother could know just how to get on your last nerve, like the way he held out a crayon then and asked, Is this your color? When I didn't answer, he held out the next one and asked again, teasing, color after color, each one closer to my face, and I thought about warning him, it wasn't funny and I wasn't in the mood, and then he held out the green crayon and asked, laughing, Is *this* your color? and got so close I felt the soft waxy tip poke my cheek.

My teeth wasn't sharp enough to break an animal's hide, but a person's skin is not as tough.

Then Scott was crying, and though my stomach already felt better than it had in days, it also sunk.

I'm sorry, I'm sorry, I said. I didn't mean to. I petted his shoulder, and he held his hand to his chest, the blood from it stained the front of his shirt. I didn't mean to, I said again even as my mouth watered.

Mom come in then. Out, she said and swept Scott up in her arms.

But—

She was already in the bathroom, prying Scott's hand open to clean the bite. Tracy, I said *go*. Just go outside. She kicked the door closed.

So that is how I come to catch my first hare, I didn't wait to see if Mom would change her mind but run out the back door and deeper into the woods than ever before. Come upon some tracks in the snow I could not identify, then a tuft of fur caught on a twig. Then a pile of scat. I rolled the pieces between my fingers and tried to recall what animal it belonged to, these pellets was much smaller than moose scat, rounder and a little flat. When I come to a place where the tracks squeezed between two trees, I took my time setting the snare. Then I hid myself in the bushes.

It was a hare. It had dark tips on its ears and big, furry feet, so I knew it was a snowshoe hare, it could move through very deep snow real easy. When I seen it, my heart stopped. I held my breath and watched it follow its own tracks toward the two trees with the snare between them. When the hare hopped, it covered so much ground with a single stride, I wished for a moment that I could move like that. Then it was between the trees, it was caught and struggling, the snare tightening round its neck.

With no knife, I had a time killing it, but I managed.

The blood come easily enough when I snapped the neck. I had my fill. The cold wind inside me stopped howling, and my own blood pulsed warm in my veins. I sat with my back against an alder, the midday sun finally inching its way into the sky and the trees all round me unveiling themselves in the weak light. The snow stained red from what was left of the hare, it was dead now but I could still hear it. It had squealed in its snare, before I snapped its neck, and I felt that squeal inside me, not just in my head but in my own throat, it tore at the soft lining there like I was the one who had screamed.

This was how I learned what I needed to know from the critters I took. Some learning, I had got from books. You open up a book and absorb the words and from that you know how to make a split stick trap or how to shelter yourself in the snow. It's like drinking, you take it in and it is part of you.

The other kind of learning, you drink it in, too. It's warm and it spreads through you, wakes up your muscles and sharpens your mind, and you can see clearly, not just with your eyes but with your whole self, and then you know what you didn't before. How a squirrel plans its route from branch to branch. How a mouse will hear you before it ever sees you. How a snowshoe hare knows to run in a zigzag, not in a straight line, to confuse its predator. Every piece of knowing makes the next hunt easier.

I watched light soak into the woods and learned what I could from the hare. But underneath the hare's experience, there was flashes of something else. The hare wasn't the only thing I'd drunk from that day, I could still taste what little I'd got from Scott, too. And with that taste come a burning shame, not my own, but Scott's. Along with it, his memory, now my memory, of waking that morning in a damp patch of my own piss. Satisfaction from the idea that come to me to hide my sheets and remake my own bed so Mom wouldn't know. Little points of anger that shot out at my sister when she wouldn't color with me, and the giddy, dangerous feeling I got when I kept goading her, like poking at a sleeping bear.

I knew my brother now in a way I hadn't before. I had felt bad almost soon as I bit Scott, but now I felt even worse, like I had gutted him and looked inside and seen things he wouldn't of wanted me to. I never felt that way when I learned what a squirrel or a vole had to teach me because how could I feel bad about being part of the natural way of things? But it was different with Scott.

Mom was waiting for me at home, sitting on the

stoop, wrapped in her red coat and a wool hat on her head. Her eyes bloodshot and her face flushed.

She stood up. Fixing to say something or maybe yell or swat at me. Her face was a fast-moving cloud, changing second to second, it couldn't settle on one emotion. Between anger and frustration and tiredness, I seen something else there, a look that happened so quick it was impossible to know what it might be. Except that for less than a second, when she looked down at the hare then right at me, it was like she seen a friend she recognized. Then the look was gone.

We don't hurt people, she said.

I know, I told her.

No, Tracy, listen to me, she said. You can hit. You and Scott are going to fight, I get it. That's natural between brothers and sisters. You can wrestle and slap and pull each other's hair. I'd rather you didn't, but I know it's going to happen. But—listen.

She drew closer, took my chin in her hand. Locked eyes with me.

You must never make him bleed, she said. And not just him. Anyone.

Okay, I said and my voice was a whisper. My gut twisted in a knot. I couldn't tell her I was sorry again.

You know the other rules.

I nodded.

Then you can remember one more, she said. Even if you break the others, you can't ever break this one. You promise?

Okay.

Let me hear you say it.

Never make a person bleed, I said.

Her eyes darted to the hare that I had brought back for Dad to skin.

Good girl, she said.

3

All that weekend, Dad roused me soon as he was awake and handed me a list of chores. At first he stuck to his guns and give me only indoor chores, but I didn't complain. I waded through piles of laundry and scrubbed the kitchen floor till it shined, cleaned every window and polished every stick of furniture and run the vacuum so much I couldn't get its whine out of my ears. The whole time wondering what had happened to the stranger. Tom Hatch. If he was healing on a clinic bed in town. Or if he'd been healed and bandaged and was on his way back to wherever he come from. Or if he was gone altogether.

Eventually Dad run out of indoor chores and let me shovel snow off the porch and even tend to some of the dogs. I brushed Homer and Canyon, clipped their nails. Made my rounds through the dog yard dropping kibble into bowls and shoveling shit. In the evenings, I wrestled with whichever racing dog we'd let be the house dog for the night. Then I settled down and done the schoolwork Scott picked up for me each day. Even though I was expelled, Dad was set on me keeping up with what I ought to be learning. I kept my mouth shut, done the work. I could still be good, even if I had nearly killed a man. Even if I'd wished him dead.

I did slip away when I had the chance. I couldn't stay gone from the woods, even if I couldn't tell Dad why. When I heard the table saw whirr to life or when Dad backed down the driveway with the plow fixed to the front of his truck, headed off to clear someone's road, I dropped my shovel or my broom and dove into the woods. Checked the traps closest to home or followed the freshest set of tracks I could find. I run a mile or two down the trail, then turned round and come home before Dad got back. In this way, I kept my belly from aching and my mind calm.

Sometimes, I got as far as the clearing where Tom Hatch had come upon me. By now the handprint he'd left on the tree was faded, you wouldn't of noticed it unless you knew to look for it. I placed my hand over it then pulled away, quick, as if it burned me.

Back home, the stranger's pack still hid under my bed. I hated to think of it, waiting on him to come back to find it. I shouldn't of brung it home in the first place. Instead of returning it to the woods, though, I drug it out most nights. Counted the money, there was almost four thousand dollars. Enough to pay for the Junior and the big race itself.

I inspected his other belongings. The tarp, a twist of jerky, a handful of uncooked rice in a bag, a tin coffee mug. I reached past it all and unearthed the book.

Like me, the stranger had folded the corners of his favorite pages and underlined whole paragraphs. But unlike me, he seemed particularly interested in details I'd barely paid attention to whenever I reread the book. *I stayed in Seattle long enough to earn the money I needed to continue north, becoming an expert at cleaning fish in the meantime.* It wasn't the kind of writing you could learn anything from, I usually skimmed them parts so I could get to the hunting and trapping and hiking bits faster. I didn't even remember Kleinhaus had stopped in Seattle for a spell.

Inside the book, the pages was covered with words, not just Kleinhaus's familiar words but Tom Hatch's handwritten notes.

If I do nothing else before I die, I will see the northern lights.

black bear = tall ears, short claws, no shoulder hump. brown bear = short round ears, long light-colored claws, shoulder hump.

Most effective snare?

"Small mistakes are magnified in the wild."

to do—1. learn about trapping 2. get map 3. best way to sharpen knife?

It had been a good few months since I'd reread Kleinhaus, and that feeling sprung up in me again, the feeling like looking at someone else and seeing your own self reflected. Except it wasn't Kleinhaus's words that spoke to me this time. Tom Hatch's handwriting was tiny, and he'd crammed his own words into every space. What I'd read so far all had to do with learning something new or reminding himself of a fact. I didn't write in my books, I liked the margins to be clean. But I had done the same kind of learning, specially at first, drinking in the words of my guidebooks and memorizing the parts of a Paiute deadfall or the shape of a lynx's tracks.

I read some of what Hatch had wrote, then closed the book, shoved it back inside the pack. But minutes later, I found myself reading again. Nodding when he come across good information about trapping or way finding. Wishing I could set him right when he got something wrong. Then shaking my head and throwing the book into the pack again. This stranger, Tom Hatch, wasn't someone I could let myself be soft about.

I couldn't go to jail. I couldn't live my life inside with no woods and no sky and no warmth in my belly.

But more than anything else, I couldn't do that to Dad. I'd seen how losing Mom had run him down. The weight he'd lost. The gumption, too, there was a light in his eyes that got snuffed out. The only reason he had carried on, I knew, was me and Scott. If I had to go away, too—if Dad learned that I had tried to kill a man—

I couldn't let that happen. Whatever I needed to do to fix things once and for all, I would do.

I put Tom Hatch's book back inside the pack. Shoved it under my bed.

Friday morning, I come inside after putting fresh straw in the dogs' houses and found Dad on the phone.

'Preciate the update, he was saying. I know you can't give too many details, but if you hear anything else—

He fell quiet a moment. Then said, Thanks again, Helen.

My gut twisted itself into a knot.

Helen? I asked when he hung up. From the clinic?

She called to say our visitor got sent up to Fairbanks for surgery day after I brought him in, he said.

I frowned, not sure if it was good news or bad. Did it

mean Tom Hatch was too far away now to bother coming back? Or that he had been patched up and might even now be on his way to us?

She say anything else? I asked.

Dad shook his head. They've got all kinds of privacy rules at the clinic, what they can and can't say. Anyway, I just wanted to know he's all right.

I fretted the rest of the day, my thoughts so fixed on where Tom Hatch might or might not be that Flash slipped out of my grip when I tried to put her in the dog run for some exercise, she darted across the snow and I had to chase her down. She pounced and bowed, stayed just out of my reach, wanting to play, but I couldn't enjoy it, I was so out of sorts. By the time I finally got hold of her and put her in the run, my head ached and my belly growled. I knew it was risky, but the minute Dad got in his truck and headed up the road to plow, I sprinted into the woods fast as I could.

I come back calmer, but that calm evaporated the minute I seen Dad. His arms crossed, a storm darkening his face.

You want to explain why you was in the woods? he asked when I got close enough.

There wasn't no explanation I could give him. Instead I said, You won't let me train, you won't let me even walk the dogs. Can't I at least hunt?

He looked past me, studying the yard and the dogs that was left, the ones that was certain not to get any exercise at all now that the only one of us who had bothered to stay on the back of a sled was grounded. It was punishment for me, all right, but I couldn't help but think it was a worse punishment for the dogs, who hadn't even done nothing.

We'll see, he said.

What about my traps? There's ones I set but ain't checked yet.

I'll take care of them today.

I kicked at a mound of snow, sent a spray of flakes into the air.

Don't be that way, Dad said. I told you if you got expelled—

He reached out to touch my shoulder. I suppose he meant to apologize even as he give me his good reasons for doing what he done. I seen his hand come at me, though, and I jerked away.

I'm sorry, Trace, Dad said. I did warn you, though.

Mom wouldn't of done it, I said.

Excuse me?

One or the other, maybe. She probably would of told me I can't race. But she wouldn't of kept me from the woods.

His mouth was a straight line, pressed so tight his

lips disappeared. His whole face like stone. Except his eyes. They went soft and gleamed in the weak sunlight.

Get inside and get after the laundry, he said. The dogs perked up when they seen him headed their way, wagged their tails and jumped their paws to his chest. Still happy to see him because there's nothing more loyal than a dog.

Forty houses in the yard, and there was a time we had a dog for every house. Now every other house was empty. Names still over the doors, signs me and Dad and Scott had made for each dog, carving or burning the names into squares of wood. Panda. Junior. Half Pint. Speedy. Slim. The first time Dad give one of our dogs away, traded Slim for half a moose the winter before, I didn't speak to him for a week even though I understood why he done it. Other dogs got traded for other things. Young, unseasoned dogs who needed good training got sold to other mushers. Four of our retired dogs, he give them to families who could take care of them. Now we only had the two retirees and fourteen racing dogs left, barely enough for a team.

I felt a wildness rise inside me. An urge to run far as I could, till my head emptied out and my skin stopped buzzing and I could focus long enough to set a snare and wait for a critter to come along, and then I could leave myself completely for a time, my eyes and ears

not my own, they would belong to a marten or a squirrel. Leave behind thoughts of Hatch, of Dad's anger at
me, of racing, even. It wouldn't do for me to go a week
without hunting. But even if I tried to explain that to
Dad, I couldn't make him understand. I would have to
find another way.

What I had told Dad was true, there come a point
when Mom didn't just let me stay outdoors all day, but
give me the run of the woods. I could stay gone overnight, even, and she never said nothing long as I told
her when to expect me back.

But that only started when I was ten. Before that,
Mom couldn't seem to make up her mind, sometimes
she shooed me outside and didn't bother to tell me,
Come in before dark, or remind me to clean my hands
before dinner. Sometimes it seemed like she couldn't
wait to be rid of me, and when I did come home I would
spot her and Scott, snuggled together in the hammock
we set up in the yard summers, or building a snow-
man in the winter. The two of them laughing. When I
got near, Scott would go on giggling and packing snow
onto the man they'd made. But Mom was like water on
the coldest day of the year, you could toss a cup of it
into the air and it would freeze before it hit the ground.
She seen me, and become brittle.

Other times, for no reason I could fathom, she would forbid me to leave the house. You have school-work, she would tell me, but no matter how many worksheets I done or science experiments I finished, I never got to the part of the day where the work was over and I could run off into the trees. At first I would bargain with her, if I made my bed and done all my homeschool and any chore she chose to give me, could I just go out long enough to check my traps? When that didn't work, I tried to sneak out, waited till she was gone from the room then run for the door, only to find her somehow on the other side of it, like she had read my mind. She could be even faster and quieter than me when she wanted. Homework, she would say and point me back to the kitchen table where my schoolbooks was.

Then I pitched a fit. Threw my pencil across the room, kicked over my chair. Lunged at her when she drew near and clawed her arms till the blood come.

Upstairs, she said in her quietest voice, the one that meant I was in the most trouble.

Once, we went more than a week that way. The two of us at odds and her only making it worse the longer she kept me away from the woods. I grew surly, then sick, my stomach hollow and cold. At night, I dreamed of running through the trees on all fours and sinking my sharp teeth into the skin of whatever I caught. In the morning I woke exhausted and pale, and hungrier than ever.

The year before, Dad had took on some help. Winning the Yukon Quest for the first time, plus a handful of shorter races, he'd started to make a name for himself, and though he hadn't yet won the Iditarod, he'd done respectable, finished in the top ten two out of the last three years. He'd got a couple sponsors who paid for some of his gear, and the number of our dogs was growing. So when a young guy named Aaron come round saying he was looking to *apprentice* someplace, Dad let him train our puppy team in exchange for doing odd jobs and helping care for the seasoned dogs.

There was others, too, the ones Dad called the *youngsters*, two guys and a girl who helped train the dogs and prep gear and food bags for races. The girl and one of the guys was both back in Alaska after going to school in the lower forty-eight, and the other guy was fresh out of high school. All three of them was interested in mushing or taking care of animals, and they worked hard for Dad.

It was my tenth day stuck indoors when Mom sent me to the woodshed to fetch some logs for the fireplace. I piled wood onto the sled and listened to the scurrying of the mice who had made their homes in the small spaces between the logs. My mouth watering. My arms sore with the effort of lifting and stacking. I hoisted one last log, turned to drop it on the sled, and there was our old barn cat, purring and rubbing against the back of my legs. I tripped over it as I turned, my arms round the log, and fell so fast I didn't have time to catch myself. I dropped like a sack of kibble, my head smacked the edge of the sled.

I was up again in a flash. The cat hadn't startled, only leaped out of the way when I fell, still within reach. Even sick, I was faster than the cat, it was warm in my arms and still purring when I put my hand round its head.

My belly was warm and satisfied by the time I looked up to see Aaron. He seemed stuck to the spot where he stood. Till our eyes locked and he dropped the bucket he was carrying and backed away, then turned, walked fast toward the kennel, faster with every step.

I understood then what it was about the movement of small things that had made our cat crazy, sent it jumping across the kennel with its claws out. With no thought in my head I pounced after Aaron, energy like I hadn't felt in days surging through my muscles, even when he broke into a sprint it was no effort for me to catch up, and when I grabbed the back of his shirt and he tried to pull away, I held fast. His eyes wide when I put my hands on him. His hands pushing as I bit into his skin.

The tires of his car spun in the snow before he managed to peel out of the driveway. Dad was off on a run, but Mom had come outside, she must of spotted Aaron from the house, seen him running to the car, his hand pressed against his neck. Here and there, between where I stood and the tracks Aaron's tires had left, the snow speckled red.

Mom didn't say nothing. Only gripped my arm and pulled me toward the house. I could of twisted away, easy, and run off, but I thought better. She was trembling all over but her hand was steady, her fingers dug into my arm till she pushed me into my room and closed the door behind me.

When I tried the door, it only opened a crack, something was tied round the knob and stretched across the hallway.

I went to my bed. Stared at the ceiling. Warm all over and heavy with sleep, not like the exhaustion I'd felt all the time I was stuck indoors but the way the cat felt after it had ate its fill and licked its paws and found a patch of sunlight to curl up in. I understood now how clever the cat had been at cornering the mice in the woodshed, what a good hunter it was, and a small part of me regretted snapping its neck.

I felt Aaron inside me, too, but he was different from the cat. I had the cat's whole life in me, everything it had learned and experienced. From Aaron, I only had a spike of fear and confusion and disgust that had drove through him when he seen what I done to the cat. And under that, a faint, warm glow as he, as I, thought of the beer I would grab at the roadhouse once my day's work was done. The last thing that must of been on his mind before I bit him.

Downstairs, Mom took the phone from its cradle, then replaced it. Picked it up again, and her voice floated up to me through the floorboards, not the words but the tone, pitched low but urgent. After she hung up, the house was quiet till Scott woke from his nap. Their voices moved together to the kitchen, and then I heard water running and bowls and spoons clattering, and soon the scent of something sweet baking. I fell asleep to the sound of their conversation, muffled by the walls and floors between us.

I think I woke sometime that night, but I may have dreamed Mom sitting on the edge of my bed, a shape in the darkness. Her arms wrapped round a pillow as she studied me.

My head was fuzzy from a sleep so deep it seemed to grab at me with sticky fingers and pull me down even as I tried to lift my head. Mom? I managed to say, my voice come out rusty.

She got up. Go back to sleep, she said.

Next morning, she was waiting for me in the kitchen. My schoolbooks missing but my pack on the table, waiting for me.

There's a water bottle, Mom said before I could ask. Her voice flat and calm as she went on, Matches, even though I know you can start a fire without them. Gloves and an extra sweater. I know you think you won't need any of it, but you might, so take it. And this.

She opened her hand and offered me a pocketknife. It was heavier than it looked, not the cheap kind you give to a kid for a first knife but a real tool with a paper-thin edge to its blade. It was the prettiest thing I ever seen and I wanted badly to pocket it. But I was afraid to take it, afraid to go out the door with the pack and the knife. Afraid that if I did, I wouldn't be able to come back.

Mom mustn't of slept all night, judging by the circles under her eyes. There was lines round her mouth and wrinkles between her brows that I hadn't noticed before, and although her own hand was steady the rest of her seemed delicate, breakable as glass. She couldn't really tell me what to do, I understood for the first time.

I was stronger than her, and faster, specially when I had got my fill of what I needed.

I planted my feet and stood firm.

She come round the table, brought the pack to me. Be back by dinner, she said.

I wasn't about to ask questions. I shouldered the pack and stumbled out the door, my knees watery with relief, though I did listen for her to turn the lock behind me. She didn't. And when I come home that evening, just as she was setting the last plate on the table and Dad was cleaning up after being gone on the trail, she only reminded me to wash my hands and keep my new knife somewhere out of Scott's reach.

Did you drink? she asked in a low voice when I come back to the table.

It was a shock to hear her ask so plain, and with Dad and Scott just a room away. What I done in the woods wasn't something we had ever talked about in so many words.

I nodded, but she seemed to be waiting on something, so I said, I caught two squirrels, plus a little beaver out near the river. I brung the fur back.

Good, she said.

After that, I had the run of the woods. I felt full and warm all the time, more patient with Scott, tolerant when Mom or Dad give me a chore I didn't like.

Mom was different, too. Though she still wouldn't go into the woods on her own, she spent more time outdoors. She was also more patient, specially with me. If I come home late or forgot one of the rules, long as it wasn't the Fourth Rule, she only chided me, there was no more sending me to my room or keeping me indoors for days at a time.

That spring, Mom started training other folks' dogs again. It was something she done before I come along, there was old pictures of her taking a pack of new pups on walks or fitting them with harnesses. Early on, she'd helped Dad teach his racing dogs the basics, and she turned out to be so good at it other people come to her to train their dogs, and not just racing dogs, neither. Soon our yard was overrun with all kinds of dogs, every single one learned to sit or heel or play dead at just a word from Mom.

She got busy fast. Soon enough, Dad suggested they take on another hand.

I don't need some kid tagging along while I work, Mom argued.

It doesn't have to be another youngster, Dad said. We're doing okay enough, we can pay someone a real wage, not just a few bucks and the benefit of experience. Someone who knows what they're doing.

They went back and forth on the subject at least a

week till Mom finally give in. But I'm the one who has to work with whoever it is, she told Dad. So I'm going to find the right person.

Mom probably met with two dozen folks before she found Masha. She wasn't the sort I expected Mom to choose, she was hardworking enough but she was also chatty, what you call *bubbly*, she never seemed to have a bad day and greeted every frustration with a smile on her face. Her disposition made her specially good with problem dogs. Maybe that's why Mom picked her.

Either way, Mom and Masha got real close over a brief time. Soon enough, Masha wasn't just helping with the dogs but Mom would invite her to stay for dinner, or the two of them would bake together or weed the garden beds. Masha always chatting away, and Mom always smiling and laughing. Something about her seemed to rub off on Mom, and even after Masha left for the day, Mom would still float round the house, cheerful and even silly.

Then, quick as switching off a light, something changed. That winter, Masha flew back to her home on account of her dad dying, and when she come back more than a month later, you could tell she felt real bad. Still, she wanted to get back to *normal*, is what she said. She was quieter than before, still friendly enough but not so fast to laugh or make a joke.

It was understandable, someone close to you dies, you feel bad. But the change in Masha seemed to trigger something in Mom. At first, she just got quiet, too, and you could imagine she was only trying to make things easier for Masha, not pry into her personal affairs or expect her to act like nothing had happened. But Mom started to grow out of sorts, she would snap at Masha or find excuses not to work so close with her. Even after Masha went home for the day, Mom would still be surly, barking at me and Scott, getting angry at Dad over small things. Or else she would disappear for the evening, close herself in her bedroom and not come out.

Then one morning over breakfast Dad asked her if she could spare Masha because he needed an extra hand to help with drop bags, and Mom wiped her mouth with a napkin then said, She won't be here. I let her go.

Dad dropped his fork. What do you mean?

I mean I let her go. I told her we couldn't use her and that she needed to find work somewhere else.

Told her— Dad stared at her. Wasn't she doing a good job?

She was fine, Mom said.

So she done something to make you mad?

No.

He crumpled his own napkin up and tossed it at his

plate. You didn't think maybe I'd want to weigh in on something like this? he asked.

Mom shrugged. She worked with me, not you.

Dad huffed. That's nice, Hannah, he said and stood up, dropped his plate in the sink. That's a great attitude. I guess you can take care of everything yourself.

Mom glanced at me then.

Tracy can help, she said.

So that's how I come to do more than just run dogs down the trail for fun. I always had my eye set on racing. By the time I was ten I was already taking small teams down the trail, my sled behind Dad's. But after Mom got rid of Masha, I started learning what it really takes to raise a racing dog right, how to train them and how to tell which pups are suited to race and which are destined just to be someone's pets.

When Fly's newborn pups was ready to move from the house to the kennel that spring, Mom laid out her tools on the kitchen table then called me over.

Grab one of those dogs, will you? she said.

I handed her a puppy and she held it against her chest and with a needle numbed the place on its foot where the dewclaw was. Switched the needle for a pair of long-handled scissors. Real deft she cut the dewclaw off. There was a little blood but not much.

You clip it off, Mom said, so it doesn't catch on

something when she's running. Better to remove it now than for it to tear off later. You want to do the next one?

I cradled the next pup, she didn't even have a name yet but we would call her Flash. She had a sleek gray coat and ears that seemed too big for her head, and even young as she was, she already showed her patient nature. I let her take one of my fingers between her teeth and gnaw.

Does it hurt them? I asked.

A little, Mom said. They say you're supposed to cut the dewclaw while they're still puppies not because it hurts less but because they won't remember the pain.

That so?

She petted the dog in my arms. Shrugged. Some pain stays with you even if you don't remember it, she said.

Then her hand over mine, this way, hold the scissors like this. Talking me through as I concentrated. After we done all four pups, we stood near the woodstove and watched them yawn and curl round each other, a pile of puppies that would grow into racing dogs.

Mom must of been thinking the same thing. She put her arm round me and said, Just imagine. These could be the dogs on your first team.

She was partly right. My first Junior Iditarod, Flash wasn't my lead but I put her on the line next to her

sister, Zip, and all the training I done with them be-
forehand, all the runs we went on together, paid off.
I didn't come in first that year but second, on the tail
of the reigning champ, a seventeen-year-old guy who
turned eighteen three days later, which meant soon as
he was done with the Junior, he turned round and done
his rookie run of the big Iditarod the following week.

I was all set to do the same. My birthday was March
first, and the Junior Iditarod was usually scheduled for
the last weekend in February. I would turn eighteen
after I run the Junior for the last time, and that would
make me eligible for the big race the first weekend of
March. It would be hard, two back-to-back races, especially when one of them was more than a thousand
miles, and there wasn't no sense in pushing myself to
race the Iditarod sooner than I was ready. But I had
dreamed of running the big race my whole life, now it
was so close I couldn't bear to miss this chance. What's
more, it would be the first time me and Dad run the
same race at the same time. I imagined him getting into
Nome ahead of me, already there waiting as I crossed
the finish line. Pride lighting up his face.

Except everything changed once Mom died. It happened in January, and most folks figured Dad wouldn't
race that year. He'd only ever missed one Iditarod, and
that was on account of he broke his leg right before-

hand and was laid up the rest of that winter. What happened to Mom made the news, partly because Dad had already won the big race twice and people knew who he was. But mostly because Alaska may be a big place but it's also real small. When something bad happens, it gets in the papers. TRAGIC LOSS FOR IDITAROD CHAMP PETRIKOFF. Soon as that come out, people started speculating. Anytime we went into the village there was someone crass enough to ask him straight out. But far as Dad was concerned, there wasn't no question.

Come that March, he was on the back of his sled, bib number 57. That year, Dad's buddy Steve Inga offered to stay behind and look after me and Scott instead of running the volunteer committee like he done ever since he retired from mushing. There wasn't no Mom holding one of the wheel dogs in place, and when Dad's team took off he didn't look back or wave to us. He stared straight ahead and vanished over the hill.

That year, we hovered near the radio, waiting for the trail report. Steve drove us into the village and we got updates from folks at the general store, the post office, ones who had their own racers on the trail. Dad was middle of the pack, not pushing too hard, falling farther behind each day. When I heard that, I knew his head was not in the race.

So I was surprised when a report out of Ophir told

that Bill Petrikoff Junior planned to push through to the village of Iditarod. That stretch of trail isn't traveled much outside of the race, which means no one really knows what its condition will be before the mushers get to it. Sometimes you get to Ophir and it turns out there's no trail at all, you have to wait for the trail breakers to come along. A newly broke trail is hard to run. It don't have time to set up, so mushers call a trail like that *bottomless*, on account of it seems like the surface will never hold, and you'll sink right through. There was reports of a big snow on its way, and if Dad pushed on and left Ophir ahead of the handful of teams there with him, he'd likely find himself running a bottomless trail.

The rest of what happened is in the papers for anyone to read. Dad took only a two-hour rest in Ophir, where the weather had got worse like predicted. Once the trail breakers had gone through, Dad was the first musher back on a sled. It was a tough slog. He lost the trail twice, had to turn his team round. Then a runner broke, and he had to repair it. By the time he got to Iditarod, he'd been passed by six other teams and he'd dropped two dogs on account of injury, left each one at the nearest checkpoint with the vet on duty.

All this must of been on his mind as he pushed through to Anvik then north to Unalakleet. I don't say that as an excuse for what happened later. Only that it was a bad race from the start, and losing so much time not to mention two dogs, it weighs on your mind. Days of riding the back of a sled, no sound but the dogs' breath and the thoughts inside your own head, whiteness all round, you can get hypnotized. Your mind goes white and your thoughts get funny. I have heard myself laughing on the back of a sled for no reason, days into a long run. Or sometimes you cry and don't even know it.

I imagine that was his state of mind outside of Golovin. The *Dispatch News* reported what happened next. *Bill Petrikoff, winner of two consecutive Iditarods, found his team coming to an unexpected stop.* It was on account of Panda. We called her that because of her markings, she had a white face with black patches round her eyes. Panda faltered, then went down. The rigging got tangled when the other dogs dragged the weight of her, till the rest of the team finally stopped, too snarled in their lines to move. Dad, who had tied himself to the back of his sled and was dozing at that point, come to and run up to the front of the team to see what was the matter. Panda was laying on the ground, wheezing, her lips and gums gray. He knew right away it was pneumonia.

All this, I know from the papers and from my own

time on the back of a sled, not because he ever told me about that day. He never said a word about it.

I hadn't yet competed in the big race, so maybe I don't have no right to say he should of done this or that. But if he had been in his right mind, he would of seen Panda panting heavier, would of seen the mucus she must of been coughing up. He might of noticed how she wasn't eating when the rest of the dogs bolted their food. Any other race, he would of put her in the basket, got her to a vet at the next checkpoint, before it was too late.

As it was, there wasn't nothing he could do. The next checkpoint was fourteen miles up the trail in White Mountain. Too far away for the vet there to do any good. He knelt next to Panda and put his hand on her side as she struggled for air.

Maybe she rolled her eyes up and looked at him. Maybe the other dogs laid down, quiet.

It was a skier who seen what happened next and told it to the papers. Some guy who lived in Golovin, just passing by on his cross-countries. He seen my dad stand up. Watched him walk a few paces. *Staggered* is what the man told the papers, *I thought maybe he was drunk*. Dad come to a stop. Then, so quick the motion startled the skier, he grabbed something off the ground, it might of been one of the wooden stakes used to mark the trail, he took it in his hand and turned and raised it above his head and brought it down. The skier said he heard yelps from the dogs. In the news, he said he couldn't be sure how many dogs Dad hit, or how many times he hit them. But he heard shrieks and howls, and then he seen Dad take Panda's body off the line, wrap her in his sleeping bag, and put her in the basket.

Iditarod rule number 42 says if one of your dogs dies, you have to notify a race official right away, then wait at the next checkpoint for someone to suss out what happened. But Dad blew through the checkpoints in White Mountain and Safety, he didn't stop till he got to the finish line in Nome. Thirty-second place, and a dead dog in his basket.

None of it looked good, specially when the skier come forward with the story of what he thought he seen. After that, you wouldn't believe how many other people claimed to of been there on the trail, too, you'd of thought the whole village of Golovin was skiing past that day. There was an investigation by the Iditarod committee, it took two weeks and when all was said and done, no one could claim that Dad was at fault for Panda dying. It was the pneumonia that took her, the committee determined. And as for him hitting the dogs, there wasn't no evidence that any dog was struck.

Still, for breaking rule number 42, Dad got suspended from racing for two years. That decision seemed to satisfy people, mostly the ones who knew my dad's name but didn't know the kind of man he is. Folks round here grumbled about the decision, said two years was too long. Them same folks, people like Steve Inga and Wendell Nayokpuk, raised a little money to give to us when Dad's sponsors started to pull out on account of none of them was keen on having someone who might of beat one of his dogs to death wear their clothes or have their name on his sled bag.

One night after all the ruckus of that year's race died down, I come home from a spell in the woods to find Dad on his hands and knees in the kitchen, scrubbing the baseboard. There was glass everywhere. Red running down the wall, at first glance I thought it was blood.

Then I seen her handwriting. Mom always spent late summers canning tomatoes from the store and raspberries from the garden, she put jars up for the winter so we'd have good fruits and vegetables even in January. She always wrote the canning date on the lid of each jar in black marker, and if she thought she'd made an especially good batch of something, she'd put a star on the lid, too. The last time Dad sent me into the pantry to fetch one of her jars, I'd seen that there was only a couple left, the jar of applesauce he'd sent me after, and a jar of tomatoes.

Dad sat back from the work of wiping the tomato off the wall, he braced his hands on his knees and heaved a big breath. He hadn't seen me come in. His back was hunched, like he was steeling himself against a strong wind, and then all the air went out of him. He seemed to shrink. He clutched the edge of the counter, as if to hoist himself from where he knelt, then only stayed there on his knees. His face sagged.

I backed out of the kitchen quiet as I could.

4

Dad's suspension would be up just in time for me and him to run my first Iditarod together, that wasn't what was stopping him. Even when he was suspended, it didn't mean he couldn't of kept training. But after his disastrous Iditarod, he had barely glanced at the sleds in the kennel.

The name Petrikoff had been left out of the Iditarod for too long. I aimed to fix that. But I had to figure out how to keep training despite Dad telling me I wasn't to go near our dogs.

Early the next week, I figured out how.

I'd spent the weekend cleaning out the shed and doubting anyone would want to live there. I hauled out the junk we'd stored inside, swept its floors and cleared the cobwebs and mouse nests from its corners. It looked presentable enough, but it was awful small. Tuesday, Dad worked the whole morning building a cot, the two of us squeezed it through the door and made up the mattress. The place was ready to rent. But no one had called about it yet.

That evening, Steve Inga stopped by, brung a big box of fruit and cookies, and a bottle of whiskey. He set everything on the kitchen table then opened the bottle.

What's all that? Dad asked. He stirred a pot of chili on the stove, more beans than meat, but the room smelled spicy and rich as me and Scott set the table.

Stopped by the post office, Steve said. Auntie of mine down in Florida sent a care package.

And the whiskey?

Dad found two small glasses and Steve poured, filled them to the brim.

Didn't want to drink it all by my lonesome.

They lifted their glasses and drained them in one swallow. We hadn't had much alcohol in the house since Mom died, Dad wasn't much of a drinker past a couple beers, but Mom liked a glass of something each night, and more than just a glass in the months right before she died.

Stay to supper? Dad asked.

Got nowhere else to be.

Steve poured them both a second shot, it went down

quick. Scott frowned as he watched them, then busied himself with dumping soda crackers into a bowl to put on the table.

Our spoons were making scraping sounds against the bottoms of our empty bowls when Steve asked Dad, You hear about Jim Lerner?

Dad shook his head.

Had a trespasser up his way, couple days back.

Somebody break in?

Didn't have to. You know Jim, he never locks his back door. Some guy wandered right in. Jim and his wife was down to the village, they come back, find this fella asleep on the floor. Passed out right in front of the fireplace.

No shit?

I swallowed, my throat suddenly dry.

A guy? I said. Like your age, you mean?

Naw, Steve said. Younger. Jim said he looked maybe sixteen. Ragged little guy. Spooked when Jim got home, took off and disappeared into the woods.

A runaway, you reckon? Dad said.

Suppose so.

I frowned at my empty bowl. From Steve's description, Jim Lerner's intruder didn't sound like Tom Hatch. Still, I wondered how long it took someone to heal from a gut wound, and how much longer it might take to hitchhike or drive down from Fairbanks.

Whether the ragged stranger who'd fell asleep in front of Jim's fireplace was headed north or south.

I offered to clean up after dinner, so Dad let Steve pour him another shot of whiskey and the two of them talked a good spell, while Scott disappeared to his room, probably fixing to read the rest of the evening away.

When Steve eventually left, Dad waved him down the driveway, then staggered a little on his way to the kennel. I stepped outside like a swimmer treading slow into a cold lake, followed him across the yard. He didn't say nothing when I picked up a bucket of kibble and trailed behind him.

Sled dogs need more food than regular dogs, they burn off so much energy. Over the summer, when we only done short, easy runs, their diet was lighter, but if I intended on getting serious about training now that there was snow on the ground, I would have to fig- ure something out. We didn't have nothing left in the kennel freezer, no salmon to add to the kibble because Dad hadn't gone to fish camp that year, and no moose trimmings because he hadn't managed to hunt. I could bring back some of what I trapped, but not if Dad was serious about me staying away from the woods.

We worked up and down the rows, him moving a little slower than usual. I paused in front of the house with Panda's name over the door. Her food bowl was still there, froze to the ground. I kicked it free, and it flew across the snow.

Dad knelt down in front of Grizzly and took the dog's face in his hands. Old Grizz, he said and his voice come out syrupy, like each word was stuck to the next. Grizz's mom was one of my first racing dogs, he went on. Got her from a guy over near Tok.

This was a story I had heard before, sitting in front of a fire, the dogs paddling their feet in their sleep. We never told ghost stories or sung songs when we was on the trail together. Instead, Dad told me stories about building his team, the first races he ever run, how he come to be one of the best mushers in the state. Early days, when him and Mom was just starting out, and everything was an adventure.

Your granddad left me seven dogs when he died, dogs he'd raced himself, said Dad. But the first three dogs that were just mine, the first three I built my team on, they was Grizzly's mom, you remember Bear. And one called Suka, and a real pretty mutt named Spruce. I drove all the way to Tok to get the dogs from another musher who decided to pack it in and move to Arizona.

I shoved my hands in my pockets. Watched the woods. Snow starting to fall.

Dad stroked Grizzly's fur. I went by myself to get the

dogs, he said. A good seven hours one way. You almost never drive on your own, so you don't know the pleasure of a long, empty road, just you and your thoughts. It's not the same as running the dogs, but your mind goes peaceful in sort of a similar way. It was late summer, almost fall. I come back under a wide blue sky that went purple, then black, and then the stars come out one by one, and a full round moon that made it seem almost like daylight again. I stopped, pulled over to the side of the road for a break, and everything was quiet. No other cars on the road. Night birds calling out to one another and bugs chirring off in the dark. I stood there in the moonlight. Then just as I was thinking I ought to hit the road again, I hear one long, lone howl. It come rolling over the hills to me. And the dogs in the back of my truck, first one, then the others, they answered back. All three of them, wailing. Like they knew they come from the wild, that those voices in the distance belonged to their brothers.

Dad stood up and let Grizz jump his front paws to his chest. The dogs all grinned at him, their ears soft. They wanted to run, but they would also just sit there, long as he asked them to, watching their own team dwindle, losing muscle, losing conditioning. Just to please him. That's how dogs are when they love you.

I stood there with my mouth dry but my eyeballs

burning. The snow was light, tiny flakes that made the air shine but wouldn't amount to much accumulation. The flakes tumbled straight down out of the sky. No wind when you want wind, when all you want is a gale to come up hard and sweep a wall of snow across the yard, or a flood powerful enough to carry everything away, the house, the bowls, the barn, the dogs. A fire to burn every last sled. Nothing left but an empty space in the trees.

Trace? Dad's voice come to me through a sticky fog, my anger thick and gluey, it clogged my throat when I spoke.

All the way to Tok, I muttered.

What's that?

You'd go all the way to Tok and back to fetch some dogs, but you won't get on the back of a sled now. You won't let me train. You don't even take the dogs on walks. What kind of musher are you supposed to be? We might as well get rid of all our dogs. Give them to someone who'd actually let them work.

I kicked Panda's water bowl and sent it sailing the same direction as the food bowl. A coal inside me, smoldering, and the only way to put it out was to run. I considered it, was close to darting into the woods and staying gone the rest of the night, I would come back in the morning satisfied and peaceful. But I would also come back to Dad's quiet anger and another stretch of indoor chores and no dogs.

So I took that smoldering coal and carried it across the snow, back to the house. My back hunched against Dad's voice when he called after me, Tracy, wait. Come on back.

Inside, I shucked my boots and coat and hat, my insides turbulent and crampish, that feeling like I was too full even though I hadn't drunk that day. It was my period, I knew I would get it soon. I couldn't count on it coming each month the way the nurse at school said most girls could. Other times, I would get it twice a month. It was too early to turn in, but I crawled into bed anyway, my clothes still on. I was asleep before I heard Dad come back inside.

I woke in the middle of the night, my throat dry. Downstairs for a glass of water, I found Dad still on the couch, he'd fell asleep, too, in front of the fire, which was just embers now. His head propped at an odd angle, he would have a crick in his neck when he woke. In the kitchen, I crept past the sleeping dogs and filled a glass at the sink. But before I could even bring it to my mouth, it slipped from my grip. The glass hit the floor like a gunshot.

Shit, I muttered.

While I sopped up the water and pinched at the shards of glass, Dad went on snoring. He always slept like he was dead. Out soon as his head hit the pillow and not moving a muscle till the alarm went off at four. The house could burn down round him, and you'd find him when the flames was doused, asleep in the ashes.

I dropped the bits of glass into the trash, a bright, glittery clatter that wasn't loud enough. My eyes on Dad.

All the ruckus had woke Homer and Canyon, along with that night's house dog, Chug. I glanced at them. Then give a whistle.

Three dogs barking ain't as loud as fourteen, but it was a nice commotion, specially inside the house. Upstairs, Scott had probably bolted up in bed, wondering what all the fuss was about. I shushed the dogs, and they laid their heads back down.

Meanwhile, Dad snored on.

The last embers was nearly out, but I felt a warmth spread through me. That hot coal still burning inside me, but it had changed. Felt more like hope smoldering in me now than anger. A feeling like that, there's two options. You can leave it be and it will burn out eventually. Or you can do something with it. Stoke it. Add fuel. Watch the flames grow.

Take it into the woods, light your way.

After she got rid of Masha, Mom stopped going to the village. Used to be, if Dad had to run to the store for groceries or supplies, she would go along to help, sometimes we'd make a whole trip out of it and end the day at the roadhouse where they served the steaks and burgers as bloody as you wanted them. More often than not, we would have a good bit to pick up at the post office, and Mom used to like making that stop, she would chat with the postmaster and the other folks who'd come in for their mail and shipments from Anchorage. *Light talk* is what she called it, conversations that wasn't about much at all, just pleasantries and gossip about what was going on in the village.

But all that stopped soon as Masha was gone. Before long, Mom stopped training other people's dogs, too. She give all her attention to Dad's team, not that he couldn't use the help. By then we had more dogs than ever, about forty in all, give or take a new litter of pups or one or two dogs close to retirement.

That didn't stop Mom from telling Dad she didn't think we needed to keep the youngsters on.

She was scrubbing the dinner dishes. I sat at the table, scrambling to finish that day's schoolwork. She'd promised that if I got it done I could spend the night in the woods, long as I took a tent with me. I preferred to make my own shelter or sleep under the sky if the weather was good but I'd take the tent if it would get me out of the house.

What she actually said to Dad was, Why the hell do we need so many people around all the time?

They work for us, Dad said. They're here because I pay them to be.

You pay them to eat our food?

Hannah, that was just tonight. They worked late, so I told them they could join us—

Without a heads-up, Mom said. Thanks a lot for that, by the way.

Dad got up from where he sat filling out papers to enter that year's Yukon Quest. He went to the sink and stood behind her, slipped his arms round her waist. She was small enough, the top of her head fit right under his chin. He kissed the place where her hair was parted. She elbowed him away.

Come on, he said and his voice was quiet. What's wrong?

She rinsed a plate.

You haven't been yourself, Dad said and the clock over the stove ticked and my pencil scratched against the paper and one of the house dogs whined. Dad's hand on Mom's belly, he lowered his voice and said, There isn't something you need to tell me, is there?

No, she spat. Jesus Christ, Bill, that's the last thing I need.

He drew close to her. It wouldn't be such a bad thing, would it? he said. Another baby.

Are you offering to carry it this time around? she said.

If it'd get you to say yes.

She sighed. Run the water. The wood popped in the woodstove. Dad kept poking at her with his hands and his words. Stroking her back and squeezing her. Telling her the timing was right and they used to talk about having a million kids when they was younger and if they had a few more they could replace all the youngsters with their own children, put all of us to work as dog handlers. He grinned and chuckled, and I wondered how it was he couldn't feel the anger building and coming off her like waves of heat.

Finally she pushed him, harder than she must of meant to. He stumbled back a couple steps. Her hands was covered in suds from the water, and she was still holding the knife she'd been washing.

Hannah—

Her hand was steady as she glanced at the knife, but soon as she dropped it, I could see her shoulders shake, her fingers tremble. She darted past Dad and grabbed her coat from the hook in the mudroom.

Where are you going?

Just outside.

Wait, Dad said. I'll come with you.

No, she said. She stuffed her feet into her boots, jammed a hat onto her head. Let the door slam behind her.

Dad grunted as he sat down at the kitchen table.

I put my pencil down and said, I'm done. Can you check my math so I can go out? Mom said I could if I showed all my work.

He got up again, went to the sink and peered out the window. Walked over to the door and put his hand on the knob, then seemed to change his mind. Back at the table, he didn't sit down, just chewed on his lip and stared at the spot where Mom had stood a few minutes ago.

Dad?

Just leave it, he said. I want you to stay inside for now. Give your mom some space.

I clomped up the stairs, unhappy at how the evening had turned. But then I went to the window at the end of the hallway and spotted Mom in the yard. She hadn't got far, just to the head of the driveway where she stood, bundled in her red coat, facing away from the house. Looking at what, I couldn't say. The trees that shielded our house from the road, or the sliver of moon hooked in the sky above the trees? Or the darkness, the spaces between the trees and the shadows that crept up the snow-blanketed yard, the stretches between each star that held nothing at all.

After a time, Old Su trotted over and stuck her nose in the pocket of Mom's coat, searching for a treat and coming up empty. Su ventured down the drive, then looked back at Mom. But Mom stayed where she was.

It was long after the hallway creaked with Dad's footsteps, long after the upstairs toilet flushed and the light switches clicked and my own room sunk under the layers of shadow and settling sounds, that I heard the back door open then close as she finally come back inside.

Day after Steve Inga mentioned the intruder at Jim Lerner's, we got a good dump of sticky snow, despite the mild temperature. It come down like someone in the sky was emptying buckets of flakes, and by the time it was over, columns of snow stood nearly a foot and a half high on the roofs of the doghouses. Dad attached the plow to the front of his truck and spent that evening and all the next day clearing driveways and side roads, earning a couple hundred dollars.

It was a lucky stroke for me. When his taillights cleared the end of our driveway, I ducked into the kennel and got to work. I hadn't yet bothered to inspect any of the winter rigs and they all had one thing or another that needed repairing. I tightened bolts and lashings, checked stanchions and runners for cracks, adjusted brake claws, replaced a bridle, which is the rope that attaches to the towline and helps with steering. When my sled was ready, I hauled it close to the door then loaded it with sandbags to weigh it down, since I wouldn't be taking no gear with me, at least not on my first run. Then I untangled ganglines and tuglines, sorted through harnesses, and stabbed my fingertips with a needle, squinting under the lamp in my bedroom, as I done my best to mend what harnesses needed it.

If Dad noticed gear had got moved round or that someone had loaded a winter rig with sandbags and covered it with a drop cloth, he didn't say nothing. Next morning, he filled a bucket with kibble then led me back out to the dog yard. The temperature had dropped some, so I convinced him to let me heat up a batch of thin broth. It wasn't much but at least the dogs would get a few extra calories with their breakfast.

Usually the dogs made a decent racket when they knew it was feeding time, but that morning they was absolutely frenzied. They yapped at us the whole time we made our rounds and only quieted once they had something in their bowls.

My bucket empty, I punched through the snow on my way back to the kennel. A cold snap had settled after the snowfall, sucked all the moisture out of the air, and the ground had gone brittle, crusted over. I broke through with every step till I reached the door, and stopped short.

Dad nearly walked into me. What? he said.

But I didn't have to answer, he could see for himself what I had already spotted. A footprint. Bigger than mine, with tread new enough to make clear zigzag patterns in the snow.

We was just over here, I said, quiet.

He pressed his own foot into the snow next to the print to show me it was smaller than his own by maybe half an inch.

Inside the kennel, a soft thud like something falling off the workbench and hitting the floor.

We would of seen somebody in there, I said, but soon as the words was out of my mouth I thought of all the places there was to hide in our kennel. Even as we'd filled our buckets someone could of been in one of the stalls near the back, or up in the loft, or behind the empty chest freezer.

Where's Scott? Dad asked me.

Still in the house, I said.

You go in, too. He put his bucket down. The morning had gone still, none of the dogs barking now.

Don't, I said.

But he was already inside, the shadows swallowed him as he moved toward the back of the building, and I strained to hear anything other than my own heart pounding. I had stabbed Tom Hatch for a reason. He had come at me, snuck up on me when I wasn't looking, and if I hadn't turned round at the right moment, who knows what he might of done? He might of squeezed my neck till my throat closed, or clobbered me with a stone. Did he have a weapon now, a hammer he'd grabbed off the workbench when he'd heard us in the kennel?

I should never of taken the money. I turned and run back to the house. I don't know if I meant to grab Hatch's pack or for what purpose, but I stopped when Scott come outside.

What are you doing? he asked.

Shhh, I said.

He come out even though he wasn't wearing a coat, his feet swallowed up in Dad's extra pair of boots. I strained to hear any sound from the kennel. Thought about the distance from Fairbanks to here, about how long it might take to heal from a knife wound. I waited for Dad to come out. It should of been me to go inside, not him. Why hadn't he ever put a lock on the kennel? Anyone could walk in, hide in the dark. I seen Tom Hatch in the doorway of the kennel, his gut bleeding, blood on the snow. Holding a hammer, holding Dad's axe.

An endless time before a shape formed itself in the doorway, and I had to blink my watery eyes clear before I seen it was Dad. He closed the door, crossed the yard. Shook his head. There's no one here, he said.

But there was. Maybe not in the kennel. Maybe still as far away as Fairbanks. But he was with us, anyhow. I carried him with me the same way I carried Mom, he wouldn't let go. Not long as I still had his money hid under my bed.

Day after we found the footprints outside the kennel, we got a second big snowfall. Dad come home after plowing the next evening and dropped into a chair at the table. Didn't bother to shuck his boots or take off his coat. He'd been gone since early that morning, and the night before I never did hear him come home, it must of been long after I was asleep.

That's the last of it, he said finally. For now.

He wiped a hand over his face. His eyes baggy. The

plowing was decent enough money, he couldn't turn it down. But I suspected that if he was going to miss out on a good night's sleep, he would of preferred to spend those hours on the back of a sled instead of in the seat of his truck.

What's this? I gestured at a loaf of bread he'd brung in with him, wrapped in plastic and unsliced.

Helen Graham made it, he said. She thought you kids might enjoy it. Nice of her.

I dropped the bread. Helen, at the clinic? You went there?

Cleared the parking lot.

Then you went in.

He peeled off his hat. Bent to untie his boots and grunted. Hand me that bottle behind the toaster, would you?

He meant the whiskey Steve had brung over, still half full. I fetched it, along with a glass, and set it before him. He was already exhausted, and a shot or two of whiskey would guarantee sleep that wasn't just deep but bottomless. I felt about six different ways at once. It would be a trial, breaking trail after two big snows. But it would be worth it, just to be on a sled and outside.

But the bread on the counter nagged at me.

So you talked to Helen?

He drained the glass, poured another.

How's—I mean, she hear anything?

I didn't know how to ask what I wanted to ask.

Dad drained his second glass. Mr. Hatch, you mean? he said. He shook his head. She hasn't heard anything since they sent him to Fairbanks. I reckon he got patched up then headed south.

South? My mouth went dry. Why south?

Dad shrugged. What his driver's license said—Oklahoma, I think it was. Or Kansas. One of them middle states.

He yawned then, and stretched, while I tried to imagine myself a grown man, someone far from home and injured, and missing a few thousand dollars. Would I still have enough on me to find a car I could drive after I left the hospital in Fairbanks? And if I did, would I use that money to stay in Alaska just long enough to find the pack I'd dropped in the woods?

Or maybe, instead, with no money and only one thing on my mind, I would hitchhike as far south as I could get, then start walking. And maybe if the weather got cold enough, I would find an unlocked door and a woodstove, and grow so warm after shivering in the biting wind, I'd fall asleep till the owner come home. Jim Lerner's description of his intruder didn't sound like Tom Hatch, but Jim probably hadn't memorized every detail about his visitor or snapped a picture. He might of got the age wrong, the shape of the man. Jim's place was north of ours. Not so far away it would take more than a day or two to walk the distance between.

Which led me to the footprints outside the kennel. There's where my thoughts got tangled up. If Hatch had spent the night in our kennel, he was gone now, he'd chose to dive back into the woods to search for his pack instead of knocking on our door to share with Dad exactly how he come to arrive in our yard with a stab wound that nearly killed him. Which meant maybe I was safe. Except when Hatch didn't find the pack where he'd left it, there was a chance he would come to the house after all. Or maybe he would give up, go back to where he come from. Or maybe he would call the VSO because he was the victim of not one crime but two.

Or maybe he was already back in Oklahoma or Kansas, safe at home in his own bed. There was too many *maybes* for me to sort.

Dad hoisted himself up then, yawned again. I can't keep my eyes open. I'm for bed.

Me too, I said too quick, it was only a little after eight, but he didn't seem to notice how eager I was.

I followed him up the stairs, the house going dark behind us as he clicked off lights one by one. Water running in the bathroom, toilet flushing. Scott, in his room reading, calling good night to us. The floorboards creaking as Dad trudged past my room.

Night, Trace.

Night.

I lay on my bed, still dressed, door cracked. Listening. Waiting. Fretting over a set of footprints and what they might mean.

It was only a handful of minutes before I heard his snores rumble up the hallway, but I made myself wait more than an hour before I got up, long enough to be sure Scott was asleep, too. Old Su and the retired dogs lifted their heads when I come back down the stairs. I crept across the kitchen. At the door, clicked my tongue at Su to follow me.

The second I drug the small sled out of the kennel and the dogs seen it, they started barking. I held my breath and watched the house. Expected a light to shine from Dad's window, him looking down to see what was all the ruckus. But the window stayed dark.

I fastened the snow hook round the trunk of a tree and laid out the rigging, then harnessed the dogs, Zip and Flash, with Su on the lead. One more check to make sure the sandbags in the basket was strapped down tight. Then I stood on the runners, reached back and pulled the snow hook loose. The dogs bolted forward, and the three of us sailed across the yard, onto the familiar trail and into the night.

We run. The air cold against my face, like glass in my lungs. The snow flying up from the ground as the dogs galloped, breaking the trail easier than I expected, sending stinging needles against my cheeks and forehead. No sound except the runners over the new snow and the breathing of the dogs. The moon overhead painted the snow with the slender shadows of bare branches. We passed the tree where Tom Hatch's handprint had long since faded. Bypassed the lake on the alternate trail, the water likely not frozen enough to hold us. Crested the hill with the two boulders on either side of the trail. Come to the place where the trees started to thin out before the river, and that's when a feeling hit me, come down so hard I lost my breath and my eyes welled up. Like someone had took away my heart but I didn't know it and had been walking round empty but not understanding why, till right then, as I stood on the runners of the sled, it come back to me. I felt it inside me, beating strong in my chest for the first time since Mom died. Alive, every speck of me. It wasn't just about the race. I hadn't run the dogs in weeks, and the previous winter I'd spent most of my time alone in the woods, no dog by my side, only the memory of Mom to keep me company. A season without my heart was long enough.

We sprinted into a clearing and I called out, Come gee! to bring the dogs round in a wide U-turn, got them back on the trail. Headed home, slower now. I hopped off the sled from time to time and run alongside it, then worked the dogs to a stop when I come to a spot where I'd set a trap the day before when I managed to sneak out while Dad was plowing. I'd left a figure-four deadfall where a set of ermine tracks made a path near a hollow log. I liked this kind of trap on account of all you need is two heavy rocks and three sticks, you carve notches into the sticks and assemble them so they hold up one rock and when an animal come along to take the bait you have laid, it triggers the trap and the first rock falls and crushes the animal against the other rock.

The deadfall was triggered, but there was no critter. The sticks was broken and scattered, and the rocks should of been one on top of the other with the ermine dead in between. But they was apart, and no ermine in sight. Could've been a marten or a wolf, I had lost plenty of catches to bigger critters hungrier than me. The snow round the trap laid thinner on the ground here where the tamaracks grew close together. I waited for the moon to duck behind a cloud, my eyes grew sharper in the dark, and I studied the places where the snow was trampled. Not by four paws, but two boots.

I stood real still and listened to the night. Watching from the sides of my vision, concentrating on the spaces between trees, the deep pockets of shadow that might hide someone. But he wasn't there. If he was nearby, I would of known. I would of felt him.

I kicked the snow clear of the blurry footprints and scattered what was left of my deadfall, my mind gnawing away at the evidence. So he had come south. Helped himself to whatever he could use in Jim Lerner's unlocked house then laid down, exhausted, in front of Jim's woodstove before getting chased off. Farther south, he didn't bother knocking on our door but headed straight for the kennel, left footprints going in that we would find the next morning. Dad hadn't bothered to look for a set of footprints leading away from the kennel, but he wasn't the one concerned about strangers trespassing, and I hadn't thought of it till later, when a new snow had already fallen and erased any tracks that might of been. Why hadn't we checked to see if anything was missing, one of Dad's tools or the wood axe, or the last hunk of meat in the freezer? A man hungry enough will eat just about anything, including a critter caught by someone else's trap.

But if Tom Hatch come to the woods without stopping by the house first, odds was, all he wanted was his pack. Not to confront me about what I done or turn me in to the village safety officer. Tom Hatch didn't want trouble, he just wanted what was his.

Except he wouldn't find it. If he was this far out, he surely didn't remember where he'd dropped his pack. But the man who'd taught himself enough to survive days, maybe weeks, in the Alaskan wild from just a book was smart enough to figure out someone had stumbled across it and took a look inside. That the most obvious *someone* was the last face he seen before his fortune changed.

I got back on my sled, aware that I had already been gone longer than I'd planned. I run the dogs hard back the way we come, and when we spilled off the trail into the yard, I was certain down to my bones Dad would be there, hands on his hips, waiting to give me a talking-to. Even when I seen he wasn't, every sound in the yard as I took the dogs off the line—every bark, every tree limb creaking, even the crunch of my own boots—made me jump. Till I realized it wasn't the house I kept glancing at. It was the trees. The kennel. The empty space of our yard, where I swore I did see him, a man taller and broader than I remembered, but him just the same, his hand still plastered over his gut, my knife still stuck in him, the hilt of it glimmering in the moonlight. I blinked, and he was gone.

I rubbed Flash's feet, then Zip's, then Su's, scratched their bellies and give them each a treat. Then reversed everything I'd done to start the night, drug the sled back into the kennel and covered it, hid the rigging and harnesses so I'd know which ones to use for my next run. My ears twice their normal size, the scurry of mice in the kennel amplified and transformed into the heavy, careful footsteps of someone who didn't belong, a figure waiting for me to be gone, or to come close enough to touch. When I was done putting gear away, I run outside and slammed the door behind me, forgetting all about my worry that Dad would wake, only wanting to be back inside the house for once, behind locked doors.

We was almost at the house when Old Su suddenly peeled away, reenergized as she galloped toward the road with her ears perked, like she was expecting someone to pull up to the house.

Come back, girl, I called to her.

She turned and trotted to me, brushing past a shadow. A dark shape, facing the road. I jumped when I seen it, my mind still on Hatch. But the longer I stared, I realized it was Mom. My memory of her, anyway.

Standing at the head of the driveway, looking toward the road.

Turn around, I thought but couldn't make myself say out loud. She stayed where she was, shivering under her heavy coat, till the moon come out again and shone down on the empty place where she'd stood.

Come back, I said again.

Upstairs, I shucked off my clothes and crawled into bed. But even though my arms and legs was worn out in that pleasant way that comes after you have been outside and active for a spell, my brain kept me awake with its chattering. I turned on the light and reached under my bed, pulled out the pack. I had smoothed out the money and separated the bills, bundled it all. Surprising how small a stack that much money made, even when a decent portion of it was ones and fives. Surprising how something so small could feel so heavy.

My stomach growled, and I thought about the deadfall, the catch that ought to of been mine but had fed Tom Hatch instead. Wondered how long he would haunt our woods before he showed up on our doorstep.

5

When Scott got old enough, he would ask could he come along when I ventured into the woods with my knife and my rules and no warning from Mom other than Be back by dinner or Don't go any farther than the lake today. Sometimes Mom would distract him with her camera, the two of them would go on their own adventure round the yard, snapping pictures, or they would stay inside and bake cookies or play their own secret games. But other times she would tell me, Let him tag along today, Trace. You can wander around on your own tomorrow.

So I would try and show Scott how to set a simple trap or explain to him that even the tiniest movement would spook most animals. But he fidgeted and whined that he was bored. So we would go walking up the trail till his legs was tired, then turn back round and head home with no catch.

Usually I tried to talk him out of coming with me, instead I would promise to show him something cool if he would agree to stay back. I taught him how to spark a fire with flint and steel, same way Dad had showed me, and how to blow across a sharp blade of grass to make a whistle. I showed him tricks with my knife.

What's *blood brothers*? he asked.

It's just a little cut, I told him. Then we shake hands, and we're blood brothers.

But you're a girl, he said.

My stomach growled. It's just a name, I said and grabbed his hand.

But Dad heard the little yelp Scott give when I cut into the meat of his palm, he chased us both inside asking, What the hell were you thinking?

What's going on? Mom asked. She was setting the table, it was nearly dinnertime.

So Dad tattled on me and Scott showed her the shallow cut bleeding on his hand. Mom give me a look. I braced myself for hollering. But she said, That doesn't look too bad, Scotty. Go wash up and put a bandage on it. You'll be all right. Can you give him a hand, Bill?

Dad nodded. Told me, And you get yourself upstairs till dinner, young lady.

Wait, Trace, Mom said. Why don't you go check your traps? Just the ones nearest the yard.

Dad threw his hands in the air. Didn't you hear me just now, Hannah? I told her to get upstairs.

I heard you just fine.

Then maybe you could back me up instead of telling her the opposite of what I just said.

Tracy, Mom said. Go on outside.

I let the door fall shut behind me and sprinted for the trailhead, left behind the sound of the two of them bickering through the open kitchen window. They was still at it, though, that night when I got home after the house was dark. I walked past their bedroom and heard their voices muffled behind the closed door.

She could've really hurt him, Dad said.

But she didn't, Mom said and her voice sounded tired.

So next time when he comes in bleeding to death, you going to reward her again instead of sending her to her room?

Mom sighed. Bill, I'm sorry. But you've got to understand, sending her to her room doesn't work. I've tried it. You've got to redirect her.

Redirect, he muttered. I don't need a lesson on how to discipline my kid. I swear, Hannah, sometimes you act like you're the only one responsible for raising her.

Sometimes I feel like I am.

What's that supposed to mean?

They both went quiet a spell. I stood outside their door, my head bent. Moonlight spilled across the floor through the window at the end of the hall, bluish-white, it coated everything, the floorboards and the bookshelf and my own bare feet.

Dad spoke real soft. Hey.

I'm trying to think of what to say that won't make me sound crazy, Mom told him.

The bed creaked.

I don't think you're crazy, Dad said.

She give a laugh. Not yet, she said and sighed again. It's just when it comes to Tracy, it's—different. We need to—

What? Dad said.

Mom went, Shh. Then called out, Tracy?

I froze. I could feel her listening for me. I crept away from the door silent as I could. Mom's ears was nearly good as mine, keen enough to hear my bare feet shuffle away from their door, to hear the tiny *click* of my own door closing.

Next morning, she was waiting for me, boots on.

Let's go, she said.

Where?

Hunting.

She might of suggested we shave our heads and fly to the moon. I stared at her as she tucked herself into an old pilled sweater, then moved toward the door.

Well, she said. We doing this, or what?

We followed the trail into the woods, walking but not speaking. A quarter mile in or so, she grinned at me, then bumped me with her hip before she took off, sprinting through the woods.

I run after her. The two of us bounding over the packed dirt, me in my bare feet, her in her clunky boots. But she was faster than she looked and I stretched my legs and pumped my arms to keep pace with her. My heart sending blood surging through my veins, it warmed every part of me and I felt stronger and faster than ever, but still she pulled away. She disappeared round a bend and when I followed, she was farther and farther ahead.

When she finally stopped and I caught up, the two of us laid on the ground beside the trail, catching our breath.

She sighed, then sat up. That felt good, didn't it? she said. I miss this.

It hadn't occurred to me, till she said it, that this was the first time I ever seen her in the woods without Dad. She always come on family walks, or the two of them exercising a new pack of pups together, but she never explored the woods with just me or Scott, and definitely never on her own.

Come on, Trace, she said. You've got your knife, right? Show me what you know.

So we pushed through the woods, looking for a good spot for me to set a snare. Then we was quiet a long time, sitting close enough together I could feel the heat coming off her body. Till a marten come along and found itself caught. I showed Mom how I used the knife she'd give me, where I knew to cut and let the blood out till whatever I caught was dead and ready to bring home to skin and butcher.

Go ahead, she said as I bled the marten.

I hesitated. It wasn't hard to recall how she had hollered the one time she caught me with Scott's blood on my mouth.

It's okay, she said.

So I held the critter close. A warm, metallic flood over my tongue, and in my head I went scurrying down the trunk of a tree to where I knew voles nested and made their burrows, I sniffed the air and smelled something curious and trotted past the vole place and into a cluster of birch trees, closer to the scent, like sticky sweet berries, and took a final step forward to taste the bit of jam smeared on a rock before the snare closed.

Most animals I found in my traps was hours, maybe days dead. When you have an animal that is dying as you hold it in your arms, rather than one that has been dead a spell, it is hot, you can feel the heat of it spread through you, and what you learn from it is as clear as if you're seeing with your own eyes. Any taste will give you a moment. But in the drink that comes with a critter's last breath, you get a whole history. Everything it has done and felt comes to you like it is happening at the exact moment you are learning it. You take in a whole life with the killing drink.

I finished. My skin buzzing with another creature's death and life, I felt I could run another ten miles and this time keep up with Mom no matter how fast she went. But I stood there, waiting to see what she would do.

She said, Leave the carcass. We'll come back for it.

We went deeper into the woods, stopping by a slender branch of the river so I could wash the blood from my hands and face. As we walked, she didn't say much, except to quiz me on the plants we found. Back then, I couldn't identify too many, I was more keen on pointing out animal tracks and piles of scat.

You need to know these things, Mom said and showed me a patch of monkshood, which looked a little like wild geranium, same color only the buds was more clumped together. You can eat the flowers and leaves of the geranium, but the monkshood is poisonous. There are all kinds of plants and roots you can eat, but you have to be able to tell the good ones from the dangerous ones.

I don't see the point in eating a plant, I said. You don't get nothing from it the way you do a critter.

No, Mom said. But it'll keep you going if you're hungry and there's nothing to hunt.

We walked a good bit, then turned round, made our way back to the marten. I slung it over my shoulder to take back and have Dad show me how to skin it.

Mom smiled.

What? I said.

It just reminds me, she said as we made our way to the trail again. There was this day, earlier this summer, you were here in the woods. Of course. I was in the kitchen. Making bread, I think. But mostly watching for you. You were gone all morning. When I finally saw you come into the yard, you had some dead thing slung over your shoulder. You've gotten so good with traps. The sun was shining in your hair, and you were already tan from being outside all the time. You looked like the healthiest person alive.

She looked down at me. Right then, she said, more than anything, you know what I wanted?

What?

I wanted to let you be, she said.

There was a churning in my head, her words tumbling over themselves and rearranging till they lined up another way. I began to lay each moment of the day next to another, like building a lean-to, at first all you have is separate branches but when you connect them, they create something whole, a safe place for you to stay. My surprise at Mom wanting to come into the woods with me. How her face hadn't changed when she watched me drink. Her own words when I told her a plant wasn't any kind of substitute for an animal. You can learn plenty of things just by watching and thinking. But certain things you can only know because you experienced them yourself.

I wanted to let you be, she'd said. But what I heard now was, *I wanted to be you.*

Why don't you come out to the woods on your own? I asked her.

She studied the trees and the gray sky peeking between branches. Her hands tucked into the pockets of her Carhartts as she walked, her cheeks red with the damp chill that clung to the day.

Who taught you to hunt? I tried instead.

Who taught you?

I frowned.

You taught yourself, didn't you? she said. You watched the woods and learned from observation. And then you caught your first animal. A vole, wasn't it? And from that, you learned—what? Do you remember?

I thought back to that day, the first animal I ever tasted, even before I managed to kill something myself. I must of been only four or five. Stepping from the warm grass of the sunlit yard into the shadowy woods and finding the vole, barely alive, its scent was what drew me to it. It fit in my two hands cupped together. And when I tasted it, my head flooded with moonlight, a stirring, a twitching in my muscles, and I poked my head from my nest then run through a warren underground till I found my way to the surface, full moon overhead, bright as daylight.

I told her, I learned that if the moon is bright enough, a vole will think it's daytime and come out to feed.

And when did you catch your next vole? Mom asked.

On a full-moon night, I said.

There you go.

I remembered, too, her finding me at the edge of our woods, and her arms round me as she carried me inside. How bright the bathroom seemed as she knelt before me and scrubbed my skin till it was almost raw and my face stung.

You didn't want me to, I said.

To what?

Drink, I said. Did you?

She sighed. When I was a girl, younger than you are now, I just did what came natural. I never thought to ask anyone about it or find out if it was the same for other little girls. My brothers never hunted, not the way you do. The way I did.

The way your own mom done?

She shook her head. I never saw her hunt. We weren't very alike, my mom and me. I used to hear stories about my grandmother, things that made me think we were the same. But I never knew her. They say she disappeared shortly after my mom was born. My own mother never seemed to know what to do with me. I think, sometimes, she was almost afraid of me.

She stopped, so I stopped, too. She bent a little so we was eye to eye, and I seen for the first time she didn't have to bend as far as she used to.

I never wanted you to feel that way, she said. Once I knew that you took after me, I wanted— She brushed her hand over my hair. I wanted something different for you, she said.

Everything between us, everything we shared, hung in the air like a held breath, I could almost see it. I was afraid to say the wrong thing and bring the whole thing down.

I couldn't help it, though. You don't hunt no more, I said.

She didn't say nothing. Just started to walk again.

You don't need it? I asked.

She kept her eyes on the trail, but her thoughts traveled her face, I could see her working through a puzzle. Finally she said, You can learn to live without it. You just need a good enough reason.

What was your reason?

You, she said. When I found out I was pregnant with you. Everyone talks about how exciting it is when you know you're going to have a baby. But no one tells you how scared you'll be.

I thought of her own mom again, someone I had only seen in pictures, a frowning, fretful-looking woman who clung to her sons but seemed to keep her distance from the daughter who was always slightly blurry, never still long enough to take a decent photo.

You was scared of me.

Not of you, Mom said. Scared for you, I guess.

What's that mean?

It started to rain then, the lightest drizzle. I could barely feel the drops on my skin, but the rain on the leaves of the trees built a cave round us, only the two of us enclosed in it together, no one else.

It's kind of your job, she said, when you're a parent,

to be scared for your kids. I worry about all sorts of things. Not just for you, but Scott, too.

Scott was not like me at all, mostly content to stay indoors all afternoon, even when the sun come out for its slim few hours in the deepest part of winter and made the snow sparkle. I ached on days like that, fidgeted and burned till I burst through the door and sprinted across the snow. There was more difference between me and Scott than just him being a boy and me being a girl.

I worry about different things for Scott, she went on. I worry that he'll get hurt.

I frowned.

That I'll hurt him.

I'm talking more about the inside. He's so quiet and tenderhearted. He takes in much more than you think he does.

I remembered the one time I had bit him, the taste of his blood on my tongue as I pulled away. The experience of him, his own experience. I knew after that day that he couldn't bear shouting if he thought it meant a fight, and that he closed his eyes when someone else got a shot or cut themselves not because he was afraid of blood but because he could almost feel their pain himself.

We was nearly back home. I could see the dog yard

and the house in the spaces between the trees. Everything quiet except the sound of the rain. Soon enough we would step out of this cave we had made, back into our regular life. But I stopped us, reached out to grab her hand. I could stop, I said. I wanted to take back the offer soon as I made it. But I didn't.

Her hand was cold in mine. Do you want to?

The rain fell harder. I didn't know how to answer her. There wasn't no part of me that truly wanted to stop hunting. But I did want to please her.

We come to the trailhead, walking slow despite the rain. The dogs barked a greeting. Smoke curled from our chimney into the slate-colored sky.

You're old enough now, she went on, you don't need most of the rules I gave you. Except the last one.

Never make a person bleed, I said automatically.

She squeezed my hand, stopped me. I'm serious, Tracy. You've broken that rule too many times already.

I flushed. I could find Scott inside me, the feelings and experience I'd took from him. The alarm going off in Aaron's head like a fire drill when he seen what I done to the cat. And before that, when I was even younger, and she'd tried to put me in kindergarten, the classroom was crowded and loud and bright, too much light, waves of color and faces and voices, I felt panic rear up in me. Then an arm reached too close, a curious hand touching me, and then a wail. And red. And hands pulling me off the little boy whose face was bleeding where my teeth sunk in.

I'm sorry, I said again.

She shook her head. It's okay. But you can't do it again. You hear me?

I nodded.

I mean it, she said. It's fine to hunt animals all you want. You don't have to stop that. But when it comes to people, you cannot break that rule. Promise me.

There was more I wanted to ask. Like why people and animals had to be different. Why learning from one could be easy, but when it come to the more complicated creature, you had to do things the hard way. If you had a way to be as close as you could to another person, why wouldn't you use it?

But we was at the house now, Dad and Scott on the other side of the door, I could hear them in the kitchen, and Mom was waiting on my promise. So I give it to her.

6

I snuck out the next night, a run with four dogs on the line that took me farther than the night before, past the lake but not quite to the river. By the time my head hit my pillow I only managed a couple hours' sleep before Dad poked his head in my room and said, Morning, Trace. Breakfast time.

He meant the dogs' breakfast, not mine. My belly was still full from my night run anyway, I'd found two traps triggered with critters I bled right where I stood. I'd found a third trap, too. Its catch missing. About two miles closer to home than the first empty trap.

My luck run out the next couple nights. For months the fridge had been making noise like a small plane about to take off, till finally it found another noise to make, and Dad spent a whole evening tinkering with it, way past his usual bedtime, trying to suss out whether it was something he could fix or if he'd have to spend the money to hire someone. I looked round the kitchen, the counter crowded with plastic containers full of leftovers and the milk slowly warming next to the three eggs we had left. Trudged up the stairs to my bed. There wouldn't be no chance to slip past him that night.

The next evening, I went to bed early, still in my sweater and jeans, and set my clock to wake me near midnight. But when I crept halfway down the stairs, I seen a light on in the kitchen. The room was quieter than it had been in a good while, the old buzzing fridge was gone, Steve Inga had helped Dad haul it away that afternoon. No replacement yet, Dad would have to fetch a new fridge from Fairbanks, which meant a long drive, not to mention the money he didn't have to spend.

One of the house dogs whined. Dad's shadow lifted its arm then lowered again, and glass clinked against glass. I could even hear him swallow. Next morning, there would only be about an inch of whiskey left in the bottle Steve had brung. I sat on the stairs a spell, listening to Dad drink, till he got up and crossed the room. A small clatter as he picked the phone up off its hook, the beep of numbers as he dialed.

Yeah, it's me, he said after a moment. Sorry to call so late.

A pause. Then, That's why I'm calling. I changed my mind. Think you can make it happen?

He give a long, heavy sigh. Said, I know. I'll deal with it some way. 'Preciate your help, Steve.

He grunted as he sat back down, and I stole upstairs. My stomach cramped and growled.

During the day, I fed the dogs and stacked wood and watched the trees, as if any second Tom Hatch would stroll back into the yard, come straight for me, asking after his pack.

When I wasn't thinking about Hatch, though, I was planning for my race season. February, and the Junior, was getting closer day by day, and then it would be time for the Iditarod before I could turn round twice. If I was going to sneak out often enough at night to train proper, I needed Dad to have fewer sleepless nights. But that wasn't nothing I could control.

In the meantime, I went against every instinct in me and volunteered to drive into the village to fetch groceries, even though the sight of trees flinging themselves past the truck's windows made me sick to my stomach.

Dad raised his eyebrows. You feeling okay? he asked, teasing. I mean, you must've come down with something if you're offering to drive into town.

Ha, I said. I'm just trying to lend a hand. But if you don't want the help— I shrugged.

No, no, by all means, he said and tossed his keys across the room to me.

Once I got to the village, I rushed through the shopping quick as I could, then run my real errand. Walked to the post office and slipped two envelopes in the out box, one addressed to the Junior Iditarod's committee and one addressed to the Iditarod's, stacks of ten- and twenty-dollar bills in each to pay for my race fees. I knew I oughtn't send cash in the mail, but that couldn't be helped.

Course, after I volunteered to drive into the village once, Dad was keen to take advantage of what he called my *unexpected willingness*. A couple days later we drove in together to pick up bags of dog kibble. We loaded the truck down with dozens of fifty-pound bags, then swung by the school to pick up Scott. When we pulled in Scott was sitting outside, fiddling with his camera.

What's up? Dad asked him.

There's something wrong with the lens, maybe, Scott said. I can't get it to focus right.

Let me take a look, Dad said and leaned against the truck, messing with the camera. I shifted from one foot to the other, ready to get back on the road. I was eager to turn in early that evening so I could get up and run the dogs again after the two of them had gone to bed. Plus, it had been days since I'd hunted. My head was swimmy and out of sorts, my belly hollow.

We holding you up? Dad said wryly. You're in such a hurry, you drive.

Fine, I told him.

We crawled our way through the village, then onto the highway. I wound the truck up, seemed to me like we was going plenty fast, till Dad looked up and said, Christ, Tracy, you can't go forty on a road like this. Someone comes along going seventy, they're going to run us right over.

I inched the truck up to forty-five.

Oh, for Pete's sake— He made a strange, choked sound, and at first I thought he was mad, but I wasn't about to go no faster, the trees already whipping past the windows quicker than I liked. But then he gasped and chortled, and I realized he was laughing at me.

What the hell? I asked as Scott joined in. *What?*

Dad shook his head, gradually got hold of himself. The way you looked! he exclaimed. He clenched his fists and his teeth, hunched forward and glared out the windshield, his eyes big as plates. Scott cackled at his imitation.

I shook my head, irritated. But a smile crept over

my face. It was nice, both of them laughing, even if it was at my expense. You going to let me drive, or sit there making fun of me? I asked.

I can't do both? Dad grinned at me.

An hour or so later, I steered the truck into the driveway. When we rolled past the trees that shielded our property from the road there was a shape waiting for us halfway between the dog yard and the house. Even though I could see with my own eyes it wasn't Tom Hatch, my mouth went dry. For a moment it *was* Hatch, the shape held something in its hands, my eyes seen it and my brain turned it into a knife, my knife, even though that was impossible since my knife was in my pocket like it always was.

The shape that wasn't Hatch raised its hand *hello*. My muscles tensed up, my foot pushed the pedal to the floor, and we rocketed forward.

Brake! Dad shouted. *Brake!*

I slammed the brake, the truck slid another three feet on the hardpacked snow, and we stopped just shy of the corner of the house.

Dad give me a look. Maybe you shouldn't drive after all, he said.

Calmer now, I could take in what was in front of me instead of what my panicked brain thought it seen. The shape coming toward us wasn't tall or broad but thin and barely taller than me, though it tried to make itself look bigger with clothes that didn't fit. Its baggy jacket wasn't warm enough for the time of year. When it got closer, I seen its pants was held up by a hank of rope.

Help you? Dad asked.

I hope so, the stranger said. Now that we was closer, you could see that even though his clothes was ill-fit he had tried to make himself presentable, he was real clean shaven and his reddish-brown hair combed, hat in his hand.

You ain't here about the room for rent? Dad said.

That's right, the stranger said. His words come out slow, like a tide creeping in.

Well, it ain't much, Dad said. But you're welcome to take a look.

Scott had already gone up to the house, but I trailed behind them round the back where the shed was. The building was about ten by fourteen foot, there wasn't much room, but the three of us crowded in so the visitor could take a look. It was clean even if it was small, and you would be pretty cozy and warm even after the fire in the stove died for the night.

When we stepped back outside, Dad said, It's pretty spare. I reckon you could find something nicer in the village. More convenient. But you're welcome to use the kitchen and the bath up at the house as you like. I got two kids, Tracy here, and you probably saw Scott before he disappeared. They won't bother you none.

This'll do just fine, the visitor said in his deliberate way. I'm not inclined to be in town.

Dad leaned on the handle of his axe and looked the visitor up and down. You got anyone to vouch for you?

I'm not from around here. But I worked for a guy down in Ketchikan this summer. I could give you his number.

Dad waved a hand. No worries, he said. Anyway, like the ad says, rent's two hundred a month.

Up at the house, Old Su nosed open the back door and come down the stairs, moseyed over. Went up to the stranger and give him a sniff, then put her snout right in his pocket.

Su, come here, I said.

The visitor glanced at me, then pushed Su away, gentle. The thing is, he said, I was hoping we could make a trade.

A trade, Dad said.

I'm a hard worker, the visitor said. And it looks like you could use someone.

Dad raised an eyebrow. We're doing fine. Don't need help. What I need is someone who can pay rent.

But one glance round the yard told you what anyone with eyeballs could see, that even with me doing my chores every day, there was plenty more still needed doing. The back stoop of the house sagged at one end and the yard was littered with half-finished projects and broken-down snow machines and unrepaired sleds. The dog yard had never looked so empty. I felt my cheeks flush.

The visitor nodded. Then said, You're a musher, that much is clear. No disrespect, sir, but if you were really fine, you'd be on a sled right now and I'd be standing here talking to myself.

Dad was quiet. Stood with his hands in his pockets. Then cleared his throat. You ever worked with dogs before?

Sure.

Where was this?

Montana.

Dad raised his eyebrows. You know Gerald Vetch?

Oh, sure.

That right? Dad scratched his beard. That meant he was rolling a thought over in his head. Gerald and me come out of the chute back-to-back the first year I won the Iditarod. We ran neck and neck the whole way through the Quest once. Every time one of us stopped, there the other one was. Real good guy. How's he doing these days?

Real good, the visitor said.

Dad gazed at the dog yard, still stroking his beard.

Dad? I spoke up.

But he was lost in his own thoughts. I often wished I could know what was going on in his head, but never more than right at that moment. I felt desperate to know if he was recalling how Tom Hatch had lurched into our yard just weeks before, or if he was reminding himself of what he'd told me, that you never knew who might come roaming through the woods. Or showing up on our doorstep.

Why don't we do this, Dad finally said. You stick around this afternoon, give me a hand. Then we'll see about the long term. How's that sound?

Fair enough, the stranger said.

Dad put out his hand. Well, what do I call you?

Jesse Goodwin.

Goodwin's hand was as small as the rest of him. He give Dad a shake, but when he went to pull away, Dad held on.

You don't mind me asking, how old are you, son?

For the second time, Goodwin's eyes fell on me. He shifted his weight from one foot to the other. Seventeen, he said.

All right, Dad said and let go. Let me show you the kennel.

Ain't you going to help me unload the kibble? I called after him.

He looked back over his shoulder. Leave it, he said. Do me a favor, take an armload of wood inside. Then you can do as you please, long as you're home for dinner.

The two of them cut through the dog yard. Goodwin put out a hand as he walked, let the dogs sniff his fingers. Dad was talking, gesturing, and Goodwin nodded. He was what you call *slight*, he looked like a strong wind might blow him away. In that way, we was not alike. But as he fell into step with my dad, watching him from behind I could almost imagine I was watching myself.

Old Su trotted away from me and caught up to him, her nose in his pocket again.

I frowned. Back when Mom trained dogs, she would reward them with treats tossed from a supply in the pockets of her coat. After the dogs she was training had spent enough time with her, they got into the habit of greeting her by sticking their noses in her pocket, searching for the treats they knew was there. It had been ages since Old Su had been trained. She was near retirement, almost as old as Homer and Canyon. And she was smart enough to know only Mom ever carried treats in her pockets. Me and Scott and Dad, we just fetched them from the big bin in the kennel. There hadn't been no treats to speak of for a good while, neither.

The last several days begun to connect themselves like dots in a puzzle book. The ruckus we'd heard in the kennel linked up to the footprints outside, to the trap I'd come upon, missing its kill but surrounded by the same set of prints. Prints that belonged to a foot only a little larger than mine. It was possible Tom Hatch was a big man with dainty feet, I hadn't took particular note of his shoes the day I stabbed him. But it was more likely that small feet belonged to a small person. A person who'd maybe spent too long in the woods, who was desperate enough to steal the catch from someone else's trap. A person who didn't mind breaking into a kennel or using treats to bribe the dogs to be quiet when he done so. A person who would walk right into someone else's home, fall asleep in front of the warm fire. Jim Lerner wasn't a musher, but he had two big malamutes, and I would of bet all the money in Tom Hatch's pack that whatever treats Jim kept on hand had gone missing that same day.

Tom Hatch wasn't haunting our woods and searching for the pack he'd left behind. He was up in Fairbanks, in a hospital bed. Or maybe on a train or an airplane, on his way back to Kansas or Oklahoma, resigned to the thought of losing a little money and a book he loved. The stranger I'd been worried about was exactly that, a stranger. Some kid barely older than me, a runaway. Or a person who come up to Alaska like Kleinhaus, thinking he could make a go of it in the wilderness till a harsh enough spell of weather taught him otherwise.

A sound tumbled out of me, like a cough. Not loud enough to make Dad turn round before he stepped inside the kennel. His voice faint, then muffled when he shut the door and went on giving Jesse Goodwin the lay of our land. Which I suspected Goodwin was plenty familiar with.

I headed back toward the woodshed, glancing over my shoulder as I walked. I couldn't tell Dad my suspicions without telling him about my trap, and that meant explaining what I was doing out in the middle of the night, staring at a set of footprints, when I wasn't supposed to be anywhere near the woods, much less on a dogsled.

In the woods, when you set a snare near a critter's den, it could be hours before that critter come back, and even then it might catch your scent and approach careful, long minutes of watching your prey turn its ears and sniff the air. In those moments, you want to lunge, grab at the animal before it decides to turn tail and run. But that is the wrong move. If you can be patient, keep your eyes open and wait for your prey to come near, you can catch it before it even knows you was watching it.

I could be patient.

I collected an armful of wood and stacked it inside, next to the woodstove in the kitchen. Stood up, and my head went fuzzy. I stumbled back and dropped into one of the kitchen chairs, lightheaded, my hands shaking. Bent double, my head on my knees, till it passed. Canyon walked over and sniffed at me, his tail wagging. Dog breath in my face, his cold nose on my cheek till I lifted my head and petted him. I was hungry, but relieved, too. The days I'd spent worrying over Tom Hatch had took a toll. I might have to worry over Jesse Goodwin, but he was here in plain sight, where I could keep an eye on him, no longer sneaking round in our woods, invisible to me.

I did go into the woods then. No dogs, just me and my knife. The traps I found triggered still had their catch. As I field-dressed a couple of minks I wondered how long Jesse Goodwin had wandered our woods before he showed up in the yard. At least a few days, I reckoned. I wiped the blade of my knife clean.

I made it back home in time for dinner, like Dad had

asked. Found him stirring a pot of leftover beans while I knocked the snow off my boots in the mudroom.

Any luck? he asked.

Got you a couple furs, I told him.

He set the table with spoons and bowls, then bustled over to the oven and took out a loaf of warm bread. Whistling.

I washed my hands at the sink. Through the window I could see Jesse Goodwin making himself at home in our shed. He'd left the door open and lit the woodstove and the little oil lamp, and his shadow danced over the walls as he moved about.

So I guess he's staying, I said. Even though he can't pay rent.

The whistling stopped. He's a real good worker, Dad said. You should've seen what a quick job he made of cleaning the dog yard. He's good with mechanics, too. Thinks he can figure out whatever's making that noise in the truck. And you heard him say he worked down in Ketchikan? He was on a boat. He'll be a real hand come summer if I can get out to fish camp with Steve. Probably clean salmon in half the time I can.

He smiled at me. That's something you won't even do, Trace.

He was right. I do not see the point in fish at all,

they are cold and slimy and you don't get no satisfaction from them, the most they are good for, far as I'm concerned, is mixing with kibble and a little rice to feed your dogs.

Dad was back at the counter, slicing the bread. Whistling again. His sleeves rolled up, his arms and face chapped from working outdoors in the cold. There was still circles under his eyes and he needed to put on about ten pounds to look like his old self. But he sailed across the room, back over to the pot, then to the table. It should of made me glad to see him so clearly happy. I shouldn't of begrudged him a little joy. But he didn't know what I knew.

Supper's about ready, he said. Can you run out and let Jesse know?

It wasn't that he asked me. He was always asking me to do all kinds of things, and half the time it wasn't asking but telling. It was the way the question fell out of his mouth, casual like. Like the way you say, Would you hand me that hammer? or Don't forget to do your homework. The kinds of sentences that come out with barely any thought, you've said them so many times before. He said Jesse's name, and it come out like it tasted familiar to him.

I hung the towel I'd used to dry my hands. What'd he say? I asked.

What'd who say? Dad said.

When you told him Gerald Vetch died about a year before Mom did, I said. What'd Jesse have to say then?

Dad turned the burner off. When he frowned, you could see the circles under his eyes, darker than ever.

Go on upstairs and get your brother, he said.

He went out to get Jesse himself.

7

Between the time Mom come on that first hunt with me and when she stopped leaving the house altogether, there was a long spell when we would run together down the trail, me at her heels, till the day I finally caught up with her, run alongside her, then pulled ahead. I thought she let me, that the next time we run, she would outpace me again. But after that, she never beat me. I always left her behind.

I would hunt or check traps while she only watched. Sometimes I would ask her for advice. But she was only interested in teaching me about plants and roots, or sometimes we would pick out a set of tracks and follow them far as we could.

When I drunk, I drunk alone.

She was full of information about what to forage, and

the woods filled with her voice when we walked together. But she skirted round the things I really wanted to know. We dug into the snow to unearth greens, clover and lamb's-quarters and rose hips, wilted but still edible. Our fingers touching as she explained what was good to eat and what was poison. When what I wanted her to explain was how she'd managed to stop hunting. Or what made her take her first drink. How she knew people was different from animals, had she bit the boy she'd told me about, the one that had got lost when she was a girl? We huddled close over the hole, shoulder to shoulder, and she spoke in her easy, patient way. Every question I wanted to ask would be an interruption. Her face would cloud over and her mouth would close, and the day would be finished, whether we'd spent an afternoon or only an hour together.

We brushed the snow from our knees when we stood. I put my foot down in her footprints as we walked, tucked my questions away to be asked some other time.

By the first week of November, Jesse Goodwin had got the old truck running, the one that had been up on blocks since before Mom died. He sat in the cab one evening after dinner, put the key in the ignition, and the engine complained for a handful of seconds then finally turned over. The sound traveled across the yard, up the shoveled path to the back stoop, which didn't sag no more, through the back door, oiled so the hinges didn't whine every time you come in or out. Into the mudroom, all the coats hanging on a new rack instead of a row of raw nails pounded into the wall. Into the kitchen, sink empty and that night's dishes drying, past the laundry room, no more piles of dirty clothes that waited weeks to get clean. Up the stairs and down the hall to my room, where I sharpened my knife and readied myself for a day in the woods.

It's funny how quick you can get used to something long as it's consistent, even if it don't sit well with you. In just a handful of days, really, I had got used to finding Jesse knocking snow off his boots in the mudroom. Jesse warming his hands over the burn barrel. Jesse in the kennel, Jesse at the kitchen table.

Or he'd be holed up in the shed. What time he spent not working or taking his meals with us he spent there, a sliver of him visible through the gap in the curtain, sitting at the small table he'd built from wood scraps, writing in his notebook, or laid on top of the quilt on his cot, turning the pages of some novel he'd borrowed from our shelves.

Tracy, come away from there, Dad said. Give the man some privacy.

I done just that. I steered clear of him best I could,

and when the two of us ended up doing the same chore, both of us feeding the dogs or shoveling snow, I give him a wide berth. But I kept my eyes on him. Dad might of trusted Jesse. I knew better.

Jesse glanced up, caught me watching him. I lowered my gaze quick, but not before I seen him give a small, shy smile.

Early November, Dad picked up a job in the village. He spent a couple days a week at the clinic mopping floors and being the handyman. It was just part-time is what he said, and temporary, he only wanted to get ahead on some bills, and now that he had a hand at home, he could take on steady work.

Being a musher is work enough, I wanted to tell him. Except he seemed to of forgot all about that.

I hadn't. Dad took to staying up later than normal after Jesse first arrived, or else he would turn in and I would creep down the stairs an hour or so later only to find the lamp lit in Jesse's shed. I couldn't know how deeply Jesse slept or whether the dogs would wake him with their excitement when they seen the sled, but I could wait and see. Once Dad took the job at the clinic, he started turning in early again, and I took that as my chance.

I drug the sled out of the kennel round midnight to the dogs' barks and howls. Glanced at the dark shed, certain that Jesse would pop his head out and ask what was all the ruckus. Then probably remark to Dad the next morning how odd it was I run at night instead of the day. I darted back inside the kennel, come out again with handfuls of snacks, and soon every dog was too busy gnawing at little chunks of frozen rabbit or squirrel to bother yapping and waking Jesse up. I felt more at ease, even though I kept one eye on the shed as I got four dogs on the line.

We run fast that night, gobbling up more miles than I'd managed on the rest of my runs that winter, and when we come back, me sweaty and the dogs panting, it was nearly time for Dad to get up. I threw out the snow hook and brought my team to a stop. Took Flash off the line and led her to her house. I'd been inclined to make Flash my lead once race time come round, and that night had settled it, she was calm and focused and even now as I got her settled she watched me with alert eyes. At least till her attention pulled away from me and landed on Jesse, already dressed for the day, unclipping Zip's harness. I hadn't even heard him cross the yard.

Zip lunged and jumped, not trying to get away but still feeling playful after our run. Jesse struggled to keep hold of her.

A queasy feeling rose in my gut, but all I said was, Keep a firm grip on her harness. But don't pull her to where you want to go. Kneel down and give her a good scratch.

Jesse squatted and held on to Zip with one hand while he stroked her fur with the other. Murmured to her, Good girl, that's right, his voice and his touch calming her till she sat with her tongue out and her ears soft.

She'll mind you now, I said. You can lead her to her house.

He walked her over to her spot, then fished some treats from his pocket. Let her lick his face after, then wrestled with her a little. I watched the two of them while I fed the dogs who'd run that night.

Zip always wants to play, I told Jesse as I filled Zip's bowl. Sometimes you just got to let her know it's quiet time. All that energy's what makes her a good racing dog, though.

You've got a real way with them, Jesse said.

That's what Dad always tells me.

He followed me over to the sled. I started winding the rigging up so it wouldn't tangle.

I'm not going to say anything, he offered.

About what?

I don't imagine you're out here in the middle of the night because you prefer to mush at four A.M., he said. When I didn't reply, he said, Your dad told me you're mad because you can't train. But I guess you found a way.

The two of them, chattering like squirrels together. Dad couldn't seem to keep his mouth shut round Jesse.

He don't got any business telling you anything about me, I said.

Jesse returned to Zip, begun massaging her feet. After I drug the sled inside, I come back out and found he had moved on to Hazel. She rolled onto her back and let him rub her belly.

You're pretty good with them, too, I heard myself say. You have your own dogs?

He didn't answer right away. Shook his head, then said, Well, yeah, at my grandpa's place. I pretty much grew up there after my parents died. Up in Maine. Grandpa had about thirty dogs, and I was practically one of the pack. He blushed under the light in the dog yard. That probably sounds silly.

No, I said. Sounds familiar.

He fished a treat from his pocket, offered it to Hazel.

I thought you said you was from Montana, I said.

He glanced up. Not from there, he said. Just passed through before I headed up this way.

So you lived in Maine?

He nodded.

With your grandparents.

Right, he said.

They was mushers?

Not really, he said. Mostly just used dogs as transportation or to haul stuff. My grandpa didn't start mushing till he retired.

Retired from what?

He was a schoolteacher. Then Jesse laughed. Said, He might have been the only musher who would recite Shakespeare from the back of his sled.

He stood up then, so I stood up, too. We was close enough, I could see the spray of freckles on his cheeks and the smoothness of his skin. I was nearly tall as he was, which wasn't very, and I was broader across. It occurred to me that if we was ever to get into a scuffle, the odds of me coming out on top was pretty certain.

Seventeen's awful young to come all that way, I said.

What do you mean?

I hesitated. He knew I wasn't supposed to be training, but he'd agreed not to rat on me without me even asking. Then again, that meant he had something on me. Wouldn't hurt to let him know I had something on him, too.

I don't know, I said. Just, you said you was seventeen. And you come clear across the country, up to Alaska. That's a lot of time on your own. A lot of time wandering round in the woods.

His eyes was gray, almost colorless in the light of the lamp in the dog yard, and his face placid as a lake on a calm day.

You ever do much trapping? I asked.

His face didn't change as he said, It's nearly morning. I should put some coffee on. He turned away from me, back toward the house. Stopped just outside the circle of light cast by the lamp, the shape of him visible but the expression on his face lost in shadow. You're seventeen yourself, aren't you? he said. Your dad told me you've got a birthday coming in March.

So?

So you spend a lot of time alone in the woods, Jesse said. A lot of people would ask about that. A girl on her own in the woods.

So? I said again.

He turned, his voice come over his shoulder. No telling what you might get up to out there. Then he scuffled away, dissolved as he moved into the shadows between the dog yard and the house.

I had stood still as stone when I'd found my trap triggered but the catch missing, the first night I'd snuck out for a run. I had strained to hear if someone was nearby. No movement in the brush, no fall of snow or crunch underfoot as someone slipped away or come closer to watch as I reset the trap. But I had made other stops that night, other opportunities for someone already roaming the woods to keep themselves hid while I drained the catch I did find.

And how long had Jesse been in our woods before that night? What else had he seen?

Just a few words and he had me fretting the rest of the day. That was how Jesse Goodwin worked, I noticed over the next weeks. I never heard him suggest an idea, not once. He never said the first word, just appeared out of nowhere to quietly go about his work till Dad noticed him. Still he wouldn't say nothing, waiting for Dad to start asking questions or building on the idea that Jesse'd already had. Then Jesse would nod and agree, make Dad feel like he was the one who'd come up with their next project. Water don't run a straight course, it winds round trees and boulders, snakes through mountain passes, tumbling downhill to reach its destination. Watching Jesse, I begun to learn sometimes it's easier to get what you want by taking your time and going round the obstacles, instead of trying to plow right through them.

That's the way the dog wheel come about. Jesse had took to lingering in the kitchen after dinner most nights, either to play cards with Dad or help Scott with his homework. That night, he hunched over the little notebook he always carried in his pocket, a stub of pencil in his hand as he scribbled, lines going this way and that.

It was Scott who piped up first. He'd pushed his math book aside to watch Jesse draw. That looks like Flash, Scott said.

I was set on ignoring whatever Jesse was doing, but at the mention of Flash I had to look up. He had drew my lead dog exactly right, somehow with just a pencil he'd managed to show the intelligent light in her eyes.

But Flash was only a detail in a larger picture. Jesse had drew something like a giant bicycle wheel without the rim or tire. The hub of it was stuck in the ground and it had six spokes, each one ended in a platform. On top of each platform was a box that looked like our dogs' houses. The Flash he'd sketched was running, attached to the end of one spoke by a lead.

What's that? Dad had leaned forward in his chair to get a better look. Some kind of training wheel?

Jesse nodded. There's a lever over here, a kind of brake. You release that, and the dogs can run in circles till they get tired. When that happens, they can hop up into the box to rest.

Dad raised his eyebrows, drew the book closer to study the picture. That's pretty clever, he said. Wonder how hard it would be to put something like this together. It'd be a good way to keep the dogs from getting antsy. Although they've been pretty calm, lately.

Jesse didn't respond, but his eyes found mine, the quickest touch. Then he looked back at his own drawing.

My face burned. I got up and run water over our dinner dishes.

Though, that's a lot of lumber, Dad said.

You could do it with scrap wood, Jesse pointed out. That's what we used in Whitehorse.

You lived in the Yukon? I asked.

He didn't bother to turn or look at me. Passed through, he said.

We've got lots of wood out back, Scott was saying to Dad.

Just need some nails and about five or six wheels, looks like, Dad said. It was clear he was already calculating the cost. The three of them bent over a fresh piece of paper, heads together, words going back and forth while Jesse's hand dashed over the page. I watched, thinking about Whitehorse. It was reasonable he would of passed through on his way north. But it was one more place to add to a growing list of places Jesse claimed he'd lived, at least for a spell.

The dog wheel was like a pebble that sent ripples through a pond. After that, it got easier and easier for Jesse to nudge Dad toward any idea. Yes, Jesse could reorganize the pantry. Yes, Jesse could repair the roofs of the doghouses with the asphalt shingles he'd found who knows where. Yes, Jesse could take the truck for a quick errand. Yes, yes, yes. Soon enough nearly everything we owned had his fingerprints on it.

Middle of November, I come into the kennel searching for the dog bootie pattern that I couldn't find in Mom's old sewing stuff. Instead of the usual jumble of camping gear and dog supplies and tools on the shelves, I found everything separated and sorted into bins. I dug through the one labeled PATTERNS AND PLANS in neat block letters and found what I was looking for. Outside, Jesse was inspecting scrap wood, picking out the best pieces for his dog wheel. That day's house dog, Marcey, jogged a stick over to him, he wrestled it free, then hurled it toward the kennel for her to chase. When he seen me, he paused. Then raised his hand, a hesitant little wave.

A softening in me, snow in a patch of sunlight. It happened before I knew it was happening, my thoughts tallying up all he'd done, the neat kennel shelves and the truck he'd got running, the clean dog yard, houses with their new roofs. Just that morning Dad had commented again on how relaxed the dogs seemed, and it was Jesse who covered for me, he piped up and said, I meant to mention, sometimes at night when I can't sleep, I'll get up and take a couple for a walk. A few minutes in the fresh air usually makes me tired enough to go back to bed. Maybe it helps soothe the dogs, too.

Dad scratched his beard. Maybe, he said.

Marcey returned her stick to Jesse. I watched him fling it again, then raised my own hand in return.

Midday, I helped Dad split and stack wood. After about an hour of work, he glanced at his watch, dropped his armful of wood on the sled, and said, I was thinking, Trace. Thanksgiving's not that far off. Might be nice to have some meat on the table.

I dropped my own logs on top of his. You going to order a turkey from the village store? I asked.

He shook his head, pulled the sled toward the woodshed. I followed along behind. Actually, I was thinking a rabbit would be good eating. Mind setting some traps?

I stopped short. You mean I can hunt? I said. Like, in the woods? The ones you're so keen on me not setting foot in?

The very ones, he said. Not racing's punishment enough, I reckon. You go on, hunt as you like. Just be careful.

Now?

Sure, I'll finish up here. Take the day.

Maybe his voice was a little too casual. But I ignored

whatever I thought I heard, I was so relieved not to have to sneak round for once.

I took the day, just like he told me. I didn't manage a hare that morning, but I left three traps along a couple paths I knew. Then I hunted for myself awhile, went out to a slender branch of the river to see if I could find a mink, and took not one but two, though the second one sprayed me a little and I had to scrub myself with handfuls of snow to try and get rid of the stench. After I had my fill, I dressed them both, then rested a spell, laid on the ground and watched the snow fall from the sky. The flakes large and languid, no wind, the day round me silent except for the trickling of the stream over stones. That kind of silence turns you inward so you grow aware of your own breathing, and the thoughts that usually bounce all round inside your head go quiet. I stayed that way a good time, till the light drained away and the early night stained the sky.

When I come back to the yard, both mink skins slung over my shoulder, I was feeling warm inside and content in my head. Till I heard the dogs bark to greet me. When you live with dogs all the time you get to know how they talk. A team of sled dogs speaks together, all their voices blend into one voice, and that's the voice of the pack. And the voice I heard then was weaker than it had been that morning.

I run to the dog yard and looked past the houses that had been empty for months, searched the faces of the dogs we had left. It took me a minute to register which house was newly empty. Flash's bowl was turned over, like she had been gone for ages.

Dad's voice come to me across the snow, flat and nearly toneless. Now, just wait before you start hollering, he said. You know Chuck Wheeler. Young musher, few years older than you? He needed a strong dog with a good head to fill out his team. He saw Flash at last year's race and liked the look of her, so he asked to lease her for the rest of the season, try her with his own dogs. It's not permanent. She'll only be gone till after the Iditarod.

I stood in front of Flash's house, picked up her bowl.

Anyhow, Dad went on. I made this deal before Jesse come along, back when I wasn't working. It'll help pay down some of them bills—

I chucked the bowl away from the dog yard, hard as I could. That's all you give a damn about, is money, I said.

Don't give me that, Dad said. You're not the one who has to worry about providing for this family.

I thought that's why you got your stupid job.

He glared. That job is what's paying— He bit his sentence in half, swallowed the rest. Then said, This was all decided a good while ago. I couldn't go back on the agreement.

She was my lead dog, I said. How am I supposed to train without my lead?

You're not supposed to be training at all.

I'm not supposed to be in the woods, neither, till it's convenient for you, I snapped. I threw the mink hides to the ground at his feet.

He shook his head. Just go inside, Tracy.

He was already turning away. I scooped up a handful of snow and flung it the way I'd flung the minks. The snowball flew through the air and hit him, exploded across his coat.

If we was only horsing round, he would of laughed and threw one back at me. Instead, he looked down at the snow stuck to the side of his coat. I hated how foolish he looked, small and stupid, and I wished he would brush the snow away.

Don't you think I'd let you race if I could? he said, quiet. But there ain't enough—

He lifted his hands.

—enough anything. Hours in the day. Time to help you with the million little things you need to compete. I can't do it all on my own.

I stared at that splatter of snow still on his coat.

I'm not happy about this, he said. I don't want to do

half the shit I end up doing. He shook his head. You'll understand when you're older.

His voice as tired as I suddenly felt, and I wanted to tell him that I did understand, as a matter of fact. I understood what it was like to worry and be scared all the time and do a thing not because I wanted to but because I didn't have no other choice.

But I couldn't say that. So instead I spat words I didn't mean at him.

You don't even want me to race. You don't care if anyone in this family acts like a musher. You barely look at the dogs, much less run them.

He finally brushed the snow away and glared at me like he was supposed to. You don't want to have this conversation, he said.

Why not?

You interested in ever running the dogs again? Spending even half an hour in the woods?

I shut my mouth.

Go inside. Now.

For once I done as he said. I kicked at a mound of snow then stomped up the back stoop, aware the whole time how babyish I was acting, but I couldn't seem to help it. I slammed the door behind me and threw my hat to the corner of the mudroom then clomped upstairs, aiming to toss myself on the bed and fume.

But Scott was crouched in front of my bookshelves, half my guides and adventure stories and both copies of the Kleinhaus book, mine and Tom Hatch's, on the floor. I scanned the room, certain he'd found the pack under my bed and drug that out, too, but there was only books, piles of them, some of them open, tossed all over, pages dog-eared.

Scott looked up. He was already trying to explain when I hurtled at him. I shoved him, hard, all the anger I felt at Dad pointed straight at him. His head smacked the corner of the bookshelves.

Goddammit, I said and meant I was sorry, but it come out angry.

Asshole, Scott said, rubbing his head. His hand come away bloody.

I didn't think. Just grabbed his head, my hand over the spot where the skin had broke. A cut on the head or face will bleed a surprising amount. You're okay, I mumbled, half to reassure him and half to distract myself from the urge I felt.

He shoved me away, though, then elbowed past me to run from the room.

I fell back against the shelves and sat there. His blood on my hand. I stared at it a good while, trying to convince myself I ought to wipe it off on my jeans, or go to the bathroom and wash. Reminding myself of the promise I'd made Mom.

And then I licked the blood away.

My head filled with pictures like flashes of lightning. They come with a flood of feeling and lit up in my mind then faded just as quick. Desire and heat and hardness rose up in me when I spotted the back of a particular girl's head in my classroom, embarrassment and excitement twisted together as she looked over her shoulder at me. A flutter of joy as I remembered the smell of Mom baking cookies, and the ache that followed that memory. A strange mix of curiosity and fear and want that pierced me whenever Dad come into the room with my sister following, the two of them connected in a way I couldn't quite understand. And lastly an odd sort of sadness when I spotted a sparrow on the sill outside my bedroom window, how it seen its own reflection in the glass and seemed to call to itself, over and over.

I shook my head, as if I could shake Scott out of my thoughts. The strange, funny, sad things that was running through his mind the moment I drunk even a little from him. At least, that was my guess on why I got what I got. There wasn't no rhyme or reason to it, other than maybe I seen and heard exactly what was on a person's mind, up at the top of their thoughts, or way down deep, when I got a taste.

I pushed myself up, Scott's experience and emotion coursing through me. My own intentions was a blur as I stuffed whatever my hands touched into my pack, water bottle, knife, the Kleinhaus book, a sweater, a hat, my flint and steel. I was down the stairs, out the door, and into the woods before I knew it. My decision made without me even deciding.

I sprinted past the lake, past the river, then cut away from the trail to make my own route through the spruce and alder. The snow deeper here where dogs' feet and sled runners hadn't tamped down a path, but I had no trouble making my way through the snow. I felt strong and fast. Free. Even freer, the farther I got away from home. I would go back, I knew, eventually, after a handful of days, time enough to clear my head and let my anger ebb. But what if I didn't? What if I just kept going north, never looking back? Things would be easier if I could be on my own, no one to keep secrets from, nothing to hide. No need to protect others from the wildness I felt inside, from the urge to give in to everything Mom had warned me against.

It was the first time, maybe, I realized I could live a life different from the one Mom had chose. Instead of hunting and running and climbing trees and living in the wild, she had somehow found Dad, and they had made a life together, me and Scott, the house, the dogs, a civilized existence. A pent-up one, too. Toward the end, she barely left her room, much less the house, the place a kind of prison she'd picked out for herself, seemed to me. If that's what giving up drinking got you, I didn't never want it.

8

Just as quick as she started going into the woods with me, she stopped. If we all went for a walk as a family, she come along like usual, her hand in Dad's as they strolled. But if I asked her to hunt with me, she found some excuse for keeping close to home. She needed to weed the garden in the summer or put up the canning in the fall, in the winter she was busy knitting, or just sitting in front of the fire, wrapped in a blanket, her feet in thick socks and slippers.

If she went outdoors on her own, it was only to stand at the foot of the driveway in the middle of the night. Sometimes I watched from the upstairs window till she finally turned round and come inside. Other times, I stood so long I got tired and finally crawled into bed, leaving her still standing, with Su at her side.

The months before she died, she barely went out at all. Till the day I stood outside her room, just the door between us, afraid to open it. She wasn't like Dad, you couldn't know just by listening if she was asleep. Outside, snow was falling in soft, wet flakes. The day warm enough the flakes melted soon as they touched your skin, a walk in the woods would mean you'd come home soaked and shivering unless you found something to warm you up. I wanted to go out. But the voices that floated up through the floorboards under my feet held me where I was.

Downstairs in the den, Dad paced and listened to Helen, the nurse who come out from the village clinic. Mom had give in after a week of arguing, she'd kept telling him she'd be fine and he kept insisting she ought to go to the clinic, till Dad finally pestered Helen into making a house call.

Finally I pushed the door open. I hadn't seen Mom in what felt like days. Her blankets, four or five of them, piled on top of her, only her pale face showing, her mouth like a gash.

Tracy. Come sit.

I perched on the edge of the bed, afraid my weight would break her. She pushed herself to sit with her back against the headboard. The effort made her breathe hard and I smelled the sourness of her breath.

Come here, silly, she said. I'm not made of glass.

I snuggled against her, her arm round me.

You're so warm, she said.

I been outside.

Today?

I shook my head. Yesterday. Last night. Before the snow started.

She looked out the window. It's really coming down.

Her hand on me so cold. What's wrong? I asked her.

I'm sick, she told me. But I'm fine. I'll be fine.

Then how come Helen is here?

For your dad's peace of mind.

We sat and watched the snow tumble down. A raven dropped out of the sky and onto the roof outside her window. It was unusual to see a bird out in a snow-storm, usually they sense bad weather coming and fly away from it, or else hole up. Find a dense tree and nest under the branches till the weather passes. The raven stood right next to the glass, so still you couldn't even tell if it was breathing, its little black eye on us.

What if I got you something? I asked.

She opened her eyes. Got me something?

Like a squirrel. Or even a vole. Something small. Would that help?

All the tiredness in her face replaced by a hardness. I told you, I stopped that. A long time ago.

I know, I said. But I thought—

I don't need it, she said.

No sound but the ruffle of feathers as the raven took flight. Nothing left but the print of his feet in the snow, soon those would vanish, too.

All I need is a little rest, she said and closed her eyes again.

I stayed next to her till she fell asleep. Whatever she was sick with, it seemed so much like how I got when I hadn't drunk in days. But it mustn't of been the same because a few days later she was out of bed, pink-cheeked and bright-eyed, no trace of tiredness in her. No sign that she'd ever been sick at all. That winter, she was full of energy. She didn't go back into the woods with me again but she spent more time than ever outside, working with our dogs, playing in the snow, riding the back of a sled round and round the yard with our youngest racers. She didn't catch so much as a cold the rest of that season, she was the healthiest I'd ever seen her. Till the night she took a walk along the road and the next we heard of her, it was from a VSO knocking on the door in the early morning, telling Dad he would need to go into town, they had already took her body to the clinic.

The first night after Dad give Flash away, I run for hours, no real thought in my head but to keep moving.

Your three priorities when you are in the wilderness are shelter, water, fire, in that order. There are lots of places in the woods to find shelter if you know where to look, hollowed-out trees or boulders where you can make a lean-to, or you can even dig a snow cave. When I finally wanted a rest in the earliest hours of the morning, I spent an hour or so on a lean-to, then made a fire and melted snow for water. The northern lights flashed across the black sky, pulsing green and white. I stopped for a minute and watched. Thought of the words Tom Hatch had wrote in the pages of the Kleinhaus book. *If I do nothing else before I die, I will see the northern lights.* He hadn't managed to stay in Alaska long enough to see the lights, they was most active in the winter during nights that stretch out so long they eat up a good chunk of the day, too. It was my doing that he hadn't reached the one goal he'd set himself before dying. Maybe he would come back to Alaska someday, not to fetch his pack but to make good on this small dream he'd wrote down. Or maybe I had ruined that for him, too.

I got up then, kicked snow over the remnants of my fire, then ventured away from my temporary camp to see what I could rustle up for breakfast. But the woods was quiet that morning. I set a snare to check after I got a few hours' sleep, but when I come back there was no catch. So I kept moving.

I didn't let myself think that first day. Not about Scott's blood, fresh on my hand, and what it give me when I licked it away. No regret about how I couldn't resist it. No anger at losing Flash, or at the way Dad had looked, stupid and mean and small with a spray of snow across his coat. No worry about Jesse, who I trusted about as far as I could toss him. Running freed me from all of that. Emptied me out. I filled the space that was left with the sky and the trees and the anticipation of whatever I'd find that day to warm my insides. I destroyed my camp and made a new one, deeper in the woods. Climbed a tree and watched the split stick trap I'd built. Waited for movement in the snow. When there wasn't none, I moved again, deeper into the wild. Farther away from home.

The second night, warm in the sleeping bag I brung along and with the coals of a fire at the mouth of my shelter, there wasn't anything to do but think. I watched the smoldering coals and remembered spotting Dad and Jesse making their way down the rows of doghouses with their shovels and spades. I had come out to help with the work, but Dad's voice stopped me before I crossed the yard. He was talking nonstop, I couldn't make out the words, just the tone of his voice and the way it rose and fell, the music of it. I remembered that enthusiasm, the way it would spark off of him and ignite something in me, a kind of electricity between us as we argued good-natured about which dog run best with which.

Dad and Jesse moved like a man and his shadow. Dad fell quiet, and Jesse spoke up. His voice wasn't very loud, even when he hollered his voice didn't carry.

Then Dad laughed. The sound of it rolled over the snow, brightened every dull metal surface and shrunk the early evening shadows. A rare sound after Mom died, a sound I didn't hear often enough.

Even I had to admit, whatever Jesse's aim was, he had made things better. In the few weeks he'd lived with us, the yard, the house, the dogs, all of it seemed more like Before than After.

I pushed Jesse from my mind as the last of my fire died, turned over to chase sleep down its narrow rabbit's hole. My belly complained. I laid open-eyed, watching stars wink at me between the branches of my shelter. I could still taste the last thing I'd drunk, Scott's worry and irritation still clinging to me. I knew it was only my imagination, but I felt his blood on my lips, coursing through me, pulsing inside my head. Tomorrow, I told myself. I would catch a critter and drink my fill, and it would bury Scott deeper inside my head, replace him with the wildness of a hare or a marten, something that would let me run unburdened with thought deeper into the woods.

But there was no critter the next day. Nothing warm inside me. I pressed on, thinking of Peter Kleinhaus. Of how, nearly starving, he come across the carcass of some animal, so long dead he couldn't tell what it had been. The bits of meat and skin left on the bones was frozen. *I found a part I recognized*, is what he wrote, *some animal's rib. There was no moment of decision, no thought at all. Only action. Only my hand to my mouth, the bone between my teeth. The animal, gnawing.*

No catch, but I dug the knife from my pocket just the same. Opened the blade.

You expect someone vanishing out of your life to change things forever, and in some ways, it does. But not as much as you'd guess. Someone dies, and the dogs still need to get fed. Shit still needs to be shoveled. You go on eating, sleeping, waking up. Snow melts, trees and grass green up, the days grow longer then shorter again. The snow comes back, nearly a year has passed, and you surprise yourself by carrying on living, despite the worst.

The first winter after Mom died was like ripping the dressing off a wound that only begun to scab over. I spent most of my time in the woods. Tried to quiet my thoughts by hunting but I passed by the place where I'd caught and bled a marten the first time Mom come into the woods with me, and I walked through the clearing where she once showed me how to dig through a pile of scat to find out which nearby plants was good to eat. Every tree I seen, every rock and fallen log, everything was like a hole in the ground you forget is there. You step in it every time, twist your ankle and think, *I have got to remember about that hole*, but soon as your ankle stops hurting, you forget again, and the forgetting is what makes you step in that exact same hole the next time.

Mornings, I would wake confused by the silent house. I squeezed my eyes closed and listened for her in the kitchen, the gurgle of the coffeemaker, the sizzle of bacon as she cooked breakfast. But there was only a quiet so complete I could hear every part of my own body, all the sounds you can normally ignore. The thud of your heart. The wet rush of your breath. The sound of your eyelids the moment they open for the first time after sleeping, the gentlest *pop* followed by the rustle of your eyelashes parting. My stomach cramped, and a warmth spread under me.

I got up, cringing at the thought that I had wet the bed. Pushed back my covers and seen the blood, a little puddle of it soaking the sheet. Smears of it staining my thighs. I put my hand between my legs and my fingers come away slick and hot, coated in red.

I didn't yet know what a period was, that it was natural and not so different from when one of our dogs went into heat. I wouldn't find out till later that most girls get it earlier than I done, sixteen is awful late. Since that day, I have wondered why Mom never told me what to expect.

I run to her room, called out, Mom! but the word fell to the floor without her there to catch it. Blood trickling down my leg. My own blood. Coursing out of me the way it had drained from all the animals I'd ever killed.

Voices outside, Dad and Scott in the dog yard. I couldn't let them see.

I barely remembered to put on clothes before I run out the back door, barefoot, into the snow. Sprinting across the yard and into the trees before anyone could see. When I was too out of breath to keep running, I walked, stumbled away from the trail, no direction in my mind but *away*. My head filled with a howling wind. Finally, legs wobbly and lungs aching, I come to a big tree with a hollow in it. I sat inside and wrapped my arms round myself. I never was one to get cold easy but that day I shivered so hard my teeth rattled.

My pants was stiff and red. I could smell myself, bright and metallic, and I wondered how long it would take to bleed to death. I could drain a smallish animal in just a few minutes. The woods was full of them, not just living animals I hadn't yet caught but the ghosts of all the ones I had killed, hundreds, maybe thousands. Then there was the blood I had took from other people. I remembered sinking my teeth into Scott's hand, remembered playing blood brothers with him when he was older. The taste of the boy from kindergarten who had got too close. The look on Aaron's face when he seen what I done to our old cat, the burnt, electric flavor fear give his blood. Even as I regretted each one, I felt a craving in me.

I knew then I couldn't go back home. I thought of our old dog, Denali, who died when I was about eight, he crawled under the back stoop and we found him a day later. Dad had said critters do that sometimes. Feel death coming and hide themselves away to greet it.

I climbed out from the hollow of the tree, still shivering, and started to walk.

I stumbled through the night, checked the traps I come across but every one was empty. I dug into my pocket, but my knife wasn't there. I pushed snow aside, burrowed down to the cold ground like Mom had showed me, places where I knew good things grew, and I ate wilted greens and shriveled berries, as much as I could find. Still my belly ached and rumbled.

Come the next evening, I sat near a slender branch of the river and considered the stains on me. All the red. All the ways it come to me. The first critter I ever caught, I hadn't wondered what to do with it. Drinking was natural to me and it didn't occur to me till later that it might not be the same for other people. By the time I understood that Mom was the same as me, I come to think of drinking the way I thought of how you touch yourself in private. You know you must not be the only one to do it, but you understand it's not something to talk about. It's the nature of the thing to be hidden.

Mom had give me plenty of advice. She'd give me her rules. But she wasn't here no more. I had to go back to figuring things out for myself. To taking what I could get, whatever way it come to me.

My fingers was numb. They fumbled with the button on my jeans.

After that, I wasn't hungry no more.

It's different when you take your own blood. Less satisfying. And you don't learn from yourself the way you learn from an animal or another person. Instead, you see and feel and hear your own life as a sort of echo, images and sounds double up on you, like placing one transparent picture over another.

I laid down, my mind fuzzy and filled with muddy memories that reshaped themselves into dreams as I drifted off. I dreamed my dogs beside me, keeping me warm. Dreamed bears and wolves and moose all running through the woods. I dreamed Mom. She was a little girl, barefoot, leaves in her hair. Running past me, sleek and swift as the caribou and foxes she run alongside. She turned her head and seen me, put her fingers to her lips, like a kiss. Or a secret. Smiled at me and waved. *Come on, come on!* I wanted to get up and follow her. I couldn't feel my feet. It took all my strength just to lift my head and watch her sprint away.

When Dad come round, I thought I dreamed him, too. Then I was flying, bundled in something warm that smelled of old campfires. Dad's voice behind me, he kept saying, Stay with me, kiddo, stay awake. So I did. I watched the dogs in front of me, Marcey and Hazel, Boomer and Grizz. Old Su on the lead. My dogs, running me home.

When we got home Dad pulled me out of the sled, carried me inside. My feet was white, hard like stones to the touch, and numb. He run water in the tub, then held me as I sat on the edge, wincing as the lukewarm water washed over my feet, full of needles. Slowly, slowly, he let the water warm. I bit my lip, my feet numb and on fire at the same time. I gripped the tub. I know it hurts, it'll be over soon, Dad said. We stayed there forever, me exhausted and clinging to him while he poured more water into the tub, more, his voice the same as the water, pouring over me, telling me he knew, it wouldn't be much longer, it will be okay, I'm here, I'm here.

Seemed like hours before he finally emptied the tub and dried my feet, then he found me some thick, warm socks and said it was all right now, he didn't think we needed to go to the clinic.

He wet a towel and drew the blanket away. I flinched.

Tracy, let me see, he said. You're covered in blood. Where are you hurt?

The stains on my pants had crusted and browned, they looked more like old mud than blood. But I was still bleeding, I could feel it coursing out of me. My feet throbbed but I stood anyway, unbuttoned my jeans.

Oh—no, no. Stop. He stood, too. I didn't realize.

He handed me the towel. I'll let you clean yourself up, he muttered.

Then he left me on my own. Closed the door behind him. I done as he said, scrubbed myself clean.

The blood kept on coming, though, it would for two days more. Eventually I learned what it was, and that it would come back. Gradually, specially when the woods was quiet and I found my traps empty, I come to see it as a gift instead of a curse.

Another night. Still no catch, the woods seemed empty of critters. My fire dead, my eyes dry with wakefulness. I watched the sky grow mottled with clouds that blotted out the stars, then finally give up trying to sleep. I dug through my pack and found the Kleinhaus book. I seen I had got the two copies mixed up, had left mine at home and brought Tom Hatch's copy with me by accident.

Still, it was a comfort to read the familiar voice. Them first lines, setting the scene for adventure. *Like most of my bad ideas, it started with desire.* I flipped the pages, skipped the boring part before Kleinhaus come to Alaska, like I usually done. Come to the part where Kleinhaus falls through thin ice and panics, only to realize he can put his feet on the ground, the water's only up to his chest. The time he gets attacked by a bear in early spring, so afraid to stop playing dead even after the bear has moseyed away, he ends up falling asleep. I thumbed back and forth through the book, reading snippets here and there, growing involved enough in the story again that I went back to the beginning to read the bits I usually skipped. I even forgot about the rumbling in my belly.

Till I come upon words that was familiar, but not because Kleinhaus had wrote them.

At age eight, I was taken in by my grandparents, long-time residents of rural Maine, retired teachers who had adopted mushing not as a sport but as a way of life. The dogs were transportation. They were farmhands. Employees, guards, companions. Occasionally, audience: my grandfather had taught English literature, and was the only musher, I reckon, who would recite Shakespeare while riding the back of his sled.

Jesse, laughing shyly as he brushed snow from his knees. The two of us handling the dogs together, me close enough I could make out the spray of freckles on his cheeks.

I turned the pages of the Kleinhaus book, barely reading, only needing to remember now. After Kleinhaus's grandparents died, he set out across the country. Spent some time in Montana, he'd worked on a cattle ranch before heading farther west. Later, he'd got a job on a commercial fishing boat in Ketchikan.

Everything Jesse had told us about his life, I could find in them pages. Every breath in him a lie.

I thought when I found the pack with the Kleinhaus

book buried under bundles of cash that it belonged to the man I'd stabbed, a stranger who had stumbled into our yard spilling blood and desperate for help. A man who would come back, I had been certain, because if he'd bothered carrying that much money into the woods, odds was he needed it. Tom Hatch never did pay us a visit, but the owner of the pack had come back after all.

I got up, rolled my sleeping bag, patted my pocket and found my knife where it always was. I had left the pack I'd thought belonged to Tom Hatch under my bed. I'd used most of the money for race fees. If Jesse found his bag in my absence, what would he do when he seen most of his money was missing? And that was assuming money was all he wanted. Before he showed up asking to trade his labor for a home in our shed, he'd watched us. From the kennel, from the edge of the trees, from the brush near the traps he'd stole from, he'd observed and waited, biding his time—for what? You don't spy on a family for weeks if all you really need to do is knock on a door and ask if anyone's seen a red backpack you lost in the woods.

My limbs grew warmer the faster I went. I pushed through brush and bare-limbed trees, waded through places where the snow had built up in drifts. Before, I'd pushed every thought of Jesse out of my head, but now he was all I could think of. Dad trusted him, but he didn't have all the information. I seen Jesse stealing up the stairs at night, so familiar with the house by now that he knew to avoid the step that always groaned underfoot. Understanding from the nights he'd seen me sneak out that Dad would sleep through anything. Maybe he would only search silently, then disappear and leave Dad to wonder where he'd got off to. Or maybe he wouldn't risk leaving anyone behind who could report him missing or describe him to the VSO.

I picked up speed. If I kept up a brisk run all the next day, I could be back home sometime the following night. Just like Dad, I didn't have all the information I needed. But I intended to get it.

The yard, full of moonlight as I come off the trail. Everything still and silent, no smoke curling from the chimney, no light in the kitchen window. I had been gone four whole days by my count, long enough that Dad had probably suspected this wasn't just me blowing off steam, that maybe I meant to stay gone this time. His truck was in the drive, he was inside, sleeping, or maybe he couldn't sleep for worrying. He would be awful mad. Time being, though, I had another problem.

The problem roused himself when the dogs woke and barked a greeting to me. I cut across the yard like a blade on ice. I heard the shed door open and close before I seen him come round the corner of the small building.

Tracy?

The distance between us halved, quartered.

Jesus Christ. Your dad's going to—

I only hit him once. My fist against his mouth, his lips crushed against his teeth, his jaw hard under my hand, the next day my knuckles would be bruised.

He stumbled back, his hand over his mouth. *Fuck.* When he took his hand away, his mouth was red.

I grabbed the front of his shirt and pulled him to me. My lips on his. He shoved at me, but I had been right, I was stronger than he was. I licked at him, swallowed. His hands on me, pushing, scratching, struggling, till I let him go. The taste of him inside me.

The truth of him inside me.

9

A clear, daytime sky. A bird cutting its way across the cloudless blue. A red building, a mound of hay. The warmth of sun on my skin, grass tickling the backs of my legs. The rake, abandoned from my chores, propped against the wall nearby.

Then the weight of another body on mine, a hand in my hair. His breath in my face.

Stop. Stop it—

The words come out strangled, I am crushed under him. His hands grabbing.

Tracy.

I push at him, it's Jesse's voice I hear but the shape I see belongs to Tom Hatch.

Stop it, I holler and stumble over my own feet, fall to the ground. It's Jesse standing over me, not Hatch.

Jesse who holds a hand out to me, concern and surprise on his face. His lip still bleeding.

Are you okay? he asked.

Panic and confusion, and me unable to tell if it was my own or if it belonged to him. Invisible fingers tugging at my clothes, a sun that hadn't yet rose touching the parts of me usually hidden. The sight of the rake, caught from the corner of my eye.

I spat on the ground, wiped at my mouth. But it was too late. A piece of Jesse inside me, and I couldn't get rid of it. He still held his hand out. I ignored it and got to my feet on my own. I couldn't look at him without feeling what he'd felt.

I'm sorry, I managed. My legs wobbly as I turned from him.

Where were you? he asked. Wait, Tracy—

His hand on my arm. I wrenched myself away, but he followed, his voice more concerned than angry. I couldn't bear to look at him, look *with* him anymore, so I searched inside myself for the thing that would make him stop.

I heard Hatch's voice, felt his breath in my ear. Heard him speak a name that didn't make no sense, that made perfect sense at the same time. The way Jesse's body felt for the brief second I let myself understand him.

Just wait, Jesse said again.

I spun round and shoved him away. Leave me alone, *Jessica*, I said.

He let go, all the color gone from his face. I had noticed early on how he never grew even a shadow of a beard, but it hadn't meant nothing to me before. In the moonlight now that face was soft. Girlish.

The house was dark. At first I could only see the hunched figure at the table with Jesse's eyes, and it stood, taller and broader than me, it come toward me, and the fear that rose up in me then was my own because it wasn't Hatch, it was Dad, a look on his face I never seen before.

Where the hell have you been?

I couldn't catch my breath. *I'm sorry* wheezed out of me again, but I was still on the grass, under the sun, under Hatch. My clothes on the ground, and the feeling of wearing Jesse's thoughts. His body—her body?— struggling. Eyeballing the rake only an arm's length away.

I went to the sink, drunk straight from the faucet. Splashed water on my face. Dad's eyes on me till I finally turned.

I'm sorry, I said again. I was just in the woods—

Just in the woods, he said.

I needed to get away for a while, is all.

I thought you were dead.

My cheeks burned. I said I was—

Yeah, you said. You say whatever you like, then you run off again, and I don't see you for hours. Days. Just like your mother. That's going to stop, you hear? No more.

This ain't the same.

Dammit, Tracy!

Just listen to me! I hollered back. I'm just trying—

But I didn't finish, my head rocked before I understood what happened. Stars flaring before my eyes, then fading. My cheek stinging. Dad's hand fell to his side, and he stared at me, his mouth hanging open.

I touched my face, but the whole side of my head was numb.

Dad's voice barely a whisper. Go to your room.

I did. Upstairs, I crawled into my bed without bothering to take off clothes that stunk of my own sweat and grime from all my time outdoors. After a time, Old Su nosed her way into my room, and I motioned for her to jump on the bed. She circled once, twice, then settled near my head, her musky breath in my face. Her fur was grayer than I remembered, her eyes milkier. I stroked her and watched how quickly she found sleep, the sound of her steady breathing almost drowning out Jesse's voice inside my head. *Stop, Tom.*

I worried that if I slept, I would dream Jesse's dreams. That I would see what must of happened after Tom Hatch attacked him.

Her. I said the word aloud and it grated against the silence in my room, tasted wrong on my tongue. I understood what I'd seen and felt, Jesse's body more familiar than not. But even as I recognized the truth of him, a knowing coursed through me. A certainty that was stronger than skin and hair and bone. Jesse's body told one story, but the inside of him told a different one. I thought of the taste of his blood on my lips, the shock of uncovering his secret. Once the shock faded, it seemed to me all that mattered was what Jesse knew about himself. What I now knew about him. It was a kind of knowledge that went bone deep, something you couldn't even question because it was part of you, the way brown eyes or stubby toes is part of you.

I looked for other parts of Jesse's story, but I couldn't get away from the weight of Tom on top of me, of the desperation that must of forced Jesse to reach for the rake nearby. I couldn't find the rest of that memory, but I imagined what must of happened next, Jesse swinging the rake, the ribbons of blood that must of bloomed across Hatch's face, the scars the wound had left. And then what? Had Jesse started his way north that very moment? I looked for an answer inside myself, but only come up with the same scene behind the red building, the barn, over and over.

When I woke a few hours later, though, Scott was the one on my mind. A memory of springtime, the world gone gray and drizzly, the only bright thing a sparrow on my windowsill, calling to its own reflection. Scott's strange sadness welling up inside me.

I pushed my blankets back and scoured my bookshelf till I found what I wanted.

Scott was sitting on his bed, papers and colored pencils scattered over his quilt. From the doorway I could see how he'd got the coloring on the sparrow's feathers just right.

You're back, he said.

Was you looking for this the other day? I asked and held out *A Guide to Common Birds*.

He nodded.

Can I come in?

He lifted one shoulder. I sat down on his bed and opened the book to the page on sparrows. It's this one, I told him. An American tree sparrow. The beak is black on top, like you've got it, but yellow on the bottom. See?

He give me a funny look, and I steeled myself, waiting for him to ask how I knew. Instead, he grabbed his eraser. I watched as he made the change, and when he was done, the sparrow he'd drew was almost like a photograph. Like it could fly off the page if it wanted.

Where'd you learn to draw like that? I asked.

You can have it, he said and pushed the picture across the quilt to me.

Thanks, I said. Then, How's your head? I reached out, and he flinched.

I'm not going to do anything, I told him. I'm sorry I pushed you.

I heard you and Dad yelling, he said.

Yeah.

Why'd you run off?

I shook my head.

Because of Flash? Scott guessed.

It was as good a reason as any. Yeah, I said.

Downstairs, the coffeemaker hissed and spat. Bacon sizzled, the scent of it coming up through the floorboards. I wondered if it was Dad already down there, cooking for us. Or if Jesse was the one making breakfast. My stomach knotted at the thought of him.

That sucks, Scott was saying. He should just let you train. At least then it would be— He shrugged.

Normal? I said.

Yeah.

I slung my arm round him and give him a squeeze. It was easy to forget sometimes that even though he wasn't keen on racing the way I was, the dogs was still a big part of his life. He helped feed and water them and clean the dog yard as much as I done, and he'd gone to every race start with me and Mom over the years. It took a lot of hands to pack gear bags for the Iditarod and sew booties for the dogs' feet, and soon as he was old enough, Scott was right there alongside the rest of us, pitching in. I forgot sometimes that I wasn't the only one with a hole in my life.

I left him starting on a new drawing and went downstairs. Dad's eyes following me as I paused to give the house dogs a good scratch then poured myself a cup of coffee. I snagged a slice of bacon from the plate next to the stove.

Been a long time since we had bacon, I said.

Been a long time since we had any extra money, Dad said.

I moved for the table but he stopped me. Put his hand on my cheek. It was tender but there wasn't no bruise, just an angry red spot. I'm sorry, he said.

It's okay.

No, it's not, he said.

We sat down and got after our breakfast, Scott joined

us before long. But the table seemed oddly empty. You seen Jesse this morning? I asked.

He poked his head in before you come down, Dad said round a mouthful of pancake. Said he wasn't feeling too good. He's going to lay low today, I reckon.

I frowned. When we ventured out to feed the dogs, I took note of the shed, the curtain drawn and a finger of smoke curling up from the chimney. All day long I went about my chores, jobs Dad give me to do and my own little projects. I still had dozens of dog booties to sew or mend. When I got out Mom's old sewing things, I glanced at Dad, certain he would remind me I wasn't supposed to be training or even going near the dogs. But he only shrugged. I sat near the door of the kennel while Dad run his saw. Pricked my finger over and over, my attention on the shed.

I thought about knocking on the door. Just to check on him. To say I was sorry. But each time, I seen his face go pale at the name I'd called him. And I felt an urge to run. I seen myself, himself, grabbing a comb, a harmonica, a wad of clothes and stuffing them into my pack, then jumping from a window onto hardpacked dirt. Images, experiences, that come to me on the taste of his blood, they played themselves over and over in my head. His legs, my legs, tired as we come to a slow-moving train, leaped into a car. He had run from trouble, would run again. I sewed booties, chipped piss from the doghouses, split wood, each job brung me closer to the shed till I stood just outside the door, working up the nerve to knock.

But the squelch of tires on soft snow turned me toward the drive. A familiar-looking Jeep rolled in and stopped next to Dad's truck. The door opened, and I seen it was Helen, the nurse from the clinic. I couldn't help the way my stomach plunged at the sight of her, even though my head reminded me that Tom Hatch was likely still miles away, still in Fairbanks or back where he belonged, somewhere in the lower forty-eight.

Hi there, Tracy, Helen called out and I nodded. Didn't make no sense for her to be here, nobody was sick.

Dad was already making his way across the yard, jogging a little. When he reached her, he give her a peck on the cheek.

She glanced at me. Everything all right? she asked.

We're fine now, Dad said, then called over to me, Trace, come say hi to Helen.

I took my time. Leaned the axe against the stump, wiped my hands against the front of my coat. Watching the two of them grin at each other.

Hi, Tracy, Helen said. Heard you had an adventure. Glad you're back safe.

Hi, I mumbled.

Come on inside, Dad said to Helen. We'll rustle up some lunch.

I know you said not to bring anything, she said. But I may have accidentally made brownies, and there was no way I was eating them all myself.

Accidentally? Dad give her a grin.

I'm not real hungry, I said, but they was already ambling toward the house, walking side by side. Not touching but familiar, easy with each other.

Come inside, Dad said over his shoulder. He wasn't asking.

Scott had put out sandwich stuff for lunch. When we come in he rushed over to give Helen a hug. Any more lynx sightings? he asked.

Not since the one that came pawing at my window, Helen said. Next time you come over, I'll show you the shots I took. There's one, he'd been drinking from the creek, and you can see drops of water still clinging to his whiskers.

No kidding!

While Helen and Dad got their lunch, I pulled Scott aside, hissed at him, You been to her house?

Like a million times, he said. She lives right outside the village.

How long has this been going on?

He rolled his eyes. Do you ever pay attention to anything other than your traps?

All through the meal, he and Helen talked like old friends, about the books they was reading and the pictures they'd took, they said things like *aperture* and *overexposure*, the words like a code between them. I tuned them out and thought about what Scott had said. A whole autumn of barely heard conversation coming back to me. Weeks I'd spent scheming on how to sneak out of the house at night and worrying about whether Tom Hatch had come back, while Dad had stood nearby and told me about the nurse at the clinic who'd struck up a conversation and laughed at the things he said, it reminded him of how easy it used to be to get Mom to laugh. In the barn, in the yard, I worked and planned and budgeted the money I'd stole off the trail, divided it up among race fees as Dad remarked how sweet it was of Helen to bring him a loaf of the bread she'd baked over the weekend. He'd have her out sometime, he'd said as we cleaned the dog yard, we could all have a nice dinner together, get to know each other. But I was only listening to myself.

I folded my arms when I'd finished eating, glowered

at them, then put my plate in the sink. Glimpsed the shed, so silent and still, Jesse might of slipped away when we wasn't looking. All at once I was certain he was gone. My chest ached and a heavy loneliness settled over me.

Dad looked on while Helen and Scott talked, a small smile on his face. For once, I could feel what he felt, even without drinking. How this, the four of us sharing a meal, must of felt familiar to him. Like home.

I pulled my chair out again, sat back down. Dad glanced at me, and his smile got bigger.

Helen lingered all that afternoon and evening, she pitched in with chores and took it on herself to shovel the front walk, then showed Scott how to make a meringue. She had Jesse's knack for quick learning, it seemed, she'd watch you do something long enough to understand, then jump in, wrangling a dog on her own or resetting a deadfall near the frozen creek. Dad had practically pushed me toward the trailhead when Helen asked about my hunting and trapping. We come back to the yard with an ermine and a squirrel and Helen took out her own knife to help clean our catch.

That's a nice blade, I told her when we'd finished skinning the bodies.

She wiped her knife clean. Thanks, she said. When I moved up here, back when I was a little older than you, my dad gave it to me. Said a girl on her own ought to know how to use a knife.

We stood outside the kennel at opposite ends of the little butchering table. Dad was up at the house, getting dinner together. Every few seconds the shape of him haunted the window, once or twice our eyes met and even from a distance I could see the eagerness in his.

You and Bill remind me a little of me and my pop, Helen went on. Back in Montana, when it came to knowing your way around the farm, Dad didn't make much distinction between boys and girls. He taught us all how to milk a cow. Drive a tractor, shoot a gun.

I cleaned the blade of my knife, then folded and pocketed it. Mom and I had cleaned dozens of critters together, had hunted for hours side by side, and I could of come up with maybe a handful of facts about her history, a few details about her childhood, and nothing at all about the time just before she met Dad. She had stood behind a wall all my life, one I never could scale.

Isn't Jesse from Montana? Helen asked.

Just passed through, I heard myself say. The words echoed in my head, in Jesse's voice.

It's a shame he's not feeling well, Helen said. Maybe we should check on him? See if he's up to dinner tonight.

No, I said too fast. Then added, He's probably asleep.

I hope he's not running a fever. There's a nasty bug going around. You know, I have my travel bag with me, I really ought to—

I'll check on him, I cut her off.

She raised her eyebrows.

Later, I said and slipped the ermine skin on the wooden stretcher.

Helen smiled. You like him?

My cheeks flushed. I tacked the legs down and spread the stretcher. After a few hours the skin would be dry and ready to work to softness so Dad could take it into the village and sell it.

It's okay if you do, Helen said. Your dad says he's a good guy.

I might of been on fire my face was so hot. I wondered if she would of felt the same if she knew Jesse's secret. If Dad would of felt the same. Would he still say Jesse was a good *guy*? People don't like learning they have been lied to. Maybe it was the same with Hatch, Jesse had lied to him, and that's why Hatch had chased him all the way to our woods. I searched inside myself for the answer, but I hadn't got that part of the story.

Helen's grin got bigger and I shot her a glare, but she was busy stretching her skin, she didn't see. It wasn't like she thought. I understood Jesse, but I still couldn't trust him. If I could of chased him off our property, shoved his pack and all his money in his arms, and be certain he would go on his way, I would of done so in a second.

Except whenever I convinced myself of that, an exhaustion rolled over me, a real, physical thing that made just standing up seem like the most difficult task anyone ever undertook. It wasn't my weariness. It was Jesse's. Now that what happened behind the barn had stopped playing on a loop in my head, I could focus on the other brief glimpses of his life I had got with one taste of him. His spent legs as he walked along-side highways and shivered under a cold rain. His heart slamming in my chest when he run down a street in the dark. A pair of men shouting after him, a freezing night in a small town, a good situation gone wrong. This was how he'd made his way north. I couldn't stitch every part of the story together, but I could hear the train whistles and truck engines and noise of passing traffic that was the sound track of his journey. To look at the handful of places he'd grown to like, see each of them for the last time.

Then I seen myself. Me, and Dad, and Scott, the three of us in the cab of the truck as we careened toward Jesse. It wasn't his calm that kept him from moving but fatigue. I felt it, I become it. From the time I had spent in the woods, spying on this family, I had noticed that even though the paint on the house was peeling and the dog yard needed a good cleaning and there was a truck up on blocks in the drive, the kids seemed healthy and relaxed. Safe. The man coming toward me, saying, *Help you?*, he should of been scary, big as he was. The closer he come, though, the more certain I felt this man wasn't dangerous or hateful. When he questioned me, suspicious as he was, his eyes seemed kind. Everything here telling me this place might be safe, at least for now. Even as the memory of so many other so-called safe situations going sour nagged at me. *Help you?* he said and I found my voice. *I hope so.*

You okay? Helen said.

I wiped at my face. Cleared my throat. Fine. Reckon dinner's ready.

I started for the house without her, wishing not for dinner but for the ermine I'd just skinned. Since Helen was with me, I hadn't drunk from it, but now I wished I'd found a way. Anything to blot out everything Jesse carried with him. What I carried with me now. Having him round was trouble, I was certain. But I couldn't send him away, neither, knowing what I knew. Not if it meant another road, another sleepless night.

10

If I do nothing else before I die, I will see the north-ern lights.

I'VE SEEN THEM, YOU KNOW. THE NORTHERN LIGHTS.

What were they like?

LIKE P.K. SAYS. ONLY STRANGER. LIKE THE SKY IS BREATHING LIGHT.

I can't wait to see them. There's so much.

SO MUCH?

World. Stuff I want to see. Stuff I want to do. Places I want to go.

Two different handwritings. Two different voices, two people talking back and forth. I could see it now that I was really paying attention, not just to what was wrote in the margins of Jesse's Kleinhaus book but how it was wrote. Both in blue pen, one handwriting smaller than the other. I'd seen Jesse draw plenty, his tiny but neat writing describing the parts of the dog wheel he'd designed, the careful letters labeling the bins he'd organized in the kennel. So one set of notes was most likely Jesse's. But the other?

It wasn't late but Dad was already asleep. Helen had stayed after supper a good while, the four of us drug out a board game we hadn't played since long before Mom died. Then we'd waved Helen down the drive. When the sound of her Jeep's engine grew faint, Dad give me a look like he wanted to say something. Instead he put an arm round me, give me a squeeze, then announced he was awful tired, he thought he'd turn in early.

I took the Kleinhaus book with me downstairs, out the back door. Jesse's lamp was lit. I walked the short distance to the shed, lining words up inside my head in neat rows then kicking them apart when they didn't come out the way I aimed. I was outside his door before I wanted to be, could hear him rustling round inside.

I knocked.

He flushed when he seen me. His eyes gray as storm clouds.

Wordlessly, I held up the Kleinhaus book.

He stepped aside then, and I come in.

He'd found himself a new pack somewhere along the way and though he didn't have too many belongings, they was all laid out on his table. His notebook and stub of pencil, a couple adventure novels, pairs of underwear and socks. Comb, harmonica.

You taking off? I asked.

He brushed past me and carried on packing.

You don't have to, I said.

His face was red, sweat trickling down the side. He had to be hot, the sides of the woodstove glowed red, and he was dressed in his usual way, a too-big sweater over a flannel shirt. I had joked to Dad once about Jesse's *uniform*, and Dad said, quiet, You ever stop to think that's all the clothes he's got? Later, he give Jesse some of his old shirts and a pair of Carhartts that was too small for him but plenty large on Jesse. Now I seen how his clothes was a sort of camouflage. Jesse was like them critters whose coats are brown in the summer but turn white in the winter to match the snow. They're just about impossible to see even when they're right in front of you.

I tossed the Kleinhaus book on the bed. I've read that book maybe twenty times, I said. You think I would of recognized parts of that story when I heard them.

He'd finished packing everything but the Kleinhaus book. Carried the pack across the small space then waited, watching me.

My dad don't know nothing about you, I told him and it come out sounding like a threat, so I added, And I ain't going to say nothing. To anyone.

He finally spoke up. Unless?

Unless what?

He stayed by the door. In case he needed to run, I realized. He'd been here before, tense and distrustful as someone used his secret like an object, something to trade for something else.

Unless nothing, I said. I ain't warning you. Or threatening you. You can trust me.

But I heard the words in my head, said by a half dozen different voices. The plunging in his stomach when it turned out not to be true.

His hand on the doorknob, wariness radiated off of him.

You like it here, don't you? I asked. You like my dad. You wouldn't work so hard to make things nicer round here if you didn't want to stay.

It doesn't matter now, he said.

I sat down on his cot, the spot farthest from him. If you corner a nervous animal, even if you got good intentions, it won't come to you willingly. Even your own dogs are likely to snap at you if they feel hemmed in and threatened.

Listen, I said. I don't give a damn one way or the other. Stay or go. But I also know you. I know you want to stay. And I know you never lived in Maine with your grandparents. You never lived in Montana. You never went anywhere in your life, till you run off from home.

Congratulations, Jesse said. You can read.

Every muscle in him tense. He didn't have no reason to trust me, specially when I had something on him. I could put us on equal ground, I realized, if I give him a secret of my own. I sighed.

I know stuff that ain't in that book, too, I told him. I know you wish you could step out of your own skin sometimes. Take it off, like a coat. I didn't get that from a book.

Jesse's shoulders dropped the tiniest bit.

I know something happened between you and Tom Hatch, I went on. Behind the barn. Something bad. He hurt you. And you hurt him back.

The wood in the stove cracked loud in the still cabin. Jesse winced. How?

There's two ways to get to know someone, I told him. One way, you learn them through their words and actions.

I dug into my pocket. It was awkward, seated on the bed like I was. But I didn't want him to spook when I took out my knife. I laid it on the foot of the cot, closer to him than to me.

He glanced at it. The other way? he asked.

I can show you.

A long silence as he studied me. I couldn't tell if he was thinking back to a moment in the woods when he come upon something he shouldn't of seen. If he already knew my secret. I thought of the day I taught him how to handle Zip, how he'd reacted when I told him seventeen was awfully young to travel clear across the country alone. *You're seventeen, aren't you? And you spend almost every day alone in the woods. A lot of people would ask about that.* His eyes, unreadable as ever. I braced my hands against the stiff mattress, held myself where I was, against the urge to take the knife and cut past my own wondering into the truth of him.

He moved slow. An eternity before the knife was in his hand, the blade open. He pointed it at me.

Not me, I said. You.

A whole crowd of thoughts clamoring in his head, each one surfacing on his face, till one finally spoke loudest. He pressed the tip of the knife into the palm of his hand and blood welled up, I smelled it the moment before I seen it. My stomach growled and I had to stop myself from lunging across the cot, grabbing the knife, and making a real cut.

Instead, I took his hand. Think about home, I told him.

I only tasted. Just enough to be able to tell him about himself later.

To watch his father, my father, climb into the cab of some big machine and steer it toward an open field, his face already beaded with sweat from the morning's work. To feel my mother's fingers stroke my hair and hear her ask, How's my girl? To step into the cool of the barn, the thick odor of cows and the stench of their shit, familiar and overwhelming. To sit in the shade, lost in a world different from my own, till I glance over the top of the book and find Tom Hatch studying me. To lay in bed and stare at a blank ceiling and wear my body like a stranger's clothes.

After, I told his own life back to him.

When he didn't say nothing, I told him how I'd finally recognized Kleinhaus's story in the one he'd been telling. How his lies had convinced me he couldn't be trusted. And that I come back from the woods because I needed to know if he was the kind of person my dad should let stay nearby, work our property. Come inside the house anytime he wanted. Become a part of the family.

He touched his mouth. The place where he'd bit his own lip still red and slightly swollen. Understanding in his eyes.

Sorry about that, I said.

What did you see then? he asked.

It's not just seeing—

I get it, he said.

I could tell he didn't, he probably thought it was just a sort of mind reading, but there wasn't no way to make him really understand. I seen Tom Hatch, I said, and he was there in the room with us, a moment we shared now, our heart hammering and the weight of him.

So you saw— Jesse started, then stopped. You felt—

Not everything, I said. That's not how it works. I get what I get in a taste. Just parts of the story. Whatever's on a person's mind, I reckon.

Jesse nodded. You reminded me of Tom.

When I socked you?

He touched his mouth, the place where he'd bled.

I really am sorry 'bout that.

Jesse got up, fed a log to the woodstove even though the fire was blazing. A tiny burst of joy, like bubbles fizzing round you when you jump into a lake, they pop against your skin. His joy. Delight at the crackling fire, at the stack of wood near the stove, the shed full of wood outside. Warmth all through the winter and never a worry that he wouldn't be able to get warm when he was cold. All that sensation washed over me in less than a second, and I understood Jesse a little more than I had in the moment before. I leaned against the wall, lightheaded.

He sat back down next to me and I shook my head to clear it.

The two of you didn't come to Alaska together, I said. Not after what happened. You come up, then—

He followed me.

He followed you, I echoed. Would he come looking for you again?

Jesse's face clouded over. I don't want to talk about him.

We can stop soon as you tell me if he might come back.

Jesse got up then, took two strides across the room and realized that was as far as he was going to get. Turned round. He run his hands through his hair, it had got shaggy over the last weeks, it stood up in little spikes. Why does it matter? he said.

It matters, I said, because I stabbed him. Could of killed him. I imagine that ain't something a man just lets slide.

His face went pale. He stopped his pacing and his hands fell. I couldn't take his eyes on me. I stood, put the knife back in my pocket. Opened the door and let winter into the shed. I was burning up. I wished he hadn't stoked the fire.

He come up behind me when I was hunting, I said, frowning, remembering. We tussled a bit. I know I got out my knife. Then he struck me. I don't recall stabbing him, but I must of. He sent me flying and I blacked out. I didn't know what I done till he showed up the next day, bleeding all over the place.

I closed the door, and the room was instantly too hot.

How could I forget a thing like that? I asked. I dropped onto the cot again. Saying what I done didn't lift the weight from me. I could claim I was only trying to defend myself, that it was Hatch who started our wrestling match when he put his hand on me. But the truth was like a seed I had swallowed, it had took root inside me. The moment Hatch touched me, I'd felt the smile on my own face. My body already acting on the realization it took my mind another handful of seconds to come to, that this stranger had just give me an excuse to let myself lose control. To do exactly what my mother had warned me against all my life.

I held my head in my hands, my face on fire.

The bed sagged a little when Jesse sat down next to

me. He put his hand on my back. You didn't mean to, he said.

But I did. And it don't matter that I'm sorry now. When it happened, I knew what I wanted.

It spilled out of me then, the way Hatch had drug himself into our yard and how I seen the recognition in his eyes when I knelt next to him. Easy enough, with Jesse silent and the two of us so close, to tell him about the panic that sent me back into the woods, the fear that Dad would come home knowing what I'd worked hard to hide from him before I even knew it had to be hidden.

I wanted Hatch to die, I said. Just so I wouldn't be in trouble.

It's okay, he said.

I made a promise, I told him. Never to hurt a person. It ain't okay.

He slid his arm round me. Yes, it is.

My ear against his chest. His heart beating, steady.

He won't come back, Jesse said after a time.

I sat up. You certain about that?

He won't come looking for you, he said. And I doubt he wants anything to do with me.

How come—

Can we just leave it at that?

His eyes on mine, plainly pleading. Behind them,

a whole tangle of thought, the history of him. Plenty more there that I couldn't see, layers of feelings and desires and fears and memories I hadn't drunk in. I had learned, the few times I had tasted another person, how so many thoughts and memories could surface at once, one on top of another, one mind thinking and feeling a dozen things at the same time. Already I felt too far away from him, in a separate room, no windows, no doors. The way I always felt with other folks, always tapping on surfaces, putting my ear to a wall to hear the mumbling going on in the next room. Wishing I could make a door, find a way inside.

Jesse traced the cut he'd made on his own palm, the wound already bloodless and ready to scab over.

I should go, I said.

What about the pack?

I froze in the doorway. Sorry?

My book, he said. It was inside a backpack.

I felt my head shake slowly. No, I said and drew the word out. No, I didn't find a pack. Just the book.

Oh, he said.

I had learned to be quiet so I could get close to the animals I hunted without startling them. Jesse had learned to be quiet for different reasons. We might of stayed where we was, staring at each other all night if he hadn't spoke up finally.

Maybe it fell out, he finally said.

I should go, I said.

Wait.

He reached past me to close the door. Then his hand on me. In my hair. His lips on mine. It was different from when I'd kissed him before, softer. Only the ghost of blood in my mouth from the wound on his lip. I felt him inside me, closer than I'd ever got to anyone else.

I got to go, I said when he drew away.

Across the small stretch of yard between the shed and the house. Making new tracks in the fresh snow that had fallen in the last hour or so. My heart thudding in my chest again. My thoughts on the backpack, still hidden under my bed. And on Jesse, and the distance I put between us with every step.

11

That week, Helen become what Jesse called a *fixture* round our place. She come out in her big Jeep or riding alongside Dad in his truck after a shift at the clinic and spent evenings helping to clean the dog yard, making cobbler for our Thanksgiving meal. Holding Dad's hand when the two of them sauntered down the trail. One afternoon, I stayed behind to help Jesse work on the training wheel and caught a glimpse of them from the corner of my eye. For the briefest moment, the figure in the red coat next to Dad wasn't Helen, but Mom. Then the sun come out from behind clouds, the day brightened, and I seen the coat was more maroon than red, the hair was a couple shades too light, and the woman at Dad's side was almost as tall as him, instead of a whole head shorter.

With Helen round, Dad's mood improved. He didn't say a word about grounding me for running off, and when I ducked into the woods to check traps he only asked, Any success? when I got back. Then, day before Thanksgiving, when I complained that the critters nearest our property had learned all my best spots for setting traps, Dad suggested, Try your luck farther down the trail.

Between homeschool work and chores, I ain't got time to get far enough out, I said.

So take a team, he said.

I didn't hesitate or ask if he was sure, I stopped what I was doing that very second and hitched three dogs up to a sled, and that's how we managed to have two hares on the table that Thanksgiving.

Thanksgiving Day, the kitchen filled with smells that reminded me of the time before we'd got rid of all our help, when Dad would invite the youngsters and Aaron to dinner and Mom was still happy and healthy, she cooked up huge meals and the room filled with voices. Usually I didn't like so many people round, but those times Mom would smile and laugh and Dad would tell stories about his adventures on the trail, everyone grinning and eating, passing plates back and forth, and the whole place bright and warm.

There was fewer of us now, but the feeling was almost the same. Helen put on soft, cheery music, and there was white Christmas lights strung round a ceiling beam over the table. The bills and books and my half-done homeschool work that was usually piled at one end of the table was gone, instead there was more food than the five of us could eat. We stuffed ourselves full, then Helen brought out the pies, a blueberry cobbler she had made and a chocolate pie made by Jesse.

How'd you learn to bake? Scott asked round a mouthful of pie.

Jesse shook his head. You pick up all kinds of skills on the road, he said.

It's good, Scott said and sliced himself a second piece.

It is, Helen agreed. I'd love to get your recipe. Where'd you learn it?

Jesse glanced at me. It's my grandmother's, he said.

That's right, Helen said. Bill mentioned you lived with your grandparents in—Maine, wasn't it?

Jesse took his time chewing.

I had an aunt who lived in Maine, Helen went on. We used to go out summers, to visit. Have you ever been to Camden?

Jesse wiped his mouth. Shot a look at the clock, then

jumped up from his chair. Shoot, I didn't realize how late it was, he said and nodded at my dad. I should get going.

I wanted to get up, follow after him. But Dad surprised me by being the one to usher him to the door. He handed Jesse the keys to the second truck.

Where's he off to? I asked.

Dad ignored me. I don't know about you all, but I could use a good walk after all that food.

So the four of us tromped along under the canopy of branches toward the lake and, all round, that kind of quiet that happens when everything is still and insulated by snow. As we walked, Scott and Helen pulled ahead with their cameras, snapping pictures and chatting. Scott still used Mom's old camera. I wondered if he thought of her each time he changed the film, same way little things would bring her back to life in my own head.

You seem awful deep in thought, Tracy Sue.

Dad kept pace with me, though he kept breaking through the surface of the snow as he walked. The trail was packed enough for me to keep on top of the snow, but Dad was heavier, he postholed up to his shin every few steps. Walking that way is tiresome, but he carried on, his face smooth and untroubled. He was happy as I'd seen him in at least a year.

I didn't mean to worry you when I run off, I said.

He squeezed my shoulder. You're old enough to know that's not the way to deal with what troubles you, he said. But I get it.

You do?

He pushed a low branch out of the way, the snow fell from it and showered us. Lot of changes this year, he said. More than just this year. And I haven't always gone about things the best way. It was a mistake, maybe, to send you to school. I couldn't think what else to do. But—

He sighed. His breath a cloud we walked through. Then Jesse come round, he said. I know you weren't keen on that. But I needed a hand.

I thought about him and Jesse making their way through the dog yard together, the way Jesse had made him laugh.

Maybe more than a hand, I said. Is that how come you let him stay even though he lied about Gerald Vetch?

We was losing light. Up ahead, Helen and Scott clicked on their headlamps. The beams bounced against the snow.

Partly, Dad said. Mostly, Jesse's a kid.

Barely, I said.

He's only a little older than you. He shouldn't be on his own like he is.

So that makes it okay for him to lie? I said and ignored the fact that if I hadn't outright lied to Dad my whole life, I hadn't never been upfront with him, neither.

Dad was quiet a good while. I thought your mom wouldn't turn some kid away, he said at last.

I frowned. It didn't sound right to me. Mom was the one who'd got rid of Masha. Who'd wanted to fire the three older kids who'd worked for us. And she was the one who'd stopped going into town so often, kept to herself, and got quieter and quieter the last few months before she died.

Dad chuckled. Don't know what made me think of this, he said and ducked under another low branch. When your mom was pregnant with you, she was determined on knitting you a little sweater. She sat in front of the fireplace and knitted, cursing up a storm. She could sew just fine, but couldn't knit worth a damn. She'd get so pissed off, fling her needles across the room. Then two seconds later she'd pick them up, go right back at it. Swearing the whole time. He shook his head. Once, she chucked the whole tangle of yarn into the fire, then snatched it out again. I come into the room, she's stomping on her handiwork, and it's smoldering and smoking, and I can't help it, I just howled, watching her dance around trying to save the thing she'd wanted to throw away.

We was nearly to the clearing where I'd stabbed Hatch. I slowed, and Dad matched my pace. I asked her once why she didn't just go to Fairbanks with me sometime, he said. Buy some baby clothes at the store, like a normal person. But she tells me, Bill, I might not get anything else right, but by god, I am going to knit my kid a fucking sweater!

His laughter rolled up the trail.

All I could do was chuckle at her, he went on. And it was contagious, almost soon as I started laughing, she started, too, pretty soon both of us was practically rolling on the ground. His smile faded a little, though its shadow lingered. She was like that, you know? She'd catch a laugh, almost like a cold. Or she'd know somehow when you were out of sorts, even before you said anything. She was just good at knowing folks.

He put his hand on my back. I guess that's why I figured she would look out for Jesse, if she was here. Whatever he's been through, to be on his own, she would've understood.

The snow was softer on the parts of the trail not sheltered by trees, I dropped through the surface of it and had to high-knee my way through the slush. The legs of my pants wet through, they stuck to me, and it wasn't no effort to find Jesse in the sensation, his own jeans stuck to his legs, his shirt plastered to his skin as he searched for shelter in a downpour somewhere between here and the place he come from.

Mom might of understood what Jesse went through but she wouldn't of known. Not the way I knew him now. There would of been a wall between her and him, same way there was a wall between just about everybody, the thing that lets each person hold back parts of themselves and only show what they want. I fell behind Dad as I trudged through softened snow. His version of Mom was different from mine. My version scolded me for hurting Scott when I bit him, and tried to keep me from the woods when I was little. My version always had one eye on me. She was moody and kept secrets and wanted the best for me, I knew, but she was also hard to figure out, specially as she begun to say less and less.

It wasn't just the secret me and Mom shared that made my version of her different from the one Dad knew. The two of them had almost three years on their own before I come along. A whole life together I wasn't privy to. I wished I had known her before I was born. Known Dad's version of her, the one who cursed and knitted and laughed easier than the mom I knew. The one who would of taken Jesse in because he was a kid and he didn't have nowhere else to go.

My stomach growled even though I still felt stuffed from our holiday meal. It wasn't food I wanted, but blood. Not from some critter caught in a snare, neither, but from Jesse. I ached for the taste of him, the experience of him. I could find him if I went looking, feel the certainty that shot through him as he fell out of a tree once that he would break his arm, the helplessness at knowing it was already too late. The undeniable satisfaction that come at a voice calling over to him, *Hey, guy,* before he looked up from his book and seen Tom Hatch.

It wasn't enough. I worried he would fade from me, and while I hated feeling the emptiness of the roads he'd walked and the way he'd strained beneath the weight of Hatch on top of him, I also hated the idea of losing the rest. The closeness of him. The thought that I might know him in a way I'd never known anyone else.

I had promised my mother that I wouldn't never make a person bleed. Maybe this was the reason she'd made me give her my word. She'd known, maybe, that one day I would have a taste of someone and it would only make me want more. But if I didn't make him—if he give it to me willingly? She hadn't never warned me against that.

The four of us turned round eventually and the sky grew velvety and studded with stars. Scott and Helen put their cameras away. The walk back, we all fell quiet, the way a group of folks will do sometimes when the setting-out part of a hike is over and muscles are just a little wore out and words get overwhelmed by what's round you, trees and snow and boulders and sky.

We'd only been gone a couple hours but Jesse was already back, just opening the dog box on the back of the truck he'd fixed up.

How is she? Dad called out as we got closer.

She's a beauty, Jesse said. He stepped away from the truck, give a little whistle, and out jumped a smallish dog, skinny and quick looking. Jesse knelt beside her and stroked her fur.

You like her? Dad asked me.

I give her my hand to sniff. She had bright, alert eyes and a mottled gray coat. Her ears perked when Dad spoke, like she was paying attention as he told me it was Jesse who'd seen the ad at the general store yesterday and who had called the musher from Nenana who was retiring. Jesse who'd arranged to meet the man today when he stopped in the village on his way south to Anchorage. Jesse who'd said it was a little early for Christmas, but maybe a new dog was the right present for me.

I hunkered down next to the new dog, scratching her chest. She's mine? I asked.

Dad took a breath. I'm sorry about Flash, he said. I am. I know you wanted her for your lead. But we've got other good leaders, and when Jesse brought it up, I thought maybe this dog would help round out your team.

My head snapped up. Say what?

Instead of answering, Dad took a piece of paper from his pocket. My stomach dropped when I seen it was from the Iditarod committee, a confirmation that they had received my entry fee. Most likely, there was a letter from the Junior Iditarod somewhere, too, either in our mailbox at the post office or on its way.

I'm not thrilled you did this behind my back, Dad was saying. But it's done.

You're not mad?

He sort of tossed up his hands, let them drop again. He wasn't looking at me, but at Helen, who give him a smile. No point in being mad now, he said. Anyhow, at least one of us should race, don't you think?

I threw my arms round his neck. Thank you, I said.

He give me a squeeze.

There was a click, the snow lit up under a flash. Helen lowered her camera. I couldn't resist, she said.

I am curious, Dad went on. How you managed to pay the fee. Not exactly a small amount of money.

I swallowed. I'd give plenty of thought to how I was going to explain this when it come up, and I still hadn't settled on a good answer. The longer I stalled the more whatever I was about to say would sound like a lie. Was Jesse wondering where I'd got the money, too? Thinking of his lost pack, the one I'd claimed I hadn't found? I opened my mouth, not sure what was about to come out.

I gave it to her, Scott said before I found a single word.

Me and Dad both stared at him.

What? I said.

Not gave, really. Loaned. I know you told me not to tell him, Scott said to me. But now that he knows you entered— He shrugged. Well, it's not a secret anymore.

Where'd you get that kind of money? Dad wanted to know.

Scott rolled his eyes. Birthday money. Payment from chores from when Mom was— I do half the papers turned in by the older kids at school. Type them up, I mean. And charge them for it. And I never spend money on anything but camera film and books.

My mouth hung open, and if Dad glanced at me he would of known right away I was just as surprised at Scott's explanation as he was. Instead, he put an arm round Scott. That was awful nice of you, son.

Don't worry, Scott told him. I'm going to make a killing on the interest rate I'm charging her.

Dad and Helen walked Scott back to the house, and Scott shot me a look over his shoulder that I couldn't read. I stayed behind, riding a whole ocean of feelings. Relief, curiosity at why Scott had covered for me, nervousness now that it was real—come March, I really would be racing, no question about it now. All of it wrapped up in an excitement like I never felt before.

That was nice of Scott, Jesse spoke up.

He closed the door of the dog box, then stood with his hands in his pockets, studying the dog he'd found for me. I couldn't tell whether he meant it was nice of Scott to loan me the money, or that it was nice of Scott to cover for me. The pack was still under my bed, but all that was in it now was a few small bills and a piece of jerky, some rice, and a tin mug. Easy enough for me to call up Jesse's memories, but impossible to know whether he knew I'd lied to him. His face blank, his eyes unreadable.

What should I call her, do you think? I asked him instead.

He come closer, give her a pat. She reminds me of a dog I used to have, he said.

In Maine? I smiled to let him know it was a joke.

I'm talking about a real dog, he said. Back home, in

Oklahoma. Her name was Stella. My dad used to say she was so smart, he ought to put her in charge of the books for the farm.

So much packed into one breath, my brain snagged on words like *farm* and *home* and *my dad*. My mouth felt dry, filled with questions that wouldn't ask themselves. Jesse knelt next to me, the two of us with our hands on the dog, gentling her, letting her lick our faces. He was so close, I swore I could smell his skin. His blood, pulsing underneath his skin.

I stood up, suddenly unsure what to do with my hands, my arms. Stella, huh? I grabbed the new dog's collar and led her to the dog yard, to Marcey, whose house was in the first row. The two dogs traded sniffs.

Stella used to disappear for hours at a time, Jesse went on while I kept my attention on the dogs. Just take off, sometimes for a whole day. But she'd always come back. I used to call them her *walkabouts*. Like she just needed to get away and be on her own for a while.

We went dog to dog, letting each one suss out the newest member of their pack.

Then one day she didn't come back, Jesse said. We looked for her for days. Put up lost dog signs. Checked with the animal shelter. After a week, Mom said she was sure another family had taken her in. Dad said maybe she'd gotten hit by a car crossing the highway.

He fell quiet as the last few dogs met their new teammate. There was plenty of empty houses to choose from, though most of them still had nameplates over their doors. I pried off the one that said *Panda* and stuck it in my pocket while Jesse piled new straw inside the house. She was smart, he said as he worked. She was a good herder and she knew dozens of commands. But she was strange, too, for a dog. She seemed to like people well enough, but she was never right there at the door when we all came home after being gone. She would sleep on my bed, but she was just as happy to sleep outside under a tree, on her own.

He stood and brushed straw and snow off his knees. The new dog circled a few times and dug at her straw bed, then laid down. Her ears perked again as he talked. I think sometimes Stella knew she was just passing through. We weren't her family; we were just some folks she lived with for a time, and when she was ready, she set out on her next adventure.

We was at the edge of the circle of light cast by the lamp, Jesse backlit and made into just the shape of himself. I realized, facing him, the light made my face plain to him. Whatever he seen on it made him smile.

What? I said.

He only shook his head. I went looking inside my-self for his lost dog, the foot of his bed where she'd slept only when she felt like it. Nothing there. If I wanted that, I would have to ask.

But he was already on his way to the shed, aiming to shut himself away for another night. I wondered what he done once the door was closed and the curtain drawn, how he sloughed his layers one by one and revealed the parts of himself he otherwise kept hidden. Imagined him slipping into bed, bare body between the sheets. A shiver low in my belly.

Night, I called to him before he closed himself off.

He paused at the corner of the shed. Night, Tracy. Then he was gone.

I rubbed my new dog's face and she rolled over, let me scratch her chest. When I was done, she watched me make my way to the house, and I called back to her, Night, Stella.

12

When you're a musher, particularly if you are getting ready for the big race, there's barely a minute goes by December, January, February, you aren't thinking about dogs. Through the fall, you have worked hard with your team and you've gone on longer and longer runs, but come winter, every day, everything you do is somehow related to the races you're about to run. You get up mornings and feed the dogs, then go over the day's chores in your head as you eat your own breakfast. You clean the dog yard and put new straw in houses. The vet comes out for prerace checkups. It takes days to pack the nineteen hundred pounds of food and gear that'll be dropped at the checkpoints by the trail committee, and you triple-check every drop bag to make sure it has the right number of replacement booties and emergency tools, and still you wake in the middle of the night, certain you've forgot something important. You mend harnesses and sled runners. Fret over the dogs who have a poor appetite and work with the ones who cramp easily. And anytime you're not home, you're on the trail, long hours and days of running, just you and your dogs, logging your miles.

Thanksgiving Day was like a door to another world that opened when Dad give me Stella and Scott lied about loaning me enough money to enter the Iditarod. On the other side of the door, there wasn't no secrets, no sneaking out at night to train. There was only a scant few hours of daylight and too much to do between the hour I woke and the hour I fell into bed, tired but happy.

For the first time since Mom insisted we didn't need youngsters round to help with our dogs, the yard was full of movement and life. I darted from house to kennel to sled, between doghouses, strategies and plans in my head, my hands never empty. I sorted through gear with Helen by my side, she wrote down what we had and how much of it, made shopping lists and packing lists. I stirred great pots of green fish and beef broth and rice then ladled it into bags Scott held open for me and we filled the chest freezer with them, at the race checkpoints I would thaw each bag and dump its contents over the dogs' kibble, thousands of calories that they would burn on the trail. I pricked my fingers mending booties till Helen brung me a thimble from her personal sewing kit. When Steve Inga wasn't busy heading up the Iditarod volunteer committee, he come out and give Jesse a hand with the dog wheel, the two of them hammering in companionable silence while Dad helped me ready a sled for a three-day run with a six-dog team. While we worked, he talked about his own experience on the trail. I'd heard most of his stories before, but now I listened with new ears, picking out bits of advice that might help me. I had run the Junior twice before and knew what to expect, but when it come to the big race, only thing I had to go on was what I'd read and what Dad shared.

One morning, middle of December, I come outside to find the dogs already on the line, pulling Dad round the perimeter of the yard. *Haw!* he hollered, one syllable striking the soft morning. I stood for a minute and watched, Dad standing on the runners of his winter rig, five dogs galloping, legs pumping, tongues wagging, ears laid back. They swung round, swallowed by the early dark, nothing but the sound of their paws digging at the snow. Then their eyes shining green in the moonlight as they circled back, disembodied till they drew closer and the shape of them formed, snouts, shoulders, ears, legs, like a hand drawing and filling them in the closer they got. Dad behind them all, bare-headed, the wind ruffling his hair. Red-cheeked and grinning.

Snow's awful soft, he said once he'd worked the team to a stop in front of the kennel. We need a good, hard freeze.

Another foot of snow wouldn't hurt, neither, I said.

He nodded. Steve says it's worse west of here. They're having a real warm spell out around Kaltag, Unalakleet.

Rough racing conditions, I said.

He grinned. Getting anxious?

No more than you'd expect, I said.

That day, Steve brung us two more dogs borrowed from a musher he knew who was taking the year off. For the Junior, I needed a team of seven dogs, minimum, and I could have as many as ten. For the big race, the maximum number of dogs I could have was sixteen, and I wanted all the dogs I could get on the line. It ain't un-common to drop more than one dog over the course of a race, they get injured or exhausted, or they just decide they're done running. I needed to finish the race with at least five dogs on the line and my odds was better the more dogs I took with me. With Stella and the borrowed dogs, my Iditarod team was up to fifteen, not count-ing Su.

I couldn't count her. Though we never did officially retire her, it was clear her racing days was over. She had got thin over the last month or so, I had stopped putting her on the line during my night runs, and she didn't jump to her feet soon as she seen you head for the door like she used to. We stopped making her take turns as the house dog, she got to stay inside whenever she wanted, and before long you couldn't walk past the woodstove in the kitchen without nearly tripping over her. She only seemed to get up when she wanted water or food, or when we all turned in for the evening. At night, she followed me up the stairs, slow but steady. I had to help her up onto my bed.

I managed my schoolwork in between prepping for the race and found time to help out with what chores I could, too, it was the least I could do considering how hard Dad was working to make the race happen for me. I felt light, relieved there was no more bad blood between me and Dad, no more suspicion of Jesse filling my head. I looked at the yard with Jesse's eyes and tried to notice the little things he had a knack for noticing, then I done what needed doing. Salted the stoop and the walk when they iced up. Darned a pile of socks. Dried dishes while Helen washed. Sometimes I would find myself at Jesse's side, the two of us cleaning the dog yard together or cooking parts of the same dinner.

All through December, we drifted together and apart, the way you see a flock of birds split, wind through the sky, then come back together to form what looks like a solid thing. We orbited the yard alone only to discover each other behind the woodshed, a mile down the trail, in a dark stall inside the kennel.

Every time we brushed elbows, I longed to pepper him with questions. About his relationship with Hatch, about why Hatch had followed him north. But other things, too. About the dreams that sometimes woke me with a cold sweat and a vague memory of running to exhaustion. About the scent of flowers that clung to his mother's clothes, he breathed it in as he stood between the soft, damp fabrics hanging from the clothesline behind his house. About this quivery feeling inside me, a pair of wings that fluttered to life when he caught me looking. About the closed-off part at the center of him, where he was hiding the rest of it, things he couldn't or wouldn't talk about. I wanted to pry him open and find answers to every question I had.

Instead, I thought of Jesse's stillness. The way he waited, patient, till someone else give voice to the idea he'd already devised, so that they felt as if they come up with it on their own. I could be patient, too.

I planted myself next to him as he greased the hub of the dog wheel and sent the whole contraption turning for the first time. Helped him lay out the gang-line for his own trip down the trail with a team of two. Watched his fingers, deft and grease covered, as he changed the oil and spark plugs in Dad's truck. Hand me that torque wrench? he asked.

I dug it out of the toolbox and give it to him. He smiled as he worked.

Something funny? I asked.

Just— He stopped, grunted as he tightened a spark plug. Then said, You remind me of me.

You when? Doing what? How? I bit off every question before it could hit the air. Waited.

I used to watch Tom work, he said after a spell. The first time I ever met him, I followed him out to the pasture and watched him mend a fence. He didn't bother with gloves, and his hands were rough. He had these thick fingers with hair on the knuckles, but they were almost delicate, the way he used them. Like a surgeon's.

I didn't realize I was holding my breath till my head went swimmy.

He asked me for a pair of pliers, Jesse went on. I knew my dad had hired him but I hadn't met him yet, till he found me behind the barn, reading. He called over to me, *Hey, guy.*

A thrill shot up my backbone, the thrill he'd felt at Hatch taking him for what he was.

He didn't know about you? I asked.

Jesse's brow furrowed and his tongue poked out between his teeth as he worked the wrench. I leaned over the guts of the truck, watching, wishing I hadn't said nothing.

But then he answered, He found out soon enough. My parents had invited someone for dinner that night, that's all I knew. So Tom shows up and my dad introduces me as his daughter, and that's that.

He wiped his hands on a rag. Grime still under his fingernails, it would be there till he showered, long after the rest of us had turned in. Some questions I had answered myself, like why he waited till there was no chance someone might walk in on him in the bathroom, or why he had said no thanks when Dad invited him to camp out with the rest of us once, not long after Helen come round. Dad chalked it up to Jesse liking his privacy. He liked it, all right. It was too hard keeping things hid in close company.

Tom didn't bat an eye, he said. Just shook my hand. Said, *Pleased to meet you.* After that, I was sort of obsessed with him. That whole summer, I barely left his side. Pitched in with his work, let him take me fishing. He taught me how to shoot a gun. How to fix cars. My parents thought I finally had a boyfriend. I guess I did.

I swallowed my question, but Jesse answered it anyway.

I asked Tom once why he didn't mind me, even though everyone else seemed to. He had this philosophy, that everyone has male and female sides to themselves, sometimes a little more of one, a little less of the other. Sometimes the two sides are balanced. So if that's the case, he said, no one should be surprised if the balance gets reversed in some folks. That someone might get a soul that says one thing and flesh that says another.

Jesse looked at me. That's how he talked sometimes. Like a country poet.

You didn't start out scared of him, I said. You was friends.

He nodded.

More than friends, I said.

He sighed heavy. Kept his eyes on his work.

So what happened?

He shook his head, and I figured he'd come up against some wall inside himself, something he wasn't ready to climb over, wasn't ready to tell me. But then he said, It went bad between us. Tom started wanted something I couldn't give him.

Hatch's breath in my ear. His hands, tearing at my clothes.

So he took it, I said.

Jesse glanced at me. Didn't say nothing.

Then what?

I left, he said. I came here to start a new life. I didn't expect the old one to follow me.

Seems like you're skipping an awful lot, I said.

He lifted a shoulder, shook his head, and I understood he was done. But what he give me was nearly good as a drink. I could use his words like a map, follow them to the hidden places I couldn't locate before. Like foraging in the woods, I lifted a rock and there he was, imagining what it might be like to be Tom Hatch, inhabit a body like his. I looked behind a tree and found him holding the Kleinhaus book out to Hatch. *I thought you might like this one, since you mentioned wanting to see Alaska.*

Su come outside for a change, walked stiffly to where I stood alone at the head of the driveway. In the same spot where I'd seen Mom so many times, when she was alive, and after that. A fierce longing come over me. I always wished she was still round, but now it wasn't because I had questions about hunting or drinking. I wanted to ask her if this was what it was like when she first met Dad. If it was right to want someone so much, you would peel their skin off if you could, open their skull, just to get closer. Had she ever got to know anyone as well as I was getting to know Jesse? It didn't seem possible that she might of ever drunk from Dad, but she wasn't there to ask, neither. It was too late. I had waited too long. No matter how old you get, your parents always get there first, and there's a comfort in that. Like an unfamiliar path through the woods where there's footprints already showing you someone has gone on ahead. Till the day you come to the place where the footprints stop.

There wasn't no longer a need to stay up till the slimmest hours of night, waiting on Dad's snores to carry down the hall so I could sneak out and run the dogs. Most nights in fact I slept like the dead, I could imagine my own snores quaking the whole house. But one night just before Christmas I found myself staring at the dark ceiling over my bed. A craving in me. I got up finally, went downstairs and stood in front of the open fridge, then wandered to the sink instead. I drank from the tap, though I didn't feel particularly thirsty. When I raised my head, I couldn't pretend anymore I didn't know what I wanted. The shed, visible through the frosted window over the sink. Jesse's light on.

He come to the door soon as I knocked, as if we had agreed on meeting. Can't sleep? he asked.

The fire in the woodstove sent our shadows flickering up the walls. I stepped inside, closed the door.

Touched his sleeve. He didn't say nothing and neither did I. My tongue would of fumbled over words, but my fingers was deft. They went searching for him, unbuttoning one shirt to find another underneath. Layer upon layer. He pulled the last shirt over his head, under that was the sort of bandage you use on a sprain, wrapped tight round him. Unwound, his breasts was small but obvious.

I stopped. Is this okay? I asked.

He didn't say nothing, but put his mouth on mine.

After, he said, Come here, and there wasn't no place to go but the cot where he usually slept alone. It was small, but it fit the two of us fine.

The room filled with the sound of our breathing. He was an undiscovered trail in the woods. A familiar landscape made strange, a mountain new to me, and I shook with my own eagerness to explore him. The paleness of him, all the parts of him that didn't see the sun. His lips, parting, his eyes, closing. His skin, softer than I expected. His breath, his tongue, the shape and weight of him. I lapped him up without drinking.

Till I come to the place where he was like me and tasted blood, coppery and familiar.

And there was the sweat of the day still on me, my own appreciation for the scent, a manly scent radiating from my own skin, my satisfaction with how the training wheel was turning out, my hunger for this girl, my hesitation round her. A jumble of Jesse that come to me all at once. And then out of the jumble, one clear moment.

There was a sweet scent in the air, something sugary and hot, the sun sending tendrils of sweat down my back, and the glow of the day not from the lowering sun but from how I felt, Tom at my side, his hand holding mine. Shouts and laughter up and down the thoroughfare, *Wouldn't you like to win your girl a prize, one dollar, three chances, everyone walks away a winner, you there, you look like a strong man, step on over.* We stop so Tom can swing a hammer, a bell rings, and he tells me to pick out a prize. I look past the stuffed bunnies and bears to the only object worth anything, a burl-handled pocketknife. There's a chorus of screams from one of the rides, and my stomach drops and soars at the same time as Tom leans over me, we kiss—

Don't, Jesse said and pushed me away.

I licked my lips. I'm sorry, I said. I didn't know—

Me either, he mumbled. I wasn't really keeping track. He tugged his jeans on then settled on the cot again. His face was pink. Did you— he started, then stopped. Did you get anything? he asked.

So I told him what I'd seen and heard, a fair of some

sort, and him and Tom Hatch. The barkers and their silly games, the stuffed animals staring at him with their glassy eyes after Tom won at Test Your Own Strength.

That's it? he said.

I shrugged. It's all a rush, I told him. It comes quick, sort of washes over me like a current, then drains off. I didn't add that now I could go looking for it whenever I wanted. That it, that part of him, was part of me. I guess this was before things went bad between you and Hatch? I said instead.

He frowned. Seemed to turn something over in his head. You don't control what you get, he said, not like a question but like a conclusion he come to.

No, I said. I told you, whatever you're thinking on—

It doesn't seem fair.

What do you mean?

That first time, you got one taste of my blood, and you found out the one thing I needed to hide. What if there are other things I want to keep to myself? Personal things? You can tell me whatever you like about yourself, and I would never know what's true and what's not. But you can know anything you want about me.

It don't work that way, I said. You could just—don't think about what you don't want me to know.

He give me a look.

Anyhow, I wouldn't lie to you, I told him.

But his pack was still under my bed. The money mostly gone thanks to the race fees, it wouldn't do any good to tell him about it now.

You still get to choose, Jesse said.

Okay, I told him.

Okay?

I won't come here for that. Not if you don't want me to. I still want to come, if that's okay. But just because I like being here. With you.

I felt the tension go out of his muscles, his whole body relaxed. I slipped an arm round him and rested my head on his chest. His heart sped up, then slowed. The blood coursed through his veins carrying all the bits that made him up, his whole history. All of it concealed just beneath the skin. Close enough to taste.

Thank you, he said.

There wasn't no reason to leave after that. Dad had stayed in the village that night, at Helen's, and both of them had an early shift at the clinic. I didn't expect neither of them home till the next afternoon. By the time the fire was dead, Jesse was asleep, one arm thrown over me. The air round us grew chilly and I burrowed under the blankets next to his warmth. Never closer to anyone, and not just because of the way we'd wove ourselves together, skin to skin, limbs wound round each other till he felt like a coat I could wear. My belly almost sloshing, it felt so full. I knew it wasn't the blood but what I'd got from it that filled me up.

Okay, I'd said, quick as you please. Like it was easy not to want to know him. I studied his face, soft in the dark. I wouldn't take what he wasn't willing to give. But I hoped he wouldn't hide himself from me just because he could.

The one exception to the busiest three months of the year is late December. Before Christmas, you take your dogs on slow runs and you look over your lists and plans, what you'll need for your drop bags. After, there's a mountain of work that'll need doing. But for a few days right round Christmas, there's a lull. Things go quiet, and you just enjoy the run.

That Christmas week, things was even quieter than normal. Old Su had barely ate anything that week, and when she come along on walks she seemed to tire out quick. Christmas Day, she barely moved from her spot in front of the woodstove, even when we filled her bowl with kibble mixed with some cooked hamburger, a treat for the holiday.

Next day, the vet come out. He listened to her heart, shone a light in her eyes and ears. Stroked her side as he explained there was blood tests he could do if we wanted to bring her to the village, but to be honest he suspected there wasn't nothing wrong, just old age.

The kitchen walls had moved closer together, the room too crowded with me and Dad and Scott plus the vet, plus Helen and Jesse, not to mention both retired dogs, perfectly healthy and lounging under the table.

Homer's a lot older than Su, I pointed out.

The vet nodded. I couldn't stand the look on his face.

What can we do? Dad asked.

Make her comfortable, the vet said. Give her a quiet space, keep the other dogs from bothering her. You can offer her food, but it's likely she won't want it.

Canyon, too, I spoke up. Su's practically a pup compared to him.

Dad put his hand on my shoulder, and I shrugged it off. I wasn't acting my age, but I couldn't seem to help it. I felt Helen's eyes on me, and Jesse's. Brushed past the vet to sit next to Su, pressed my hot face into her fur.

I slept downstairs that night, curled next to Su where we'd moved her bed to the den in front of the fireplace. The next night, Scott joined us, all three of us snoring while the fire faded, till either him or me woke and added another log. We took turns helping her stand as she drunk from her water bowl. We brushed her fur and rubbed her belly. She didn't make no sound, just watched us with soft brown eyes.

The third day, she wouldn't stand up, not even with help.

I'm going to take her on a run, I told Dad.

He give me a long look. Then nodded.

Outside, I hitched a small team to the rig, then put some blankets and straw in the basket. When I come back in for Su, Dad was petting her and talking in a quiet voice. I backed out of the room, waited by the sled.

Dad come out after a few minutes, carrying Su. Together we clipped her into the basket, though she wasn't likely to try and jump out. I whistled, and the team pulled us into the woods.

All round, the trees wearing snow like robes, trunks furred with it, limbs coated. It was a wet, sticky snow, and we went slow, breaking trail. Tiny crystals of snow hovered in the air, never seeming to land. I hopped off the runners and jogged alongside the sled, traveling in a cloud of my own breath, it crusted on my eyelashes and the ends of my hair.

When we got to the lake, I was shocked to find it still hadn't froze over.

I slowed the team and threw out the snow hook. I had to pee.

After, I walked out onto the shelf of ice that edged

the lake, a plate solid enough to hold me for about ten feet, then the ice thinned. The rest of the lake held a collection of little floes. I plucked a small rock from my pocket and tossed it at one. The rock hit the surface then slid into the water. The surrounding floes bobbed from the ripples, then stilled, the lake once again calm and anonymous.

Back on the sled, I passed by the place where the river made a waterfall as it emptied into the lake, the spot that never seemed to freeze over no matter how cold it got. We begun to climb, till we reached a wide shelf of land that overlooked the lake. We'd buried a number of dogs in that spot over the years, their graves marked with cairns made of stones.

I tied the sled to a tree and give the dogs on the line a treat. Unclipped Su and lifted her out of the basket. Carried her to the spot where the land ended and looked over the lake. She wouldn't sit, so I laid her on her side, then curled myself round her.

The water coursed south from the lake to the river. The sun drifted across the sky.

The seconds between Su's breaths grew longer.

Somewhere round twilight I sat up and wiped my eyes. I watched Su in the rapidly growing dark, looked for her flank to rise. It did, just barely. I said her name, but her eyes stayed closed.

I made the cut small. I didn't want to hurt her, even if she was nearly gone.

I drunk. I took Su in and bounded down the snowy trail, and the delight that flooded my body was complete and overwhelming, pure, undiluted happiness. I felt the tug of the harness and saw no other dogs in front of me, felt the whole team watching as I led. I bolted my food, barely tasting it, and I scratched at my own ears, and I napped in front of the woodstove and in piles of my brothers and sisters and teammates. I watched white snow fall across the black-and-gray world and the frigid air sent a shot of electricity through me, and I howled, the only way to give voice to my want.

After, I wrapped Su in one of the blankets from the basket. Most winters, we would of let the body freeze then buried it come spring, when the ground thawed, but this season had been warm enough, I had little trouble digging a hole big enough.

She run with me all the way back home, and when we spilled into the yard Jesse was there, busying himself with the new dog wheel. He looked up when I slid past him, and our eyes met. Up at the house, Helen was at the window, and inside Dad and Scott would be rustling up dinner. I threw out the brake. Behind me, I could hear Jesse jogging over to help take the dogs off the line.

If I could stop when I wanted and not tell the rest, this is where I'd choose to end. I'd conjure up the hard freeze that was on its way, let the ice and snow set us just as we was that day, when a quiet happiness shot through me, something more like *rightness*, and I couldn't tell if it was my own feeling, or Su's, or Jesse's. A recognition of coming back to a place where you know you belong. Where you know you are wanted and loved.

13

There's some things you just don't talk about, except to talk round them. Mom never told me that in plain words but she taught it to me.

Like when I wanted to know why I heard her in my head, even when she wasn't nowhere nearby. Because you know me, she said.

I don't, I said.

Her breath plumed and hung in the air between us. Then it was gone.

When you were born, she said, it was in the open doorway of the barn, with twenty-two pairs of canine eyes watching. You came out big and heavy. And always hungry. Some women have trouble getting their babies to take the breast, but that was never a problem with you. You were voracious. I fed you till I ran dry.

She looked in my eyes.

Then I fed you more.

My heart loud enough in my chest I wondered if she could hear it. Is that how come I'm like you? I asked her.

She looked up at the clouds. The air was brittle and made her eyes water. I don't know, she said.

What about Scott?

He was never as hungry as you were.

I stared at the ground. Our footprints in the snow nearly identical, if someone come along they wouldn't be able to tell one set from the other. But I wasn't done growing yet, I might of got taller, my feet could of grown longer. I could of turned out nothing like her.

You told me it was wrong to make a person bleed, I said.

She nodded. That's right, she said. But you didn't make me. I gave it to you. She took my hand. She'd forgot her gloves, my hand warmed hers. Sometimes I'm sorry I did it, she said. Sometimes I think if I hadn't, you might not be like you are. She give my hand a squeeze. But sometimes I'm not sorry at all.

Because it means we're the same? I asked.

We had come off the trail already, crossed the yard, and now we was back at the house. Standing at the edge of the driveway together.

Because, she said, it means I'll always be with you.

14

In the days before the Junior, I vibrated with nervous energy. I had packed and shipped my drop bags full of food and extra gear for the big race, attended the Iditarod rookies' meeting, argued with Dad over the things he suggested I ought to pack that I thought I wouldn't need. I had worked my team hard but smart over the last few weeks and now it was time for them to rest, we only went on the shortest, slowest runs in the last week before the Junior.

I had run the Junior twice before, it was familiar, and so with the big race still a week away I tried to focus on what was right in front of me. Seventy-five miles one way from Knik Lake to Yentna Station for a mandatory ten-hour layover, then back the way I come for a total of one hundred fifty miles. Four days after

I finished, I would celebrate my eighteenth birthday. That's when I would let myself start worrying about the Iditarod, I decided.

Day before the Junior start, the weather was clear and cool, twenty degrees. Over the course of January and February it had finally started to seem like real winter. We'd got a couple decent snowfalls, but now the snow had settled, the trail I'd been running was nicely packed. Everything set for a perfect race.

I spent the morning double-checking my sled bag and the gear I meant to take. The dogs could tell something was going on, they barked and jumped and play-bowed as I walked up and down the rows greeting them and handing out treats.

Jesse found me in the kennel afterward. Nervous? he asked.

Not about this one, I told him. But next week— I shook my head. I don't know what's in store.

But Bill's told you all about the race, Jesse pointed out.

Yeah. He also told me no two mushers ever run the same race.

He frowned. What does that mean?

I think it means I'm fucked.

Surprise made his face completely naked for a second. I understood that he usually hid himself from most folks because he had to, but in that moment I realized he was choosing what to reveal even when he was with me. Long as I couldn't drink. Over the course of a few weeks he had told me about himself, narrated his own life like it was a series of adventures, funny stories full of interesting characters that glossed over the shadows I'd seen in the brief tastes I'd got from him. His time on a commercial fishing boat down in Ketchikan turned out to be true, also the month he'd spent working in a seafood plant in Homer. He told me about growing up on a dairy farm and tagging along after his father, pestering after him to learn how to milk a cow or replace the spark plugs on the tractor. How he'd hoped one day he would inherit his dad's land so he could keep the farm going. He might of, too, he didn't have no brothers or sisters.

But once he started living the way he was meant to live, things changed. He didn't have to explain to me how he'd knew words like *girl* and *she* and *her* didn't fit him, no matter what other people said, or why giving himself a buzz cut at thirteen felt so good. *You'll look ridiculous in your Easter dress*, his mother had said, and I felt the sting of her words, all the lightness and joy gone out of him when he seen the disappointment on her face.

I had learned more about him than I ever thought I

could without his blood, it was enough to make me feel like I knew nearly everything.

His surprise at what I'd said wore off and he laughed. When he stopped, he was himself again. The self he wanted me to see.

Trace! my dad hollered from outside. You 'bout ready to go?

I'd said I wasn't nervous, but my belly done a flip. I grimaced.

Jesse glanced out the kennel door, then stepped closer, give me a quick kiss. Good luck, Tracy Sue.

He hung back as I made my way across the yard, and when he come out to help load the dogs into the truck, I noticed he'd left by the kennel's back door so it would seem like maybe he come from the training wheel or the woods.

Once we'd loaded the dogs and tied the sled to the roof, we was off. Dad steered us down the drive and I watched out the side-view mirror, Scott and Helen and Jesse waving to us. They would come down to Anchorage for the Iditarod ceremonial start but I had told them I would be less keyed up if it was just me and Dad at the Junior start. They waved and waved, till we rounded the corner in the drive and they fell out of sight.

We rolled into Wasilla for the final vet check, and

then that evening we went to the mushers' meeting, a roomful of kids and their families, there was fifteen of us signed up for the race. I recognized a couple faces from previous Juniors. There was pizza, then a talk from Dr. Jayne about proper care for dogs on the trail. There was older, seasoned mushers who spoke on speed and sled care and the right clothes to wear. Then, finally, the bib draw. Since I had got signed up for the race late, I didn't get to draw at all, just got the bib that was left when every other racer had gone. I got number 3, and that meant I would be the third racer to leave from the start.

Lucky number three, Dad said to me later that night, after the meeting. We'd made camp and got the dogs bedded down, then rustled up dinner and sat by the fire with cups of hot cocoa from the thermos. Talked about the kinds of things you talk about when it's dark all round, the fire crackling and your dogs sighing in their sleep. The sort of stuff you don't remember later except to recall the feeling of it, and the sound, two low voices in the glow of the fire.

After we turned in, when the fire was embers and the two of us warm in our sleeping bags, that's the conversation I remember.

His voice come to me out of the dark.

Trace?

Yeah.

About Helen. He paused. I didn't go looking for someone who—what I mean is, I don't want you to think— He fell quiet again.

I don't, I told him after a while.

Don't what?

I sighed and stared up into the night. No wind or even a breeze that night. Not a cloud over us, the sky empty except for all the stars shining down, each one pinned to its lonely spot. I had spent more than a dozen nights at Jesse's side over the course of two months, had met him out on the trail, him coming and me going, us timing it so we'd find each other in the woods. More than once I'd woke up forgetting he was next to me, I'd freeze, heart pounding, hand already groping for my knife, till I realized it was him, and he was only there because I'd said he could be. Just as often, though, I woke to the warmth of him beside me and found myself nestling closer, the way our dogs would curl round each other in their sleep.

All critters like warmth. And if you spend years waking up to a warm body next to your own, seemed to me when that spot went cold, you'd long for a way to make it warm again.

I don't think you meant to find someone to take Mom's place, I said.

One of the dogs huffed in its sleep. Another stood, circled on its bed, then laid down again.

I like Helen, I told Dad.

Me too, he said. I could hear the smile in his voice.

How come? I asked.

He shifted in his sleeping bag. She's got a way about her, he said. Makes you feel at ease. And she's open. Always interested in trying new things, always willing to be up front about what she's thinking. I like that.

Is it the same way you felt with Mom? I asked.

He cleared his throat. Your mom was a lot of things. But she wasn't exactly open. Specially the months before she died. She got quiet. Secretive. Used to be, we was always pretty honest with each other, but it got so I knew she was keeping something from me. You know she used to go walking at night? Not just the one time, but almost every night, for a while.

I remembered standing in the hallway. Watching her bundled in her coat at the mouth of the driveway. Old Su nearby.

She thought I didn't know, Dad said.

It made you mad. Her going off like that.

Not mad, he said. Well, maybe a little. Worried, mostly.

I thought of him rolling over in his bed, her side cold. Of him staying up, waiting for her to come back.

Wondering if she wouldn't. When she did, when she eased the back door closed behind her and crept up the stairs, did he want to holler at her the way he done when I run away? It never occurred to me before that the reason he was so scared then was because he'd gone through the same thing with her.

That's not to say I like Helen better than your mom, he told me. Or that Helen's supposed to be some kind of replacement. I still love your mom. I still miss her. You understand, kiddo?

I nodded then realized he couldn't see me. But my throat was thick and my tongue stuck, the whole of me heavy with worry. I hadn't never taken anything from Dad, not a drop, but at that moment, I knew him. Felt him in my bones. Wrapped in my sleeping bag, I was also hunched over the kitchen table, my eyes burning with sleeplessness, my head snapping up at every sound the house made. My whole self weighted down with dread and fear. I should of said then how sorry I was. How I never meant to do that to him.

Instead, I rolled over, curled myself round the feeling like a small boulder I would carry with me.

Heard Dad say to me, Night, Trace.

The race didn't start till ten, but I woke early, made a fire right away and started the dogs' breakfast. Dad woke while I fed the dogs, and he rustled up breakfast for us humans. We ate in silence, watching the stars fade. Another clear, crisp morning, about fifteen degrees. Good day for a run.

The Junior starting line ain't near as chaotic as the Iditarod start. For one thing, there's fewer mushers, just fifteen of us that year compared to the fifty or sixty mushers that usually run the big race. Still, fifteen mushers with as many as ten dogs each, plus the parents and handlers and volunteers and spectators, it makes for a decent crowd.

I shut it all out as best I could. Focused on my dogs as I bootied them, then took hold of their harnesses and led them one by one to the gangline. The Junior requires at least seven dogs to start the race, you could have as many as ten on a team, and it was a good idea to bring the maximum in case you had to drop a couple dogs over the course of the run. But in just a week I was going to be running most of the same dogs in the big race, and I wanted as many fresh dogs as I could get for the Iditarod. So I'd brung a team of only seven to the Junior. Chug and Boomer in the wheel position, and just ahead of them, Grizz and Marcey as my swing dogs. I had learned over the last couple weeks that Stella and Zip run well together, so I'd paired them right behind Peanut on the lead.

My belly give a little tug as I settled my team, I thought of Flash and hoped the musher Dad had loaned her to understood that she was a natural leader. Then I pushed thoughts of her aside and concentrated on my own lead. I give Peanut a good pet and a talking-to.

Dad finished rechecking my basket, making sure the sled bag was secure.

A crackle cut through the air, I winced as the sound system squealed. Then the announcer asked the first couple teams to head toward the chute and the starting line.

Reckon we ought to get over there, Dad said.

Volunteer handlers was already heading our way. They grabbed hold of the dogs' harnesses and behind us another volunteer hooked a snow machine to my sled, it would do the job of a tag sled, which is meant to slow the dogs down and keep them in place till the starting line countdown reaches zero. The announcer's voice introduced bib number one, a racer from Bozeman, Montana, and my team jerked forward, closer to the start, as the first countdown begun.

Dad had hold of Chug at the wheel position, and I thought of Mom, all the years she had stood in that same spot as Dad waited out the seconds before the start of another race. He looked back at me and his face nearly cracked with how big his smile was. I couldn't help but smile back. I briefly wished Scott was there, and Jesse. I pictured the two of them helping to handle the team, or standing close to the start and cheering, the way they most likely would the day of the big race. Warmth rushed all through me, and if I had felt even a little nervous that morning, all the nerves went out of me. My head went as calm as if I had just spent the last few hours running through our woods at home. I breathed deep and stepped onto my runners. Held on to my handlebar. My dogs yipped and danced and tried to wriggle free from their handlers.

The sound system crackled again. The announcer told us, bib number two is rookie Quentin Trefon, from Bethel.

I barely heard the countdown. My team surged forward, and we was at the start.

Bib number three is veteran musher Tracy Petrikoff, running her third Junior Iditarod.

Dad winked at me.

I winked back, then focused. A small crowd just beyond the starting line, a blur of faces smiling and chatting, a few hands fluttering as folks waved. I spotted Wendell Nayokpuk from the village general store, and somewhere Steve Inga was organizing the day's volunteers.

Ten, the announcer started the countdown.

The sun had rose above the trees and the light bounced off the snow and made my eyes water. I wiped at them with one gloved hand.

Nine, eight.

Took my hand away, and there he was.

Seven, six.

At the far end of the crowd, standing off by himself. The scars on his face red and angry against skin that hadn't lately seen enough sun.

Five, four.

All sound fell away except the beating of my own heart in my ears, it grew slower and louder and replaced the announcer's countdown as I stared past Dad and into the face of Tom Hatch.

Three.

Dad, grinning. Hatch, turning away for a moment, then turning back. His eyes found me, and he raised his hands and started to clap.

Two.

The sled strained under the power of seven dogs eager to pull. My whole weight on the brake. A river of sweat underneath my coat and damp at the edge of my wool hat. Hatch's eyes on me. Pinning me to the runners where I stood. My whole body frozen, my heart a panicked bird inside a cage.

One.

Go.

We lurched forward. I hadn't stepped off the brake, but still the dogs surged, struggling, and I remembered how to use my legs again, I lifted my foot, and we sailed past Dad, he reached out to touch my shoulder. *Proud of you, Trace,* his voice come to me from the top of a canyon as I fell, the dogs went forward but I was going down, tumbling down past the sea of faces at the starting line, till I come to Tom Hatch. I plummeted past him, our eyes locked, and he smiled at me.

Good luck, musher!

Then we was on the trail. I looked back over my shoulder. The next team already at the line, and the crowd had swallowed Dad, I couldn't find him. But Tom Hatch was there. Still waving.

15

I turned, and his hand struck me. I staggered but there was nowhere to go, his hands was already clutching me, the only thing to do was to find my knife.

This time, he didn't throw me aside. I stepped forward and suddenly found myself on the ground behind the barn, Hatch's warm breath in my face. *Stop, Tom. Stop it.* I glimpsed the rake out the corner of my eye.

Then I come back to the yard, myself again. My belly full.

The sun shone and sent shadows dripping across the snow. I gripped my sled's handlebar, but I was barely on my runners. I was in the woods, behind the barn, Hatch coming toward me, toward Jesse, again and again. I was a hare, a marten, chewing at its own leg, pulling at the noose round its own neck and only managing to make it tighter. I turned, Hatch reached out. I seen the rake. The knife in my hand. The hunger that rose up in me, the instinct to protect myself, they was one huge tidal wave that swept me toward him. Then it slammed down.

I fell. Shit! I exclaimed and got a mouthful of snow. I spat and hung on to my sled and bounced over the hardpack on my belly, my feet kicking. I kept my head up, tiny pellets of ice peppering my face. I could see that Grizz had somehow managed to cross the gangline to run on the same side as Marcey and now they was tangled, while the rest of the dogs paid them no mind and kept running.

I didn't bother calling out again. The dogs wouldn't stop no matter how much I hollered *Whoa!* I hauled myself onto the left runner, arms straining, then balanced there on my knee. Threw the rest of my weight on the brake.

When I'd worked the dogs to a stop, I peeled myself off the ground and checked the team while a musher wearing bib number 5 zipped past. Got the dogs settled with a snack, then took a look round. While my head had been back in the woods and behind the barn, the dogs had kept us on track. I spotted an orange trail marker about twenty feet ahead, then squinted at the sun, done a little math, and realized my team had managed nearly twenty-five miles in about two hours. We kept going at that speed, the dogs would be wore out long before we reached the Yentna Station layover.

I had planned to rest the team after four hours on the trail, but I had also planned to stand on my brake and keep them at a steady eight or nine miles an hour once they got past their early race jitters. They needed a break. I checked their feet then let them be, they curled up and dozed, only waking when another team or a race official on a snow machine passed by.

At first I busied myself digging through my sled bag, looking for gear I didn't need. I gnawed on a piece of jerky that tasted like old leather in my dry mouth. I considered stepping away from the trail, seeing if there was any animals nearby I could take, some way to get something warm inside me and banish the image of Hatch from my head. But we was in a wide-open area, the nearest trees dotting the horizon, and I didn't want to leave my dogs. Another team passed, then another, one musher waving, the next calling out, Everything good? I nodded, then watched that team run into the distance, till they vanished.

I watched Hatch over and over, first his hand reaching out to me, then his hand waving, the smile on his face as he seen me at the start line. A predator's grin.

I paced while my dogs slept. The crowd at the Junior start had been bustling but not overwhelming. Had Dad seen Hatch, too? And if he had, did it matter? I imagined the two of them running into each other, Dad exclaiming over the stranger he'd ferried to the clinic, asking after his injury. Shaking Hatch's hand and wishing him well. Hatch smiling and nodding, thanking Dad for his help. Then climbing into a truck or making his way toward the road to hitchhike north with the certainty that when he reached my house, far as he knew, it would be empty. Maybe he was wily enough to hang back the way Jesse had done, watch the yard from the protection of the trees long enough to learn that Scott and Helen had stayed behind.

Why he had come back, I couldn't be certain. Was he looking for Jesse? If he had been hanging round, he could of easily heard through village gossip that Bill Petrikoff had taken on a hand, a young guy who'd just showed up one day. Or maybe he knew about the money in Jesse's pack? The money I had took for myself.

Whatever he wanted, it was my fault either way. Once I'd stabbed Tom Hatch, I should of never left home. I should of been always on the lookout, because he was my responsibility.

Stella woke up when another team slid past. We'd

been stopped nearly an hour, enough time for the dogs to feel refreshed. Stella stretched and yawned, then looked at me with her head cocked, as if to ask, *What now?*

I could forge ahead, like I'd planned. I had about fifty miles ahead of me before Yentna Station. But once I was there, like all the other Junior mushers I would have a mandatory ten-hour layover before I could turn round again and finish the race. That was ten hours I couldn't waste. Ten hours, then another eight or more back to the finish line, then the hours it took to pack the dogs and the sled and the gear, and the time on the road, and when we finally reached home, Hatch would be long gone. Leaving what in his wake? Thanks to Jesse, I had seen the kind of violence he was capable of.

But if I turned round right now and let my dogs run hard as they pleased, I could be back to the starting line in less than a couple hours. Hatch had a head start, but not much of one. Me and Dad, we could catch up with him. Get home before he could do much damage. All I had to do was drop out of the race.

My stomach sunk. Another team passed by, the musher wearing bib number 15, he raised a hand from the back of his sled, and I raised mine back. After that, the trail was empty. Nothing but emptiness round me, endless white space, a mountain in the distance. It's what you call a *paradox*, the way that kind of emptiness can fill you up. As much as racing was about training your dogs and caring for them, planning and strategizing, it was also about appreciating this place, the rise and fall of the land, the barrenness and fullness of it.

The dogs had realized we was nearly ready to hit the trail again, some of them stood and barked, eager to do their job. We had only run a couple hours, they was still a fresh team and none of them showed signs of reluctance to get back into the race. We was in last place now, but the nearest team had only just passed us, we could catch up. I knew my team, and with a good rest that night, I felt like we still had a chance to run a respectable race, maybe even pull ahead. It wasn't crazy to think we could still win this one.

If I run, though, it would be the kind of running a hare does when it catches the scent of a wolf in the air. A jagged, all-out kind of running, the woods and snow a blur. Nothing on its mind but finding its home, somewhere safe. But there wasn't anyplace safe. Not with Hatch nearby.

Peanut whined when I opened up my sled bag instead of getting on the runners and pulling the snow hook. I pushed through layers of gear and food and extra clothes to find what I was looking for, not letting myself acknowledge that I had already made up my mind. Only solving the problem in front of me, then the one after that.

First problem was figuring out how things could go wrong. You don't just turn round and go back to the starting line because you changed your mind, and I wasn't about to tell Dad I come back to the start early because of Hatch. If I could get through the next day or so without having to confess what I done, Dad would never have to know. So I needed to create a reason for dropping out of the race that he would understand.

I had seven dogs on my team, and to stay in the race, I needed to finish with a minimum of five. If things somehow went horribly wrong, if I had to put three dogs in my sled's basket on account of injury or sickness, I would be justified in turning round right here. I wasn't about to injure none of my dogs on purpose, they needed to be in their best shape come the big race, never mind that no matter how many critters I had bled with my own hands, I didn't think I could intentionally hurt any dog, much less one of my own.

Instead, I dug through my sled bag, growing more frantic as I searched for the surprise Dad must of left me. My first Junior, I slid into the Yentna Station layover and made straw beds for my dogs, fed them and cared for them, then rummaged through my gear to find my own dinner, a plastic bag of frozen moose stew

I would heat up with my little pocket stove. What I found was the stew, plus a treat: Dad had taped a dark chocolate candy bar to the bag, along with a note in his slanty handwriting. *Good luck Trace, I am Proud of you. Run hard and have Fun!* I haven't never cared for chocolate one way or the other, but I ate that bar, the bitter sweetness on my tongue a reminder of how hard Dad had worked to help me get where I was, of how much it meant to him that I had wanted to race, that it was something that linked us together.

Ever since then, he always slipped a chocolate bar into my sled bag right before a race, when I wasn't looking.

I finally found it, wrapped in my extra pair of socks, a bar of plain dark chocolate with no filling or nuts inside.

The dogs had already had their treat, but Marcey was never one to turn down any type of food you give her, and some you didn't. Once, when she was house dog, we left a plate of burgers on the counter and she managed to knock the plate to the floor and eat every last patty. Boomer wasn't such a pig, but he would still eat nearly anything, plus he had a sensitive stomach. I snapped the chocolate bar in half and offered both dogs a piece. Marcey practically swallowed hers whole while

Boomer held his between his paws and daintily bit off smaller pieces.

Both dogs weighed enough, the amount of chocolate I give them wasn't likely to do real harm, just make them sick. By the time we got back to the starting line, they would probably be shaking and panting, maybe even vomiting. For now, they both sat on their haunches, licking their lips and waiting to see what I would do next.

I walked up the line to my leader. When I'd needed a replacement for Flash, I'd settled on Peanut because of his sharp sense of direction, he always seemed to know the way to go, even on a trail new to him. But he was also a trial. Ornery and obstinate, downright difficult when he wanted to be, of all our dogs he was the most likely to wriggle out of his collar and run off if he was feeling restless. It wasn't much of a stretch to imagine he might experience one of his ornery moods just a few hours into a race and give me the slip.

The moment he heard me unclip his harness, Peanut bounded away, springy with energy after a snack and some rest. I whistled, and he come racing back, then passed me, headed in the right direction now, back the way we come. Good boy, I called after him. He paused, looked back with his tongue hanging out, his ears perked. When he seen I didn't mean to follow right away, he barked, then took off, a dog on the loose.

I tried to take my time clipping Marcey, then Boomer, into the sled's basket. No telling exactly how long it would take for them to start showing they was sick from the chocolate, and I needed evidence that I couldn't possibly of kept racing. But Hatch was on my mind, him and the minutes that separated us, each one adding to the next, till we was hours apart, him ahead of me, and me scrambling to catch up. My hands shook as I put Grizz in the wheel position where Boomer had been, now it was up to Stella and Zip to lead. The dogs had been patient enough while I'd dosed Marcey and Boomer, but when I stepped onto my runners they went crazy, barking and jumping and tugging on lines. I pulled the snow hook and let them take me west long enough for them to run out their back-on-the-trail jitters. I scanned the horizon and seen I was alone, no other teams or race officials in the distance.

Then I hollered, Come gee! and we turned, headed back the way we come.

The sun dropped out of the sky trailing pink and orange, till there was only a thin band of light on the horizon and a half moon hanging in the sky. The early evening seemed to fill the dogs with adrenaline, they pulled with real enthusiasm over a trail dotted with dozens of paw prints and runner marks. Time to time, I hopped off the sled and run alongside uphill, when I jumped back on, my heart was pounding not just from the small effort but from how close I was to home. To the truth.

The trail back seemed twice as long as when we'd run it earlier in the day. At every small rise, I squinted into the distance hoping to see a snow machine's headlights, but it was more than an hour before I finally spotted a race official. Both Marcey and Boomer was shivering and panting in the basket.

I threw out my snow hook then waved my arm.

Got a little turned around, didn't you, musher? he said when he pulled his ATV up next to my sled.

You seen a loose dog? I asked. My leader got away, and now I got two sick ones in the basket.

Marcey picked that moment to start retching. She made a hacking sound, nothing come up yet, but it got the race official's attention.

I haven't seen your runaway, he said, but I'll radio to the other officials. Meantime, we'd better get you back to the start so the vet can take a look at your dogs.

Can you have someone find my dad, too? I asked. Bill Petrikoff. He's camped out near the start.

You're Petrikoff's kid? He frowned, shook his head.

Well, that's too bad, you dropping out. Y'all have seen enough bad luck for one family, I'd say.

Don't worry, I told him. I'm running the big race next week. That'll put us back on track.

He grinned. That a girl, he said. Follow me.

His radio squawked as he turned his ATV round. I whistled at the dogs, and we fell in behind the official, following him down the trail at a too-slow speed for my taste. I practically bounced on my runners, more anxious the closer we got to the start.

When we finally reached our destination, it wasn't no longer a start but a finish. Race volunteers had already erected the big arch with its banner that read JUNIOR IDITAROD FINISH! in giant, bold letters. For the second time that day, I had to stand fast against a wave of regret. I imagined the next afternoon when the first musher come gliding across the snow, greeted by a cheering crowd. Parents whose faces would beam with pride. I ended my run with Dad jogging over to meet me, wearing a look of concern.

You okay? he said and put his arms round me.

I don't know what happened, I told him, it must of been something they ate.

I gestured at the two dogs in the basket, both of them had got diarrhea by now and my sled bag was sprayed with shit. The vet had already come over and was unclipping Boomer from the rig.

And then Peanut— I said.

He's in the truck, Dad said. Steve found me when Peanut showed up about half an hour ago. What happened?

I shook my head. I didn't have to pretend to be upset, standing under the finish arch with two of my dogs being ferried away by vet techs while fourteen other mushers was gathered round the bonfire at Yentna Station by now, chatting about the day's run and the condition of the trail. My eyes went hot and my throat filled with a stone I couldn't swallow.

Dad hugged me again. We were worried, Trace. I know Peanut likes to run off, but— His turn to shake his head.

I cleared my throat. Can we just go home? I asked.

It took longer than I'd hoped. The vet checked Marcey and Boomer, then give them both something to make them vomit. She frowned as they horked up half-digested kibble and asked, Any chance they got hold of some chocolate somehow?

Then we packed up camp, I worked so fast I had the tent down and my sled bag cleaned up and stowed in the truck before Dad had finished tying my sled to the top of the dog box. I sat in the cab of the truck watching him talk to Steve Inga and trying to not scream at him to hurry up. Finally, he settled behind the wheel.

You know, the roadhouse is still open, he said. We could drive into the village, get something to eat—

No! I practically shouted the word. I mean, I really just want to go home. If that's okay.

Sure it is, he said and turned the truck onto the highway.

We was closer than ever to home, closer with every mile we drove, yet it already seemed too late to me. Too much time had passed, wasted on packing and talking and running part of a race I never should of signed up for. I gripped the handle of the passenger side door so hard my whole hand went pale. I could see home before we was anywhere near it, different versions of it. All the windows of the house dark while a shadow emerged from the woods and got closer, closer. Tom Hatch standing over Scott's bed while Scott slept, Hatch slinking room to room, searching for Jesse's pack, startling at Helen's voice asking what he was doing there. Bodies left bloody on the floor by Hatch's own hand. That same hand pounding at the shed door till it burst open, Jesse shouting as Hatch pounced, finally finding what he'd come north to find.

When we pulled into the drive, I threw open my door and got out of the truck even before it had stopped.

Tracy! I heard Dad holler at me, but I was already running round the back of the house, I threw open the door and tracked snow across the kitchen. Homer and Canyon both sprung to their feet, barking, bringing Scott down the stairs, already in his pajamas, Helen looking up from her book in the den, a shout of surprise dropping out of her. Both of them unmarked, unharmed. Alarmed by an intruder but the intruder was me, there wasn't no one else.

Where is he? The words fell out of my mouth before I could stop them.

Where's who? Helen asked. She put a hand on my cheek. You're so flushed. Do you feel all right?

Jesse's in the shed, Scott told me.

But Jesse wasn't in the shed, he was at the door, frowning and glancing at Dad. I heard the truck— he said.

I shrugged Helen off, pushed past Jesse and went back outside. Run to the middle of the yard, that panicked-rabbit run. I turned, scanning the perimeter of the woods. Trying to hear the sound of someone approaching over my own panting.

Tracy! Dad was calling after me.

The kennel. I remembered the night we found Jesse's footprints outside the building, a good place to hide till the middle of the night when no one would expect a visitor. I sprinted across the yard, pushed the door open so hard it slammed against the wall and swung back at me. I held my breath and listened as I crept across the room, listened for someone else breathing, floorboards creaking, anything, as I went stall to stall only to find each one empty.

You want to tell me what's going on? Dad spoke up from behind me.

Jesse was in the doorway. The two of them staring at me, wanting answers that I couldn't give.

I— I started, and all at once felt lightheaded. I staggered. Helen, who had followed Dad to the kennel, rushed over to me and put her hand on my forehead again.

You've got a fever, she told me then put her arm round me. Is this why you came home early? she asked Dad, then said, Come on, let's go back to the house and get you into bed.

I let her usher me outside, confused and tired. A sort of terrified calm rushed through me, the resignation a critter feels in its last moments, when it sees your knife, feels your hand round its neck, and some part of it understands everything will be over soon.

When we got to the shed, Jesse peeled away from the group. I went after him, seized by an idea.

I seen the man from the fair, I told him.

Jesse's face as confused as Dad's.

The man who won the strength game, I tried again. Understanding lit his eyes.

What's she talking about? Dad asked.

Jesse shook his head.

But when I let Dad and Helen lead me to the house, I glanced back at him. Mouth pressed into a frown. He'd got my message.

Upstairs, Helen took my temperature then give me a couple pills from the medicine cabinet. I tried to insist that I needed to help take the dogs out of the dog box but I didn't try very hard, truth was I could barely string words together I was so exhausted from the day and the panic and the strange disappointment of coming home to find everything and everyone just as I had left them. Dad would take care of the dogs, Helen assured me. What I needed now was sleep. So that's what I got.

I didn't wake till noon the next day. The house quiet, no sound but the radio someone had left on. I stayed in bed, watching snow fall past my window, long enough to hear that the Junior had wrapped up just before eleven that morning, a seventeen-year-old musher from Big Lake had come in first, second went to the rookie from Bozeman, and a girl from Nome had placed third. I expected to burn a little at that news, and was surprised to find I didn't care.

I finally crawled out of bed close to one. My face still flushed when I looked in the mirror, I didn't feel hot except to the touch, my palms was clammy. Before I'd left for the Junior, I had took two squirrels, it should of been enough to get me through a few days before I needed to find something else warm. I felt sick, but it didn't feel like the same kind of sick that come when I hadn't drunk. I splashed water on my face and brushed my teeth, then went outside to find the truck gone.

I knocked on Jesse's door, then pushed it open when there wasn't no answer. He was gone, too, his bed made and a book he'd borrowed open and facedown on his small table. The woodstove dead but still warm to the touch.

I went back outside into snow that come down thicker now, big palm-sized flakes wafting from the sky. The yard eerie with quiet.

Now, I thought. A silent message from me to Tom Hatch. Come right now, when it's just me and you.

The thought threatened to send me into a panic again. Even though I knew he was close, he had the upper hand. But I had tricks. Tools. Years and lives I had drunk in, everything the animals I'd killed had taught me. Hatch didn't have none of that. I breathed deep. Slowed my thundering heart.

I waded through new, shin-deep snow to the trail-head. The nearest trap was only about a mile down the trail and with any luck I would find a catch.

The day muffled with mounds of snow, it clung to the trunks of trees and blotted out the sky. But there was a grinding in my head, like metal chewing on metal, a sort of screaming that made it hard to think. I tried to clear my mind of Hatch's face. Smiling as he raised his hand and waved. *Good luck, musher!* The look of recognition in his eyes the day he landed in our yard. His brows knitted together, his face too close to see in detail, as he pressed himself onto Jesse.

I tried to be Jesse. Went looking inside myself for what I knew of Hatch, the kind of man he was. Methodical. Handy. Patient, till he wasn't. He had courted Jesse in his way, but then something had gone wrong, his patience had run out and something else had took over, landing the two of them behind the barn. Later, they had come north, Jesse first and Hatch after him. I could piece that much together. Then I walked into the story with my knife in my hand and my mind washed away with a tide of blood.

Nearly five months, Hatch had stuck round after Dad took him to the clinic. He'd spent at least some of that time in Fairbanks, recovering from his wound. Time he must of spent puzzling out where Jesse might of gone. Then what? Had he come back to the village, started hanging round the roadhouse and the post office, chatting about nothing to folks till it wouldn't seem odd when he asked about the family whose yard he'd collapsed in? He'd discovered enough to show up at the Junior. And if he knew anything about my family, he knew who Dad was and probably figured that odds was Iditarod champ Bill Petrikoff Junior would be in Anchorage come the first Saturday of March, along with his kids, gearing up to run the big race. Leaving his property empty. If anyone stayed behind to keep an eye on things, it would probably be that young man Petrikoff had took on, the one who didn't say much and lived in the shed out back.

My trap was empty, so I hid myself in some brush and waited, the thoughts in my head churning and grinding against each other so loud I felt certain every animal in the woods would hear and stay away. But after a spell, a fox come slinking out of the trees. About ten feet from the creek, he stopped short. Sniffed the ground, then circled round a spot in the snow that didn't look no different from any other spot. I held my breath. His ears, each one big as a plate, facing forward. He stopped, lowered his head. Waited. Then launched into the air and come arcing down, face-first into the snow, his hind legs and tail the only parts visible till he resurfaced with a mouse between his teeth.

I should of took that fox. I was hungry and cold and feverish and if I went much longer without some kind of warmth I would get even sicker. But I sat and watched it hold the mouse between its jaws and crunch down on its body, and its reddish-orange coat made me think of Mom's coat, the only bright thing against the whiteness as she stood at the mouth of the driveway. Till she turned back, come inside the house. Never passing the house to go into the woods the way I would of done.

When the fox slinked off, I stood, too, pocketed my knife, and headed home, my stomach aching worse than ever but my mind certain.

16

Sometimes I would catch Mom watching me. I would look up from sewing booties for our dogs' feet or chipping frozen piss from their houses, and there she would be, hands shoved in the pockets of her coat, her eyes on me. A strange expression on her face, or no expression at all. When Dad was irritated with her he would call her *temperamental, fickle,* words that sent her into a rage but only meant you couldn't predict what mood she might be in.

Sit with me, she would say other times and I would perch on the edge of the couch near her till she put an arm round me and pulled me close. I don't bite, she whispered in my ear. I had come into the den more times than I could count to find her and Scott cuddled up in the same spot, reading together or her teaching him how to use her complicated-looking camera. There was always something between them, I understood, invisible strings that kept them close, while if anything tied me to Mom, it was only her understanding that I was different from Scott, that my needs was different. That's what I thought for a long time.

Tell me about your day, she said when I still smelled like snow and wet wool after hours in the woods. So I described the windless afternoon and the trees furred in hoarfrost, how the brief sun that day had found diamonds in the snow, they glittered loud as a song in the soundless wood.

She stroked my hair while I talked. You're so warm, she whispered.

Her moods would last days, weeks sometimes. She would grow paler than normal and stay in bed long past morning, and Dad would ask if she was feeling all right. Then, one night, I would wake to find her gone, her red coat floating in the dark while I gazed on her from the window that overlooked the driveway.

I only had a few days before the Iditarod ceremonial start, but a few days was more than I needed. The trick is to go just long enough, and not too long. By the next day, my stomach yawned and snapped like a fish on a bank gasping for water. By afternoon, it clutched like a fist, and that evening as the whole family sat round the dinner table, Dad complimenting Jesse on how tender and juicy the burgers was, the meat stuck to the roof of my mouth, dry as sawdust. When I finally got it down, my belly lurched and I got up from the table and run to the toilet.

When I didn't come back out, Dad knocked on the bathroom door and said, Trace? You okay in there?

The taste of vomit was thick on my tongue. I flushed, then leaned against the sink and splashed water on my face, drank from my own cupped palm. Seen in the mirror what Dad would see when I opened the door.

Jesus Christ, kiddo, he said and put his hand on my forehead.

I don't got a fever, I told him.

You look like death on toast.

Thanks, I said and give him a weak smile.

No going off in the woods tomorrow, okay? he said. I think you need a day in bed.

I'm okay, I said. I need to check my traps.

Jesse can check them for you.

But—

Do as I say. He put his arms round me and rested his cheek on the top of my head. I closed my eyes and let my whole weight sink into him.

Go on, now, he said. Rest up. You don't want to miss your big race.

No, sir.

His eyes on me as I climbed the stairs. For that moment, I changed my mind. I didn't want to listen to my own stomach gnaw at my insides. I wanted to push past him and run to the woods, drink the first critter I found. Then put my dogs on the line and run, because I had a race to train for. I wanted to slide into the yard after a hundred miles and be greeted by Dad's smile, the way he always raised one hand, not a wave but like saying, Here I am, always waiting on you to come back. Over the last couple months, he'd worked just as hard as I done to get me ready for my first Iditarod and even though I knew he'd understand if I dropped out on account of being sick, I also knew that if I didn't race, at least a part of him would be disappointed.

Trudging up the stairs, I glanced down at the kitchen and seen Scott and Jesse, both of them watching me head to bed at seven o'clock. My eyes found Jesse's. Concern on his face, concern for me. When I got to the second floor, I heard him ask Dad, Everything okay?

No, I thought. But it would be. I would make sure it was.

The next day, I didn't get out of bed till Helen come

round. She took one look at me and become the nurse she was, took my temperature and shooed me back into bed, piled blankets on me and give me something to rub into my skin, something else to swallow with water. When I heard her tell Dad she thought he ought to take me into town, I pushed my blankets back and hauled myself to the bathroom, my knife in my hand. Made the smallest cut in the crook of my arm. Watched myself in the mirror after, as the color come back to my cheeks, the dullness gone from my eyes. Rolled my sleeve down, over the cut I'd made.

When I opened the door I found Helen about to knock.

I was just going to check on you, she said. You aren't nauseated, are you? Dizzy?

Matter of fact, I'm feeling pretty good, I told her.

You do look better.

She put a hand against my cheek. I knew she was only feeling for fever, but my stomach dropped when she touched my face. Her hand so unlike Dad's, which was broad and calloused. Unlike Jesse's, which roamed over me, urgent, as generous as his touch was, it was always wanting something, too. Helen touched my cheek, and I thought of all the times Mom had done the same.

I'm okay, I said.

I know you're probably itching to get on a sled, Helen said. But please do me a favor and don't go outside today. Give yourself a day to mend.

I nodded. Can I give you a hand in the kitchen?

She smiled. Of course you can. It's nice of you to offer.

I sat at the table and watched more than I helped, Helen give me vegetables to chop for a salad while she readied dinner. She moved like a bird about the room, lighting in one spot then sailing across the room to fetch something from the pantry. When Dad come in from feeding the dogs, the two of them beamed like kids to see each other. A surge of warmth come over me, though no one had thought to stoke the fire in the woodstove that evening. When Helen left after dinner, I waved as she pulled her Jeep out of the drive, sad to see her go, though her being round made things more troublesome for me.

One sip of my own blood wasn't much, and by the next morning I felt woozy and looked pale enough to play up how sick I was. When I didn't get out of bed round my usual time, Dad come in to check on me.

How you feeling, Tracy Sue? He pushed my sweaty hair out of my face. Seems like you were getting better, and now this.

I'm fine, I said. I'll be on the back of a sled tomorrow morning.

He sighed. Looked round my room, the soft glow of the lamp in the corner, the bookshelves he'd made me, filled mostly with books he'd either suggested or give me when I wanted to learn something new, the rocking chair he'd built Mom when she was pregnant with me. She'd used it when Scott come along, too, then it got moved to the den somewhere along the line, but after she died I drug it up to my room. Sometimes I would sit in it, rock back and forth, and think of her with a baby in her arms. How she must of worried over me, over Scott. *Sometimes I think if I hadn't,* she'd told me, *you might not be like you are.* How loud I must of cried to make her decide to do what she done.

Dad rearranged my blankets, fluffed one of my pillows. He seemed distracted, or hesitant, and finally after he hadn't said nothing in more than a minute, I said, What?

He sighed again. I don't want to tell you that you can't run your race, he said. But—

I know, I interrupted because I didn't want him to have to say it neither. I know I'm too sick to run. My voice cracked. Silly, the way my eyes stung when I had made this decision myself. But saying the words out loud somehow made it more real.

I'm sorry, kiddo. Dad stroked my hair.

It's okay, I said and swallowed the sob that wanted to come out of me.

We sat in the dark for a time, neither of us saying anything. Till I cleared my throat. You should run, I said. Before Dad could tell me it was against the rules or he wasn't ready, I went on, I read over the rulebook, and if it's an emergency, the race marshal can approve a substitute musher. The fee's already paid, the team is ready, and anyhow, people want to see you race again.

Trace—

And Steve Inga is practically best friends with everyone who's ever been involved with the race. He could talk the marshal into okaying a sub.

He shook his head. Even if Steve finagled that, he said, there's no time. The mandatory meeting's on Friday—

So? It's Wednesday. We shipped the food drops before the Junior. All you need to do is pack your sled bag and go.

Dad frowned, but I could see a spark in his eyes. He was thinking of reasons to say no, but there was just as many reasons to say yes. I knew he just needed a push.

There hasn't been a Petrikoff in the big race since Mom died, I told him. I was too young, and you was suspended. But both of us is eligible now. If Mom was here—

I didn't need to finish what I was going to say. I could see it in his face, in the way his whole body changed, his muscles seemed to relax even as a sort of excitement pulsed off of him.

Please? I said, for good measure.

He held up a hand. If I race, that means Helen is going to come out and check on you. I might see if she can even stay here, long as you're feeling poorly.

Fine, I said and sunk back into my pillows, tired and relieved.

Dad smiled at me. Guess I'd better go pack, eh? You want some breakfast before I do?

I shook my head. I think I'm just going to sleep a bit more.

He give me a kiss on the forehead before he left the room. I did sleep afterward, not just for a few more minutes but for the whole day. When I woke it was long past sunset and the house was quiet. I trembled while I dressed, my skin cold now and my head swimmy. I longed to head into the woods, slice open the vein of some lively critter. But I still had work to do.

Jesse had turned in for the night. The beam of my flashlight bounced off the shed's walls as I slipped off my boots and climbed onto the cot next to him. He woke with a jump, then relaxed when he seen it was me.

You're freezing, he said. His voice seemed smaller in the dark.

I snuggled closer to him. I hadn't come out to the shed since before the Junior, even before I'd left for the race I had often been too busy to visit, I ended most of my days by falling into my own bed and not waking till Dad poked his head into my room and let me know coffee was on. I had missed the shed filled with the orange glow from the woodstove, missed the closeness of the room. Waking up to find Jesse next to me. I would miss him again, but if my plan worked, I wouldn't have to for long.

What happened? Jesse asked.

We hadn't had a chance to talk private since I'd made Dad drive me home from the Junior and busted into the house, expecting to find Hatch. It took me a second to realize Jesse was asking about the message I'd give him that night. *I seen the man from the fair, the man who won the strength game.*

Hatch was at the start, I said now. He waved at me. I was certain he meant to come out here while me and Dad was gone. But he didn't. Or maybe he did, and he seen the three of you, and decided to wait.

Jesse frowned. You think he's waiting till the Iditarod to come back and—what, exactly?

You tell me, I said. You know him. Why would he

of stayed in Alaska so long past the time it took him to heal?

In the dark, I didn't have to close my eyes to see Hatch gazing at me the way he'd gazed at Jesse. Or feel his hand in mine. Or his weight on me, his breath in my ear, the rake an arm's length away, my fingers straining for the handle. *I came here to start a new life. I didn't expect the old one to follow me* is what Jesse had said about Hatch coming north. I couldn't imagine a man who would cross so many thousands of miles to chase after someone who didn't want him. Then again, I didn't know the man. Not like Jesse done.

You're right, Jesse said. He's figuring Bill will race, he'll be gone, and as far as Tom knows, you and Scott and Helen will go down to Anchorage with him. Maybe that's what the Junior was about—he staked this place out first.

Seeing if you was still here, or if you moved on, I said.

And now he thinks after Bill leaves, I'll stay behind. Alone, Jesse said. He pulled his gaze away from the ceiling to give me a look. Is that why you're not racing?

I'm sick, I reminded him.

He rolled his eyes. Then said, Fine. So we wait for him. And when he comes, we'll be ready.

I'll be ready, I said.

What?

You can't be here, I told him. I can't do what I need to do, plus keep you safe.

He sat up. What you need to do?

I didn't answer, only watched the fire, so close to dying the wood had stopped crackling, there was only embers left. No sound from the dog yard outside. Silence growing thicker between us, so dense that when Jesse finally spoke, his one syllable barely broke through.

Oh, he said.

I kissed him then. Tired of talking, tired of thinking and convincing. I had more work ahead of me, but for now all I wanted was to sleep a bit, next to his warmth.

He wasn't done, though. If one of us is staying behind to deal with Tom, he said, it should be me. I can talk to him. Get him to leave, once and for all.

Has that ever worked before? I said. All the times he found you as you was coming north? You just talked, and he stopped?

Jesse's face flushed. No, but—

He went quiet. Light behind his eyes, his brain puzzling something together. His mind worked fast, I could almost hear it clicking and whirring like some kind of efficient machine.

Fine, he said after a spell. But I should still be the one to—get rid of him.

I sighed. Then pounced, I wound my legs round his and pinned his arms to the mattress, my teeth pressed against the soft skin of his neck, where a vein throbbed. I could feel his pulse speed up under my tongue. He tried to pull out of my grip, but I held on for a few seconds to prove my point.

I haven't drunk in days, I told him when I let go. I feel like shit, but I could still do that. Hatch is stronger than you, too. But I'm at least as strong as him. If one of us has a shot at dealing with him at all, it's me.

I could tell Jesse was irritated, but he was also coming round to my point. I don't like it, he said anyway.

Don't matter if you do, I told him. Only one of us needs to have this on our conscience, and it might as well be me, since I'm the one who nearly killed him the first time.

He chewed his lip, wanting to protest. But he said, If you think that's what's best.

I closed my eyes, pulled his blankets round me. The mattress creaked when he lay down again. I was so close to sleep. But I spoke up one last time.

Stay in Anchorage, I said. At least for a while. Helen will bring Scott back home after the ceremonial start, but you tell her you're volunteering with Steve for the rest of the race. And don't come back till Dad finishes.

But—

Promise, I said.

Outside, one of the dogs howled. Another joined in, then another. They sang like that for a long minute, baying at no moon, just checking in with each other, harmonizing briefly then falling silent again.

Okay, Jesse said and that settled it, the dogs begun to sing again and I floated on their voices, lifted up, up, soaring into the night even as I sunk deeper into sleep.

The morning they left I bundled up and stepped outside to watch Dad recheck the bindings that secured his sled to the dog box. The team was already inside, each dog probably already curled up and dozing, they was so used to the road trips that took them to each race start.

Helen come out onto the back stoop and put her arm round me. I'll be back right after the official start, she said. Or maybe I should stay here? How are you feeling?

Go, I told her. Otherwise, Steve is going to have to be Dad's date for the mushers' banquet.

She grinned and give me a squeeze. Soon the trucks was loaded up, Jesse behind the wheel of one truck with Scott in the cab next to him, and Helen waiting on Dad in the second.

Dad come over to where I stood. How you feeling? he asked.

Pissed off.

He chuckled, then got serious. I know. This isn't how I pictured this day.

My stomach cramped, and I winced.

I'm not so sure I ought to go myself, Dad said. You've been sick an awfully long time.

He took off his hat, and right then I was convinced he would shuck his coat, too, tell Jesse to take the sled down and let the dogs out. I had gone too far, got too sick, and now he wasn't going to race.

If I don't feel better after the weekend, I told him, I'll have Helen take me to the clinic. Okay?

Mean it?

I swear, I said.

I'm calling Helen from the first checkpoint, he said. She better tell me you made a full recovery or that I'm getting a bill from the doctor. One way or the other.

Yes, sir.

Good enough, he said, then a look of surprise struck his face. Hell's bells, Trace. I nearly forgot! Happy birthday.

A laugh fell out of me. For months, I had pinned my hopes on this birthday, it was the whole reason I was even able to enter the big race. But I'd got so preoccupied with Hatch and Jesse and convincing Dad to race, I had forgot all about it.

I didn't even make you a cake, Dad said.

How about you just win this race? I said. That would be a pretty good gift.

A win for Tracy, he said and give me a hug. I'll do my best.

Then he was walking away, leaving me where I stood. He climbed into his truck, the engine already running to keep the cab warm. Jesse rolled his window down and stuck his head out, give me a look. He started to say something, then changed his mind. Whatever he'd wanted to say, odds was he couldn't say it in front of Scott, anyhow.

I waved one more time, then darted inside, through the kitchen and up the stairs to my room, before the trucks rolled down the driveway. Even from inside the house I could hear the engines grumbling then growing faint as my family pulled away. I could see them leaving. Dad's truck first, then the one Jesse drove. I could see it easily enough from my bed, blankets over my head, eyes closed. Didn't need or want to see the real thing.

When I woke, it was Friday. I reached over to my bedside table and found my knife. Sliced across my palm and licked. Enough to wake me up and make me feel for the first time in days like I might want to do more than trudge from my bed to the bathroom and back. I put on boots and a sweater, tucked my hair under a wool hat, then struck out across the yard and onto the trail. Jesse and Dad both had checked my traps early on but they hadn't reset any since I was too sick to mind them. So I hunted, still feeling slightly woozy, till round midmorning, a snare I set caught a small marten near a squirrel midden where it liked to rest.

Once I had something warm in me, there wasn't much to do but wait, and think.

Next morning, I watched the ceremonial start on television, sharpening my knife as Dad's number was announced and the crowd clapped and cheered to see his team sail down Fourth Avenue. The real start happened the following day, fewer cameras round and no television coverage, just mushers and their families, handlers, volunteers. A few busy hours as the mushers left the chute one by one, then everyone scattered.

Helen had planned to drive back to the village that same evening, after the official start, and Scott spent the night with her so she could drop him at school the next day. Late Monday afternoon, her Jeep come trundling up the drive as I was working my way through a small stack of wood.

Scott leaped out of the Jeep, already chattering at me

about the start and the mushers he'd met, the movie he and Helen had caught while they was in the city. It wasn't till his stomach complained loud enough all three of us heard it, and he run inside for a snack, that me and Helen was alone.

I split a log and it fell to the ground.

I guess you're feeling better, Helen said.

Once I'm done being sick, I said, I bounce back fast. No kidding.

I stood another log on its end.

Jesse called last night from Skwentna, Helen said. He didn't want to call here and wake you up, but he asked me to tell you that Bill came in with the early leaders.

I frowned. What's Jesse doing at Skwentna?

Just eighty-three miles from Anchorage, Skwentna was one of the busiest checkpoints, since most teams hit it the first night. I pictured Jesse there, antsy and wondering what was happening back here, if Tom Hatch had showed up yet.

Helen waved a hand. Oh, who knows where he is now. Steve's got him traveling all up and down the trail. Jesse's going to have a front-row seat to the entire race, from what it sounds like.

I went back to chopping to hide the relief that come over me.

Helen went on, He also said to tell you Bill stayed six hours at the checkpoint. He's using the Tracy Strategy, is what Jesse said.

Hearing that made me smile. Dad had planned to check in at Skwentna and get through the vet check, then grab his food bags and hit the trail again, quick. His strategy was to run fast early on, get as much distance from the other mushers as he could.

But I had planned to run my race slow and steady. Since it was my first year, my job wouldn't of been to try and win but to learn the course, finish strong, and look toward the next year, when I could run as a seasoned musher. I had read how long-distance runners pace themselves, going slower the first half of a race to conserve energy so they could speed up toward the latter half, and I thought that plan could work for a team of dogs. I'd meant to try it out over the course of the Iditarod, just to see. Weeks before, I'd asked Dad what he thought. Might just work, he'd said. Then added, Every musher's got to come up with their own way of running a race. Now he had decided to run my race for me, in more ways than one.

Helen took her coat off, laid it over the hood of her Jeep. Started gathering the logs I'd split, stacked them on the sled till it was full then drug it over to the woodshed. When she come back, I swung the axe, then told her, Appreciate you bringing Scott home from school. I reckon I can drive him tomorrow morning.

You don't have to worry about that, Trace, she said. I thought I'd stay the afternoon. I've got a night shift tonight at the clinic, but after that I thought I'd hang around for a couple days. I figure you could use the company. Besides, you've been sick—

I feel fine now.

She nodded. You're still on the mend, though. I don't imagine you'll want to keep the house up and run Scott around while your dad and Jesse are away.

I appreciate it, I said again, but I can manage.

I really don't mind—

I do.

She put her hands in her pockets. I kept my eyes on her, waiting for her to look away, but she didn't.

I told your dad I'd look in on you, she said. I know you're old enough to manage on your own, but you don't have to, Tracy. I really think I ought to stay. I'd like to.

She was growing roots right in front of me, every second I let her talk they sunk deeper in the ground. Truth is, I wanted to let her stay. A wildness come over me, a recklessness sent the words battering at my lips, clamoring to get out and let Helen in on my secrets, all of them. Tom Hatch, Jesse, how both of them come to be here, and why. What I was, what I was capable of.

Instead, I thought of Tom Hatch. Conjured up the same images I'd worried over when I seen him at the Junior. A knife in his hand, a gun, his weapon pointed at Scott and Helen. I found a hardness inside myself, like a wall, and stood behind it.

It don't matter what you like, I said. Fact is, you're not my mother, Helen. I'm eighteen. I don't need a mother. I don't need you.

The smallest smile on her face as she watched me. I piled the rest of the logs on the sled and waited for her to move, prayed she would leave. An apology on my tongue that I couldn't give voice to.

Finally she tugged her coat back on. Opened the door of the Jeep. Before she got in, she said, Fine. I'll bring Bill's truck in the morning, and you can give me a ride back to the village when you take Scott to school.

I took the axe in hand again.

Call me if you need anything, Tracy.

I didn't look back, just listened as her tires shuffled over the soft snow.

The second day of the race, when Scott called after school to ask if he could spend the night with the Lester kid's family, I told him it was fine. Then, trying not to sound too eager, I added, Do you think his mom would be okay with you staying a couple days, actually? I'm not feeling so hot again, and I don't want you to catch nothing.

Sure, Scott said. Or I could just stay at Helen's—

No! I snapped. If Helen got wind I was sick again, she would come back to the house, no matter how rude I had been to her before. I added, I just mean, Helen's awful busy, and she's done so much for us. Let's give her a break, what do you say?

All right. Let me ask Chris's mom if I can stay a couple days.

I watched Homer and Canyon, the only two dogs still at home with me, pace the kitchen while I waited for Scott to come back to the phone. Concentrating on the click of their toenails on the wood floor, counting their steps to keep myself calm. Finally, Scott was in my ear again, telling me Mrs. Lester said he was welcome for as long as we needed, and could she do anything for me?

No, thanks, I told him. Be good.

And just like that, I was alone. I would be, till Hatch showed up. All I had to do now was be ready.

17

A biting wind kicked up and whistled round the corners of the house. I hunted and checked traps, but with the wind so harsh and no dogs to pull my sled quickly down the trail, I stuck close to home Tuesday and didn't bother to go out at all Wednesday. I tried to read, but my eyes wandered away from the page, my ears perked for the sound of another person nearby. I kept the radio on for race updates. If Hatch was smart, he was listening to the radio, too. He would know that Dad had dropped back a few spots but still blasted through the Finger Lake checkpoint and on to Rainy Pass. But the next stretch of the race, from Rainy Pass to Rohn, could be treacherous with glare ice. Then there was the Dalzell Gorge, a two-hundred-foot drop followed by a stretch of trail that crisscrosses over a half-froze creek. And if he got through that, he'd have to deal with the Farewell Burn next, all gravel and sandbars. Three hard stretches, three chances for Dad to run into bad luck, scratch the race, and come home early. Hatch couldn't risk waiting much longer.

Thursday morning I wore paths in the snow all over the yard walking from the house to the barn to the shed to the dog yard. Anxious and desperate to be in the woods. I went down the trail as far as my first trap, but come back fast as I could, the yard still empty. I took Dad's shotgun from the cabinet where he kept it, made sure it was loaded with the safety on, and propped it in the corner of the kitchen. I honed my knife.

That afternoon, Jesse called from the McGrath checkpoint to say he'd heard that Dad had left Nikolai round one A.M. just ahead of the start of a light snow. He was still running near the middle of the pack but he planned on taking his twenty-four-hour layover at McGrath, get some rest, and let the mushers ahead of him break the trail. He'd dropped Fly back in Rohn on account of fatigue, but the rest of the team was running strong.

What about you? Jesse said. Everything okay?

If you mean have I had any visitors, the answer's no, I told him.

He was quiet a spell. Then, Maybe he won't come.

Or maybe Hatch was in the woods right now, watching the house. Or prowling up the trail, a low rumble in his throat as he got closer. I thought it, but didn't say it.

The wind kicked up even harder, moaning through the yard. Homer and Canyon, who usually barked themselves silly four or five times a day till we let them out, curled up on the couch and didn't seem interested in moving any farther than their food bowls. I rolled from room to room like a tumbleweed. Built a fire in the woodstove, then another in the fireplace, just because I didn't know what else to do. Sat down in front of the fire to sharpen my knife, then got back up after a few minutes to check a sound I thought I'd heard outside.

Scott called to see if it was okay to come back home. He wouldn't say it, but he sounded tired of his friend, cranky and out of sorts, ready for his own bed and books and dogs.

Just give me one more night, I told him and hoped it was all I would need.

I tried to read.

I thawed some stew for dinner.

I whittled some, and thought about what I would do with Scott if Hatch didn't show up tonight. Let the curls of wood fall to the floor.

Swept the floor.

Round eight thirty, I opened the door to let the retired dogs out, and the wind cut through me, fired bits
of snow like embers at my cheeks. The dogs whined
and hid just inside the mudroom, till I shoved them
both toward the door. Just go! I hollered and my voice
was lost in the gale.

I waited with the door closed, fed another log to the
woodstove, then opened the door again and whistled.
Canyon come sprinting back inside and dropped onto
the floor like he'd run the whole Iditarod, but Homer
didn't follow.

Goddammit, I muttered and pulled on a coat.

The wind whipped across the snow and sent it swirl-
ing, it become a thick curtain impossible to see through.
I slid my feet forward to feel for the first step on the
back stoop, my hand out. In a brief moment when the
wind died and the air cleared, I spotted Homer, standing at the end of the driveway.

Homer! I shouted but the wind snatched my voice
away.

I started toward the driveway, hoping he wouldn't
suddenly decide to bolt. If he did, he was on his own.
There wasn't no searching for him in whiteout conditions.

Of course I should of known, even before I got to her, which dog it was. Should of known that if I tried to pet her fur my hand would go right through her.

When I reached Old Su, she looked up at me, barked, then trotted away, down the drive. I blinked and expected she would vanish, or at least be lost in the tumbling snow, but she was still visible, every now and then the snow let up and I would glimpse her, twenty feet away, forty, now nearly to the place where the driveway cut through the trees.

I run after her.

I got a break from the wind when I reached the trees, protected for about a quarter of a mile, till I reached the end of the drive and stood on the shoulder of the highway. The wind slicing through my coat.

Su was there, maybe a dozen yards away, walking south along the side of the road, toward the village. Except she wasn't alone. Even in the dark, with no light or moon shining down and the snow flying, I could make out Mom's red coat.

I followed her. A car trundled by, moving slow, and for a long moment its headlights lit the road. She paused on the shoulder, silhouetted, waited for the car to pass.

She never did talk much about how she'd hunted when she was a little girl. She'd told me about running wild in the woods, disappearing for hours or even days and coming home with tangled hair, covered in dirt. In blood, too, most likely, though she never mentioned that part. She'd only said she'd been a wild thing. Till she decided to tame herself.

She took a few more steps, then stopped short. Crouched down. Minutes had passed, or hours, I couldn't tell. The evening had cinched tight, the snow had nowhere to go, it filled my eyes and blotted out everything but her.

All the questions I should of asked her but never did. All the ones I did ask, only for her to dodge a straight answer. Why hadn't I insisted on answers, like how, exactly, she had stopped herself drinking? Or why people and animals was so different, and how she knew. What had happened to the boy who'd got lost in the woods when she was little. Why she wouldn't go into the woods alone. Where she went when she snuck out at night. I remembered holding those questions back, afraid she would spook and scurry away, shut me out.

She knelt on the shoulder of the road. This far outside the village, in this weather, in the dark, she didn't have to hide herself.

Why the trash bin in her bathroom was so often filled with scraps of tissue soaked red.

Why she was so often sick, and so quickly well again.

When I thought of how she died, I used to wonder what she was thinking when the truck hit her. If time had stretched out as she flew through the air, as flakes spun round her, like floating in a sea of snow. And I wondered what she was doing out, middle of the night, walking along the highway's edge.

She hunched over the body. You'd find them flattened in the middle of the road or thrown to the shoulder, those that had met their end crossing the highway. Long dead. Long cold.

I had roamed the woods for days at a time with no catch. I knew what it was like to go without. How you become desperate enough you will take whatever you can get. How you look at your own arms, the cuts you've made, dizzy with the loss of blood, and realize you've already taken too much. All you want is something warm. And if there's nothing warm, then you will settle for anything that will stop the ache inside you.

I didn't know I was crying till a sob wrenched itself from me. I covered my face and wept, aching for her. Aching after her. She was just a few feet from me, close enough for me to ask her anything, but I didn't have no more questions. I only wanted to tell her to stay. Not to hide.

But when I took my hands away, she was already gone.

No moon, no beams of light from cars driving toward me as I turned round and headed for home. Nothing but snow, thick as a wall. The driveway, soft with accumulation. If I hadn't been blinded by the storm. If my own head hadn't been filled with longing for her. If my eyes had seen what was in front of me instead of what was inside me, I might of noticed the fresh tire tracks, leading to the house.

Sometimes I think maybe she never did get hit by that truck. I went to her funeral so I know full well she is nothing but a pile of ashes that Dad scattered in the raised beds where she used to plant her garden. But sometimes I let myself believe she tricked us all, that whoever those ashes was, they wasn't my mother. That my real mother had planned all along to take to the woods that night. She didn't head for the highway like usual but down the trail, till she come to a clearing in the brush and boulders and snow, where she could see the rolling land and the mountains, and she let herself be pulled onward, into the wild. She descended then climbed, and every step took her farther from her old life. Closer to what she always knew she was. What she knew she'd always be. What she'd told me time and again I could run away from the moment I chose to, the moment I had a good enough reason, when all along she'd known what I know now, that you can't run from the wild inside of you.

Taillights stopped me at the bend in the drive. Two red eyes that flickered in the dark, in the blowing snow, before they went out completely and I heard a car door open and close. I slipped and nearly fell as my feet found a new direction, away from the house and toward the kennel. I'd missed him on the road, the same snow that now hid me from him had blocked his headlights, or I'd been too distracted by ghosts to notice them. And now he was on my doorstep, or working his way round the corner of the house, searching for the shed. Quiet, grateful for the wail of the wind to mask his approach.

I reached the kennel and pulled the door closed behind me and the constant noise fell away, the whine of the wind muffled by the walls, and for a moment I felt like I'd gone deaf. I could hear my own heart, thudding hard in my chest.

I needed to move, but I was stuck. Pulled in so many directions at once, I couldn't move at all. My mind like a moth inside a clutched fist. It's contrary, the way some critters will go still when a predator is nearby, instead of running or hiding or fighting back. But I understood it now, the way every possibility can seem like a mistake, so you end up not making any decision at all.

I shook my head, like to clear it. That wasn't me. I had the advantage, Hatch thought I was inside the house. I could come from behind, ambush him before he even knew what happened. But Dad's gun was propped in the corner of the kitchen where I'd left it. My eyes darted round the barn. Dad's workbench, with the big saw. Dozens of harnesses hung from nails. Axes, hammers, even the wrenches and screwdrivers in Dad's toolbox, the whole kennel full of tools that could be used as weapons but none of them a sure thing. I was strong, I had pinned Jesse when I felt half dead, and now, after several days of hunting and drinking, I was better than well. But I was still a girl. Stronger than most, but I wasn't sure I could kill a grown man if it come down to a hand-to-hand fight. I needed distance to kill Hatch, and certainty. I needed the shotgun.

The wind died all at once, a lull in the storm. I held still, my ears aching from listening so hard. Quiet outside. He could be inside the house by now, or in the shed. Anywhere.

I waited for a surge in the wind then opened the kennel door. A gale caught it, nearly wrenched the door from my hand. I gripped hard and pressed my whole body against it to get it shut. Then stood with the wind wrapping itself round me, bits of ice and snow biting at my face. I turned. Let instinct and memory lead me in the direction of the house, invisible in the flying snow. Everything invisible.

I cleared my head and felt my senses sharpen. Tried to think of Tom Hatch as a creature I was hunting. To feel him out there, wherever he was. Just another animal.

A dog started to bark. Homer.

I inched forward, skirting the dog yard, I thought. I couldn't see the light of the lamp or feel whether the ground under my feet was ice or snow. Couldn't tell if Hatch was across the yard or inches away. I put my hands out, certain I would bump into him, I flinched at the thought of it. The wind shifted, pushed at me like a palm, urging me forward. Something inside me give way and I broke into a run, hoping I was headed the right direction. Moving blind through the snow. Closer to the house, to the gun. Fast as I could, till I run directly into Hatch.

His hands grabbed me, his fingers round my arm, his other hand clutched my coat. I think he shouted. His voice taken by the wind. I tried to pull loose, but he held fast, fingers digging into my arm. He towered over me, so tall his face seemed miles above me, too far away to make out in the dark and the storm. His body pressed against mine, same as when he'd took Jesse behind the barn.

My free hand in my pocket, fumbling.

His hands searching. The palm of his glove, sudden and rough against my cheek. His hot breath on my skin.

I drew my knife out, windmilled my other arm from his grip. Unfolded the blade. I understood without thinking hard that the blade wasn't long enough to slice through all his layers and still pierce the skin.

Tracy? The voice faint in the wind.

No! I heard Jesse say, his voice ringing out inside me.

My knife the only bright thing in the white and the black. It gleamed as I slashed, a straight line across his neck that opened like a mouth.

Tracy, said Helen.

She didn't fall. Her arms dropped, then she raised one hand, put it to her neck. For a second I seen her clear, and she seen me. Then the wind rose again and the snow hid her from me, so the memory I have of her looking down at her own palm, studying the blood that run out of her, I know I must of only imagined that. I had sliced a hundred necks, drained the life out of countless animals by knowing exactly where to cut. It is a fast way to kill, only a matter of seconds, the blood stops going to the brain and the animal is quickly gone. No time for Helen to gape at me, a question in her eyes.

But plenty of time for me to understand what I done.

I folded in half and let loose a stream of vomit, it splattered against my boots and the snow on the ground went yellow with it. My insides heaved, everything solid in me coming loose and the earth rising up, the ground itself rolling and cracking and opening under me and swallowing me. I wished it would.

She was only a shape on the ground. Her eyes filling with snow. A black puddle growing under her.

I tell myself what I done next, I done on account of I owed her something. After taking her life, I meant to carry her with me, like a burden.

I knelt next to the shape of Helen. Crouched over her. Drank.

18

I find myself in a cool, dark barn, my fingers round the udder of a cow, and my pop's hand over mine, his breath tickling my ear as he tells me, *Giver her a squeeze, the milk'll come slow at first, there she goes—* The musty, pleasant smell of the barn and the solid flank of the cow and the milk hits the bucket with a metallic hiss and Pop lets go, he don't smile easy but now he grins and a joy wells up in me so intense I nearly topple over.

The sun setting over fields of hay behind my family's house and lighting everything orange and yellow and the queer longing it fills me with, unexplainable and palpable.

My brothers and sisters, shouting from other rooms, fighting or laughing, the stench of my oldest brother's room, dank and sharp, like dirty socks and sweat and something I can't quite place. The hothouse heat cut by a cooling breeze, the five of us lined up on the screened-in porch and trying to sleep but waking each other with pinches and fart sounds and giggles till Ma pokes her head out and tells us, *Settle down,* her voice dressed up in its stern outfit but still amused underneath.

The quiver in my belly when the boy with black hair brushes past me in the hallway at school. The heaviness of my private parts, a dampness, when I think about him, touching myself.

A thunderstorm raising the hair on my neck, the feeling of my ma's arms round me.

Other things, everything. A fish flopping on a grassy bank, pride and regret at the shot that killed my first deer, the warm tang of beer on my tongue, my whole self buzzing with coffee, bleary eyed, the words in my nursing books fuzzing together. My own hand stopping a man's blood, pressed against his chest, and the mothball smell of the closet I hide myself in, giving into a minute of crying the first time a patient dies on my watch.

I cry, too, overwhelmed, at my first sight of Alaska, the mountains here grander than anything I've seen back home.

And I make the bed I've slept in, a bed that isn't mine but where I have come to feel at home. Voices float up through the floorboards, children who don't belong to me but who I care about, have grown to love, the boy who is generous and kind and easy, and the girl who is wary but quick, who wears her longing for her mother on her sleeve. And then he steps into the room and my pulse quickens and I could stay here, in this room, be part of this family, forever, if they see fit to let me.

Days and months and years of love and hate and want and boredom and fear and contentment. A life-time in one drink. The last drink, her last heartbeat. Her lifetime coursing through me, no longer coursing through her, as all round us the snow swept the land and howled like a wounded dog.

19

In the morning, I woke to the sound of a dog whimpering. I sat up, my whole body sore down to the bones, and snow cascaded off of me. Homer rose, too, licked my face, he had curled himself next to me in the night.

The sky was clear and blue, by the faint light and the position of the sun just above the trees I could tell it was still morning but late, near about ten. Sometime in the night the wind had finally died, there was drifts about three feet deep against the barn and nearly burying the dog houses. I was lucky, the drift that had formed over me and Homer had acted like a blanket, kept us warm as I'd slept.

The new snow had all but erased Helen. The only

part of her visible was her eyes, froze open. The light in them gone.

At first, I stayed pinned to the ground, wanting to look away from her but unable to. There was a wave rising, towering above me, weighted with the reality of Helen, dead beside me, and my knife, coated in her blood, and Dad, oblivious on the trail, and Scott, at school now but home by four thirty that day. The hole I had tore in their lives. A wave, building and building, it would crash down on me soon and when it did, I wouldn't be able to swim against it, it would carry me away, useless and flailing.

But I could do something now. Before it crashed. I couldn't right what I done, but I could move.

I wrenched myself up from the ground and led Homer inside, fed both dogs. Then drug out a sled, the one I'd meant to race with that year, and got out the rigging I'd need for just two dogs. Two retired dogs who hadn't pulled a sled in ages, but the memory of it lived in their bones, they was still strong.

I went back inside and forced myself to eat a bit of breakfast, a cold hunk of leftover elk meat that stuck in my throat. Then it was back outside with both dogs now, I put them on the line and instantly they began to bark and tug at the sled. I took them round the perimeter of the yard a couple times to get the eagerness out of their legs, then gee'd them toward the house and cut through the middle of the yard, where Helen waited.

I knelt, pried my fingers under her. There wasn't no give to her. Her body stiff, her clothes froze to the ground. I strained and felt something pull in my back. She tore free all at once, I tumbled back under the sudden release, and hit my head against the edge of the sled.

Her eyes filled with sky. The kindness in her face was gone, everything gone. I thought of the way I had sent her off a few days before. *You're not my mother. I don't need a mother. And I don't need you.*

A wail grew inside me. I choked it off before it could escape.

I took my glove off and tried to close her eyes, but the lids wouldn't stay shut. Instead I fetched an old blanket from the barn and covered her. Wrapped her as careful as I could.

Even bundled that way, she was near impossible to move. However much she'd weighed in life, death had doubled it. I panted as I drug her, the blanket bunched in my fists. Pulled her onto the sled, then stood with my hands on my knees, catching my breath. Went round and lifted her legs, spun her on her back till she was mostly on the rig. I fumbled with knots as I tied her body down with the same ropes we used for securing gear. Perversely glad that it was such a great effort. I deserved to struggle. Killing someone shouldn't be an easy thing.

On the trail, I could almost convince myself it was just another run. Except the quiet of the woods didn't cool my mind and send my heart thrumming like usual. I remembered Hatch, the possibility of him, and waited for the hair on my neck to stand up. But the threat of him seemed distant now. Inconsequential. Not a word from my vocabulary, but Helen's. All I could hear was her voice—

Tracy?

—and feel her concern, she'd carried it with her as she'd drove out to the house to check on me, despite the poor weather and the way the truck had fishtailed, her worry when she'd found the house empty, the impulse she'd felt to check the shed, a suspicion inside her, paired with amusement and nostalgia for her own young infatuation, that there was something growing between me and Jesse.

I shook my glove off and sunk my teeth into the flesh of my own hand, deep enough to draw blood. Pain shot up my arm, electric and bracing. I couldn't get lost in Helen now. I had work to do.

The sled spilled out onto the lake and the dogs carried me over the ice, and all the breath went out of me. Ice, solid as stone, thick, and my mind like a panicking bird, throwing itself against a wall. No chance of the sled breaking through. No tools in my basket for chipping away at what had to be a good four or five inches of ice. It hadn't occurred to me how cold it had got after an early winter of strangely warm days, and it had been ages since I come to the lake, I had trained and hunted most of the winter in other parts of the woods. I had imagined the water swallowing Helen like a throat, the floes of ice holding her under till the spring melt. Till I could find a way to tell Dad what I had done.

I drove my two-dog team across the ice, north, more out of habit than hope. I remembered, the day Old Su died, dropping a stone into the water and how the ripples had sent the floes bobbing. I steered the dogs back toward the middle of the lake, searching for a crack, for a dark spot where the ice was thin enough to punch through. I remembered, too, the shape of the tool my dad, Helen's dad, used to drill a hole in the ice, our hands round our hot mugs as we sipped and waited, the tug on my line when I caught a fish. I squeezed my eyes shut, shook my head. Tried to ignore Helen's life, playing out inside me and distracting me.

We traveled south, the dogs fresh and keen.

The sound of a blade on ice, feel of the frozen air

on my face as I spun, then toppled, landed hard, my brothers laughing at me.

North again.

Round in circles, the dogs galloping and their tongues wagging, and me on the back of the sled trying to hold down the panic rising inside me, trying to ignore what I'd took from Helen, every memory she had of ice. Solid ice, all around.

I finally brung the dogs to a stop near the west side of the lake. Leaned on the handlebar and wrapped my arms round my head. With no more sound of the runners or the crunch of eight paws on ice, it was even louder inside me, the memory of Helen's brothers laughing, the whisper of her skates' blades. She shouted, *Hey, Pop, watch!* and I felt the toe of her skate catch the ice, her head, my head, turning before my body did, my whole self suddenly spinning. I shook my head again, plugged my ears with my fingers.

Stop it! I hollered.

My voice bounced against the ice, then the day was quiet. I opened my eyes, seen my dogs looking over their shoulders at me. Heard water churning. Falling. Finally able to think straight, I could see the lake in front of me instead of the Montana lake in Helen's memory. No more laughter and shouting in my ears. Instead, I heard the rush of the waterfall, west of here.

The little cove where the river emptied into the lake. The water there never completely froze over, no matter how cold it got.

Let's go! I called out. The dogs lunged forward and we followed the sound.

It didn't take long to reach it, a jagged shelf of ice round a hole at the base of the waterfall, maybe two feet wide. I undone the ropes that held Helen on the sled and pulled the blanket away. Twisted the fabric of her coat in my hands and hauled her out of the basket. She landed hard, her head thudding on the ice, and a cry startled from me.

The dogs watched as I drug her by the feet toward the water. Their breath condensing on the air. Sliding her across the ice wasn't no easier than dragging her over the snow, I coughed and wheezed. She stuck to the surface of the lake and I heaved her toward me. Took a step back, toward the hole.

The scrim of ice cracked underneath me, then give way.

The cold gripped me, I gasped and my insides turned to ice, then I bobbed to the surface, sputtering and gulping air, my arms and legs flailing and splashing and the water and cold like a vise round me, crushing my chest. My whole body a heart, slamming itself round but stuck in one place. I wrenched my head back to keep it out of the water. Seen the sky. A bird flying overhead. Gliding across the quiet of the day till that quiet was broken by the splashing and gasping of a girl about to drown or freeze to death.

The thought calmed me down enough I stopped struggling. Sunk again, so tired, nothing under me, it would of been so easy to go under and not come back up. Easier than admitting to Dad that Helen was dead, I had killed her. Boots heavy on my feet, clothes weighing me down. Quiet now, for the bird. For me. Helen laid on the ice, staring unblinking at the sky and waiting for me to join her.

Instead, I kicked. Rose up, grabbed the edge of the ice. It broke off in my hand. I kept kicking till I was on my belly, my forearms on the ice now, my coat sleeves freezing to the surface of the lake. I wrenched them free, kicking, inching forward onto the shelf of ice, my cheek on the lake now, my shoulders. A cracking sound under me, straining. Half out of the water. I couldn't go back in. I kicked harder, my eyes on Helen's shoulder. My fingertips brushed the top of her head. Kick. Kick. Still holding my breath. I exhaled. Flung my arm forward. Grabbed Helen's coat. Pulled myself across the ice till I laid at her side.

Funny how warm I was then. How far away everything was. The dogs was barking, they'd been making a ruckus the whole time I was in the lake, I realized now. They would be how Dad would find me, days from now, following their hungry barks till he come to the lake.

Helen's eyes on the sky, unable to follow the bird's path. It was far away now.

I'm sorry, I said between chattering teeth.

I hauled myself up. Not shivering but quaking, my whole body racked and shuddering as I scooted away from the water then hauled Helen toward me, till we was on thicker ice. An hour, two, a whole day, it seemed, to strip her of her coat, her pants, her socks, and boots. Another whole day to strip myself, a week to crawl into her clothes, not warm but dryer than my soaked-through clothes, at least. Do this. Just do this one last thing, and you can go back home. Like this never happened. Except it had. Would continue to happen. Always.

I pushed at her bare feet and she was a plank of wood scooting headfirst toward the water, till the ice broke under her. I inched myself back toward the sled. For a long second, she floated. Till she begun to drop, feet first. Her eyes the last thing visible before she disappeared under the water.

My teeth clacking so hard my whole skull felt about to shatter. My bare hands stuck to the ice and I peeled them off, one then the other, as I crawled to the sled. The ice creaked, panic squeezed the breath from me, till I realized it was just the normal twanging of a froze-over lake. My arms and legs dumb, hard to work. Fumbling to pull myself into the basket. Under the blanket I'd used to cover Helen.

I might of fallen asleep then. I might of got a whistle out first, something to tell the dogs it was time to go home. That's where they went, back down the trail, without me to encourage them or holler them faster. They raced through the woods under snow-crusted branches, the day noontime bright and glittering, the kind of day you ought to spend outdoors. I stared at the patches of sky, struggled to keep my eyes open. Afraid of what I'd see when they closed. But when I couldn't keep them open no more, when I finally did drift off, I didn't see nothing. There wasn't nothing left.

Back at the house, still more to do. I left the dogs on the line and attached to the sled, tethered to a tree so they wouldn't run off, while I hauled myself inside and crawled out of Helen's clothes and into the shower. Lukewarm water likes needles all over me at first, till my skin begun to warm and I finally stopped shaking. I was lucky nothing was frostbit.

Downstairs, I built a fire in the woodstove, stoked it,

then fed Helen's clothes to it, piece by piece. Her Carhartts smoldered while her wool socks burst into flame instantly. I would have to take her boots to the burn barrel, they would smoke something awful. I held her shirt to my face, remembering how after Mom died I had sometimes hid in her closet, where her blouses and sweaters still hung, and pressed my face to the fabric to catch the scent of her, clinging like a ghost to her things. Helen's shirt smelled faintly of sweat, of metallic cold air, of dog and fabric softener and things baking. When I took it away, it was damp, and I threw it into the fire.

Back outside to take the dogs off the line. I left the sled parked in front of the barn, the gangline strewn across the snow, while I fed the dogs again then rubbed their paws and checked them for cuts since I hadn't took the time to fit them with booties.

The ground where Helen had laid all night was rusty with the blood that had run out of her. No puddle, I'd disturbed the snow when I drug her onto the sled. But there was enough red spotted on the ground to tell something had bled there.

I fetched a rake from the barn and tried not to think about how it was the same kind I'd seen through Jesse's eyes. Used it to comb the red out of the snow.

Exhaustion was creeping over me, ready to fell me like a tree. But it was after noon now, only a few hours before the Lesters would bring Scott home from school, and there was one last thing to do.

I climbed into Helen's Jeep and found her keys where she always left them, in the ignition, like anyone was welcome to use her car if ever they needed to. I turned the Jeep round, got it onto the highway, and drove. A half hour south I pulled to the side of the road and got out, locked it with the keys still in the ignition. A VSO or a state trooper would come across it sooner or later and start wondering who it might belong to. By then Dad would of already reported Helen missing, I imagined. People would search for her, police and co-workers from the clinic and folks from the village, she was well liked. They would find her, eventually. But not till spring.

I run back home.

When I got there, I finally crawled into bed. Certain I would plummet into sleep, every bone and muscle and inch of skin shredded. But when I closed my eyes, it only made finding Helen easier. I searched for sleep and found her life, lived it moment by moment and all at once. I stared at the ceiling and seen Helen, not a breath or pulse in her, just a pair of eyes under the ice.

———

At first, I thought it was a dream. A hunger gnawing at my stomach, my trip to the refrigerator automatic, not an option but a routine. Then a checklist, one intention lined up after the next, an evening full of plans: Snack. Homework. Drawing. Anything good on TV tonight? Dinner, maybe I should offer to make it so I don't have to eat Tracy's cooking—

I sat up in bed, my head pounding. Thoughts like bubbles continuing to float to the surface, then burst open, exposing me to—

Scott? I hollered.

His footsteps on the stairs, irritation pricking his skin, how he hated yelling, why couldn't people just talk in normal voices?

I clutched my head. These thoughts wasn't mine, but they couldn't be his. I wasn't looking for them, hadn't drunk him in ages. And the thoughts I'd got from him before wasn't like this, clear, loud, happening inside me soon as he had them.

What's up? he said when he poked his head in my room.

Concern that my sister looked sick again. Exasperation, there was always something going on with Tracy, trouble all the time. Hunger still scratching its nails at me, my shirt too tight at the armpits, I didn't know why I picked this one to wear today, and a washed-out feeling, all I wanted to do was hide in my room a bit and draw or read in quiet, it had been too many days away from home and too many hours with a friend I now realized I only sort of liked.

Nothing, I gasped, and I got up, shoved past him and shut myself in the bathroom.

With a little distance, Scott was fainter but not gone. I could still find him, except there wasn't no *finding*, he was there, present inside me without me needing to conjure him up, and the feeling and thought and impulse and experience wasn't old but new, *now*. It didn't make no sense. The taste I had got of Scott when we was younger was like the taste I had got of the first animal I ever caught, the chipmunk that wriggled out of my hand and bit me. Before I drained it I only got fleeting impressions, the briefest sense of its fear and the instinct that drove it to protect itself. A taste only gives you moments. I had got moments from people, too, thoughts and memories that was on their mind when I drunk. From Aaron, from Scott. From Jesse. Sometimes I could suss out what was on his mind even without drinking, we was so close, but I hadn't never heard his thoughts, loud and unfiltered inside my own head. I had drunk from hundreds of animals as they died warm in my hands, lived their lives. But their lives hadn't opened me up to every other critter in the woods.

Never make a person bleed, that's what Mom had told me, what she'd made me promise.

I had broke that promise plenty. But I hadn't never drunk from a person as they died. Not till Helen.

I crumpled to the floor as Scott knocked and asked, You okay, Trace?

Go away, I said and closed my eyes.

He went away, the floorboards creaking underfoot and the hinges on his bedroom door complaining. Still, he was there. Inside me. The closest I could be to anyone, hearing the voice in his own head narrate, feeling relief at taking off the too-tight shirt and pulling on a sweatshirt instead. He was there, a room away, yet louder than my own thoughts.

20

Dad didn't win the Iditarod that year but he done all right, come in eighth with a team of fifteen, no more dogs dropped after Rohn. He finished in nine days, fourteen hours, twenty-one minutes, and three seconds. He didn't tell me how running this particular race brought back the memory of Mom, aching and comforting at the same time, how the distance of months and the changes those months had brought somehow made the loss of her not exactly okay, but tolerable. He didn't tell me, because he didn't need to.

The whole of his existence rushing at me before he even come inside the house the day he returned. At the sink, I scrubbed a plate for long minutes, even though I had polished it clean, concentrating on not sensing Scott, who was in the den, shoveling ashes from the fireplace. Unprepared to be pummeled by the pleasant fatigue and the gratitude for home that preceded Dad inside.

I staggered, dropped the plate into the sink full of water, and gripped the edge of the counter.

Whoa, there, Dad said when he seen how my legs buckled. You're not still feeling poorly, are you, Trace?

Concern reaching for me like hands, and numbers clicking through his mind, he always forgot if the clinic's phone ended in an eight or a nine. And an absence tugging at him.

Helen leave this morning? he asked as he led me to the table.

I dropped into a chair, my stomach plunging. Grateful this openness didn't go two ways, that he couldn't know what was in my head, because along with the dread of him discovering Helen was missing, and the guilt over what I done, now I understood I wouldn't just feel my own loss and regret and horror at what I done. I would feel his, too.

It didn't make sense. Dad and I had always been close in the way of two people who work alongside each other or who like the same things. The dogs brung us close, racing, the woods, even the times he showed me what he knew about hunting or shelter building. All that linked us together, but not the way drinking would of. Yet now I was as close as I could get to him. I had the same sudden access to him as I had with Scott.

She wasn't here, Scott was telling Dad. I haven't seen her since Chris Lester's mom dropped me off Friday. Did she come back after you got sick again? he asked me.

I didn't tell her, I mumbled, then added that I didn't feel so well now, I thought I would try to nap a bit, and I stumbled up the stairs, leaving Scott and Dad downstairs to wonder about Helen. While their unspoken thoughts and feelings trailed after me like tendrils of smoke.

I stopped in the bathroom first. The only way I had been able to get Scott out of my head the night before had been to sleep. I was wide awake now, despite how I felt, like someone had wrung out my guts. I rummaged round inside the medicine cabinet till I found an old prescription bottle, a picture of a truck on its side with a line drawn through it. *May cause drowsiness. Alcohol may intensify this effect. Use caution when operating a car or dangerous machinery.* I swallowed two pills without water, then flopped onto my bed, didn't bother getting under the covers.

My dreams was my own, no one else's. I know because I dreamed of Helen, her body sinking slow into the icy water. Her eyes, filled with snow.

I skipped dinner, though I woke enough to hear Dad describing the race to Scott. He recounted each leg of the run from Willow to Nome, though he didn't sound as animated as he'd done in previous years. He was distracted, worry fretting his brain, plucking at it like fingers that couldn't still themselves. Till finally, in the middle of a sentence, he got up and dialed the phone. His fifth call to Helen that day. I listened to ringing through his ears, till her answering machine picked up. *Hello, you've reached Helen Graham's residence. I can't come to the phone right now . . .*

Think maybe I'll drive out there, he said to Scott.

Can I come?

The whole house suffused with their distress. *Suffused.* I rolled the word round in my head, not a word I would normally use, but a Helen word, a word I had got from her. I closed my eyes and buried my face in my pillow, didn't stir when Dad knocked on my door, and when he and Scott was long gone, I went downstairs to find the note he'd left me on the table. *Gone to Helen's, back soon. Love you.*

My head finally my own for a spell. Clear. The thoughts inside it only my own. My arms and legs limp with relief. I roused them, shoved my feet into my boots and went outside. For the first time since my trip to the lake, I sought out the trail. Run into the trees.

I needed to find a way to disconnect myself from Dad and Scott.

I stayed in the woods long past when I should of come home, at first hunting, setting snares, then waiting in the sublime silence of the woods, reveling in it. Near about midnight, it begun to snow, slow, soft flakes that wafted to the ground. It covered the tracks of animals and masked the sounds of them in their dens. I rose finally and plunged deeper into the wild, looking for traps I had set. I found one triggered, then another, the animals already dead but I drunk from them anyway. Filled my head with random minutes from their lives. I was quickly full, but I kept running, searching, and when a vole darted across the trail I was quick, I snatched it before it vanished in the underbrush. Its whole short life rushed through me. Then the silent wood again, and my silent head. Escape, finally.

When I come home, I found that Dad and Scott had returned with company. The Village Safety Officer's car was parked outside, engine still running against the swiftly dropping temperature. The snow had stopped.

Stepping inside the house was like turning on three radios all at once, all at full volume. All three minds, Scott's, Dad's, and the VSO's, exposed. I waded unwillingly into the stream of their existence.

There you are, Dad said, and there was relief I was

home and irritation that I had gone out without telling him. Worry about Helen, weighing heavier on him now that he knew she hadn't showed up at work, neither, something the VSO had told him, the VSO whose attention was like a mirrored ball, each face reflecting upon a detail, a scrap of information, a face, my face, marking me as an unknown, noting that he would have to make time to ask me questions, the way he had asked Scott, whose fear had escalated though he was trying to tamp it down, a boy sitting on the lid of a cage that contained a rabid bear, willing and eager to eat him whole.

Stop it, I hollered. Or only whispered, since the three of them ignored me.

We found her Jeep about thirty-five miles south of here, parked on the shoulder of the highway, the VSO told Dad. This was after someone at the clinic went to her house to check on her. She'd missed— He glanced at the small notebook in his hand. Two shifts. Coworkers said that wasn't like her.

Dad shook his head. No.

We sent search and rescue out, in case she broke down and got lost somehow.

She wouldn't of left the highway in that case, Dad pointed out.

The VSO nodded. Still, worth a look. Didn't find any sign of her, though.

So, what now?

I had crept across the room, nearly to the stairs, but now I felt every face of the VSO's attention turn to me, the glare of it hot as the sun.

When did you last say you saw Ms. Graham?

I swallowed. Winced under the weight of all their focus, all three of them hanging on to me like I was a hand about to pull them from a ledge. I breathed deep.

She dropped Scott at home last Monday, I said slowly, wading through their thoughts to find my own. Then I give her a lift back into the village when I took Scott to school Tuesday morning, after she dropped off the truck. I guess that was the last time.

And she didn't come back to your house?

Not after Tuesday.

And she didn't call to check on you?

No, sir.

His brown eyes lingered on my face and I made it blank as I could. I felt suspicion like spider legs skitter all over my skin. Then he nodded.

Well, you think of anything, you tell me. Or your dad.

Will do, I said.

Dad's hand found me, his arm slipped round my shoulders and give me a squeeze. Go on upstairs, both of you, he said. And try not to worry. VSO Chappel here will help us. We'll find her.

His hope as palpable as his doubt. I ducked my head as he kissed the top of it, unwilling, unable to look him in the eye.

She really didn't call? Scott whispered to me when we got to the top of the stairs. That doesn't seem like her. She's a nurse. She was worried about you.

Well, she didn't, I said.

He trailed behind me as I tried to ignore him, his words tugging at me. Why would she walk away from her Jeep? Where would she have gone? She wasn't far from here—why didn't she come home if she needed help? Do you think she got hurt?

My head on fire.

Why aren't you more *worried*?

I spun round. Shut *up*! Just shut up!

He blinked. The color went out of his face, and then a storm gathered where his worry had been. Not a thunderstorm, but a soft, ceaseless rain. Drops that found no place to land, just fell through a bottomless crater.

I'm sorry, I said. I'm just—scared. I'm worried, really. I just don't know what else to do.

His face softened a bit. He wanted me to stay, to sit in his room till he fell asleep, the way I used to do some-times, right after Mom died, when a nightmare woke him and he called me to his bedside. He hadn't done that in ages. I guessed the nightmares had stopped. His whole self latched onto me, digging blunted claws in, wanting me to comfort him. And still, from downstairs, Dad and the VSO radiating their selves up at me. Made sense for Dad to think after me, I felt concern for me tugging at the corners of his mind, the parts that wasn't focused on Helen. But I nagged at the VSO's thoughts, too. He felt me like a distraction, kept trying to swat thoughts of me away like a tiresome gnat. I hated knowing he hadn't brushed me aside. Like there was a searchlight looking for me, edging closer in the dark.

Scott's thoughts hopeful, pleading with me not to leave him.

Night, Scott, I told him and turned away from the disappointment I didn't need to feel, it was so plain on his face.

I closed my door, then wadded up a blanket and shoved it under the space between the bottom of the door and the floor. It seemed to help a little.

I'd stashed the pills from the bathroom under my pillow. I took three this time and hoped it would be enough. Then I waited for sleep, staring dry-eyed at shadows.

When I woke, it was still night. The house quiet, my head quiet, too. Mom quiet as she sat on the edge of my bed, weightless. No red coat now that she was indoors, instead she wore her fuzzy white robe, her hair wet.

I was a lot like you when I was your age, she said without saying anything.

I remembered the day she come to my room to warn me away from strangers, not because the strangers was dangerous but because she worried I might be. Hikers, hunters, folks who had lost their way. People get lost in the woods all the time, she said. Like that boy who had disappeared from the village where she'd growed up. *I even went looking for him*, she'd told me.

Was you the one who found him? I asked her now.

She reached into the pocket of her robe. Her fist clenched when she took it out again, she dropped a knife on my bed. Not a pocketknife like mine, but a kitchen knife, a small one with a serrated blade, the kind you would use to cut your dinnertime steak.

She drew her hand away, the hand of a child, and the mom fresh from the shower with dripping hair was gone, in her place was a girl younger than me, bare chested and wearing only a pair of boys' shorts, her hair a tangled mess, her fingernails crusted with dried blood. Her lips smeared with it. A wild thing.

You drunk him? I asked and realized it wasn't a question because I already knew the answer. You done it as he died.

She fiddled with the knife, not looking me in the eye.

And after? I said. You knew him, but did you know—everybody?

She was herself again, pale and frail looking. Too tired to keep her eyes open. I thought of all the times she spent days in bed, shut away from everyone. Of the pills I'd found in the medicine cabinet and used myself to plunge into sleep. To escape everyone else's thoughts.

Thought of the years and years she must of lived with other people inside her head.

Now she wore her red coat. Her lips too red, and there was blood on her face. She wiped at it with the back of her hand.

Vomit at the back of my throat. I swallowed it, and my stomach burned.

Scott was awake. I knew it, not because I could hear him get up and cross the hall to the bathroom or because his light clicked on, but because I could feel the pressure in his bladder, the groggy half-woke murmur of his brain remembering the remnants of the dream he'd been having, something about a lynx that stalked outside Helen's house.

My eyes went hot, and I squeezed them shut.

Does it stop? I asked Mom, my voice cracking.

But I knew she was gone even before I opened my eyes again.

Jesse made it home the next day, skinnier than ever but happy and full of stories from the checkpoints he'd worked. He'd caught a ride with Steve Inga, who stayed to dinner, and the kitchen was lively with conversation, even livelier if you could hear what wasn't said, the silent commotion that happened inside every person's head. Some of the talk and thought was about the race, but most of it centered on Helen. They laid out their facts and memories like puzzle pieces, tried to fit them together into a picture that would tell them what might of happened.

I stayed in my room, still feigning sickness. Took four pills that evening, and sunk into a heavy sleep.

Late the next morning, Dad roused me.

Come on, he said. Pack a bag. We're going camping.

I would of been confused if I couldn't of felt the aimless desperation in him, the need to move, to get out of the house. I rummaged round my room, collecting what I would need for a night or more on the trail. Stuffed clothes and gear into my pack then found one of the straps broke when I tried to shoulder it. Shit, I muttered. Stuck my head under my bed, found Jesse's pack, the one I still hadn't told him I'd found before I even knew he existed.

I had done my best to avoid thinking about Tom Hatch. Wasn't all that hard, actually, with Helen taking up most of my thoughts and the rest of my head filled with other people's existence. It was possible Hatch was still round, still planning to show up on our doorstep one day. But every day that passed, the likelihood seemed smaller. Everything seemed small under the shadow of Helen's death.

I repacked my things in Jesse's old pack, then strapped it to the sled Dad had already drug from the kennel. Threw a tarp over it when Jesse materialized in the yard, heading my way.

Need a hand?

He followed as I fetched Boomer from the dog yard and led him back to the rigging laid out in the snow. Though I had drunk too many animals to count at the moment of their death, not to mention Old Su as she had faded in my arms, there wasn't no cacophony from the dogs inside my head. But I didn't even have to try to sense Jesse. His voice was casual but his thoughts was tremulous with anxiety and curiosity, invisible fingers poking at me, prodding for information.

He didn't show, I said.

Jesse shook his head. I was going to ask if you're feeling better, he said.

Only because you don't want me to think you're more worried about Hatch than you are about me.

Whoa, Jesse said and grabbed my arm, firm but gentle. Why would you say that?

I stared at the ground, trying to wade out of the soup of him. He was too close.

Sure, I'm worried about Tom, Jesse said, quiet. But either he showed up and left, or he showed up and—you took care of it.

The unspoken question not just in his eyes and his inflection, but hovering in the air between us, a tangible thing.

Dad come over, guiding Marcey by her harness. She had long recovered from her chocolate treat, was back to wolfing down any food you put in front of her. She grinned with her tongue lolling, danced up on two feet, and I wished with everything inside of me that my mind could be as simple as hers. Eager to run, not thinking about much else.

I think two on the line will be enough, Dad said as he clipped Marcey onto the gangline. We're not going too far.

I'm ready when you are, I told him.

What can I do? Jesse's voice dropped to a whisper as Dad stepped onto his own sled.

I knew Jesse meant what could he do to help me. To mend things between us, since he sensed something was off. But even with that worry, hope shimmered round his edges like light creeping into a dark room round the edges of a door. With Tom out of his life and a new family of sorts, here, Jesse was finally starting to believe maybe he could have what he'd been searching for ever since he left Oklahoma. Since before that, even.

But at the center of him, still, a box with a lid shut tight. A part of him I still couldn't reach.

I rubbed my forehead, squeezed my eyes shut for a brief moment. Dad whistled to his team, and they sprung forward, pulling him toward the trailhead.

Nothing, I told Jesse and tried to sound like myself. Everything's okay. We can talk when I get back.

I hopped onto my sled's runners and called out, Let's go! to Marcey and Boomer before Jesse could say anything else. Followed Dad onto the trail, not needing to look back to know Jesse watched till I was gone.

The deeper we dove into the woods, the quieter my head grew. The woods closed round me and the runners of the sleds hushed against the snow and the dogs breathing, their feet churning, we traveled in a cloud of our own breath, under the bowed limbs of trees and sky growing lighter with the burgeoning day. Dad's head was quiet, too, the fullness and emptiness of the woods had the same effect on us both, our worries didn't exactly vanish, instead they was like the land after a big snowfall, everything buried, the shapes of things still discernible but all their hard edges blunted.

I was warm in my coat and hat but when we hit the lake and crossed its icy surface, a spike of cold shot through me. I begun to shiver almost as hard as I had the day I pushed Helen into the water. I gripped my handlebar, thankful Dad was ahead of me and couldn't see how badly I shook.

We made camp after dark. Dad was quiet as we ate next to our fire, preoccupied with thoughts of Helen now that we wasn't moving over the trail. He didn't know what to do, and he gnawed at his not-knowing, a bone he couldn't chew through or leave alone.

Where's the farthest you ever gone from here? I spoke up.

Hmm—? His face emerged from the shadows as he leaned forward into the circle of light cast by the fire.

Training out here, on your own, I said. How far out have you gone?

He sipped hot chocolate from his thermos, his mind mulling over the question now, distracted for the moment. Like I'd hoped. His cheeks was still windburned from the race, and his hair had got shaggy. I noticed for the first time it was starting to gray, the white in his beard wasn't from frost.

Long time ago, Dad said, I took a small team all the way through the mountains. You know those two peaks, the ones that look almost like a pair of blunt teeth?

I nodded.

I followed a pass that took me right between them. Come out the other side. But the only descent I found was a chute that makes Dalzell Gorge look like a playground slide. So that's the farthest north I ever went from here. This was, you must've been about four or five. Two babies at home, I didn't fancy plunging head-first down the side of a mountain.

The flames of the fire lapped at the night round us. Dark as pitch now but in the morning the sun would be up earlier than ever, we was gaining more and more light and in a couple more months the days would grow warmer and the snow would soften, the trees would bud and the grass green up and, for a time, making your way off the land would get easier. Then the snows and ice would come again. Collecting water, finding something to eat, staying warm would all get harder, unless you knew what you was doing.

Dad wedged his thermos in the soft snow and put his hands out toward the fire. You know, he said, before Scott come along, before you was even born, I always figured on having a couple sons who'd run the dogs with me. I had it all pictured. We'd have a big kennel, a couple hundred dogs. Three or four of us all racing together.

You sorry it didn't turn out that way?

He shook his head.

Nope. You come along, and you was so good with the dogs from day one, like you could read their thoughts. You were a natural. In my wildest imagination, I couldn't have conjured up a girl like you, Trace. It didn't even matter when Scott got older and it turned out he wasn't all that interesting in mushing. Don't get me wrong, if he'd showed more of an interest, I would've taught him, too. But you learn pretty quick your kids are going to be drawn to their own thing. And it don't really matter, long as they're happy. I imagine Scott'll go off to college once he's done with school here. Maybe study photography, maybe writing. Maybe he'll write for a newspaper or a magazine. I could see him coming home, covering the big race one of these days when you're running it.

The dogs was bedded down in the straw we'd laid out for them. Now Zip stood up, stretched, then moseyed over to lay with her head in my lap. I stroked the fur above her eyes, the velvety softness of her ears.

What about me? I asked. What do you imagine about me?

Dad took a stick in his hand, poked at the fire till its embers flared.

I guess I always picture you on a sled, he said. Figure you'll take over the property one day. Run a proper kennel like I thought about doing. Maybe you'll be the one with sons and daughters racing along with you. A hundred dogs.

I nodded.

Who knows? he said.

I tilted my head back. The sky, endless, empty. Starless that night.

Who knows, I echoed.

We turned in when the fire begun to die. Dad's brain chattering, the edges of his thoughts growing fuzzier the closer he drifted to sleep. Still, I knew what he was going to ask before he give voice to it.

Trace?

Yeah.

You sure Helen didn't come check on you at all?

I could of told him then. About Tom Hatch, how stabbing him was a mistake I might of ended where it started, if only I hadn't gone back into the woods and found the pack full of money. A pack I assumed belonged to Hatch, so it was easy to claim the money as mine. Except that wasn't even the real reason I kept the money. I kept it because I thought I needed it, because the only thing that mattered to me was racing and the money would pay my racing fees. It also made me beholden to Jesse, though, so that when Hatch showed up again, it wasn't just a matter of finishing what I'd started the day I stabbed him. It was also a matter of owing something to Jesse. I owed him protection. I didn't just owe it, I wanted it, wanted to protect him and keep him nearby. Close. I couldn't let anyone hurt him because he was mine.

And so I had feigned being sick, I convinced Dad to run my race, I hid Scott at a friend's. I planned and waited, and made certain everyone I cared about was safe, and then I had finished what I'd started. And then Helen's voice spoke my name through the windstorm, her eyes found me in the blowing snow. Her blood blossomed red between her fingers.

Trace?

I cleared my throat. I'm sure, I said.

The wall I had been building all my life between us, this was the final brick. Cemented in place, I couldn't never take it back. I had my own regret. My own horror at what I done. Worse, I had his confusion. His fear that something terrible had happened. It had, of course. There wasn't no coming back from it.

He sighed. Okay, he said, his voice small in the dark. Good night, kiddo. Love you.

He did. Love like a wildfire, like a monsoon, like a tsunami, love that consumed him, that existed like a physical thing, something with breadth and depth and heft. I felt it when he was near, different from the way he loved Helen, or Mom. It was the love you have for something you have made, something that is still part of you. It was overwhelming, its endlessness, I couldn't bear the weight of it. Yet I feared it would vanish if he knew what I done.

It is like this, life is just a greedy vulture. I have read about how vultures will eat and eat, no matter how full they are, they will keep gobbling up whatever's in front of them. Life gobbles up one thing and that just makes it greedier, so it starts swallowing other things, too. It starts with Mom. She walks into the night and never comes back. The dogs are next, one by one they are taken. Then our way of life. Then Dad, the way things used to be between me and him. And if you think there's a way to get used to that kind of loss, all you have to do is live long enough. Nothing stays.

I found it the next morning. Searching for the small knob of flint I needed to spark against my knife blade to make a fire, rummaging through the unfamiliar pockets of Jesse's pack, thinking idly how I would have to mend my own pack when I returned home. I emptied it, then cursed. Held it upside down and shook it, and what fell on the ground wasn't my lost flint, but a knife.

I had took out the tin cup and the bag of rice, everything inside the pack, left it all in my room. But the knife must of been wedged under a seam inside the bag this whole time. A nice pocketknife with a pretty burled handle. I frowned. Picked it up, turned it over in my hand.

And remembered spotting it among the cheap fluffy prizes lined up on the shelves of the Test Your Strength booth, *Everyone walks away a winner, you there, you look like a strong man, step on over.* The ringing bell, then Tom telling me to pick out my prize, he'd won it for me. I look with Jesse's eyes past the stuffed bunnies and bears to the only object worth anything, a burl-handled pocketknife. And there's a chorus of screams from one of the rides, and my stomach drops and soars at the same time as Tom leans over me, we kiss—

My nose running, I wiped it with the sleeve of my coat. Then opened the knife. The blade sharp but stained a rusty brown, he hadn't bothered to wipe it clean, likely because he'd been in a hurry. The blade itself emblazoned with the name of the manufacturer, the blood would of been harder to clean from the engraved letters. GOODWIN KNIFE CO.

I dropped the knife, it made a hole in the snow.

I hadn't let myself think about the day I'd stabbed Hatch more than I absolutely had to, but now I called it up. There was the chattering in my head from the squirrel as the life drained from it.

There was the bloody handprint on the trunk of the tree, and the grass, dewed with blood.

There was Hatch, his hands already on me when I turned.

And here, I always run into a wall, a blackness that descended upon me when Hatch tossed me aside and my head struck the hard root sticking out of the ground. I had tried to search for him inside me, some part of him that I had taken in, but I'd never found it.

Because it wasn't there.

Instead of putting my effort into looking for Hatch, I put it into what I actually seen that day. Like the blood. It was already glistening on the blades of grass and smeared across the tree's trunk before I spun round.

On Hatch's hand when he'd reached out for me. Hatch was already bleeding by the time he come to me. Already weak. Too weak to toss aside a girl who was small, sure, but muscular and heavy. He hadn't lunged at me, he'd staggered. Hadn't grabbed me, but clutched at me, needing help. Because he was already in trouble before we met.

I knelt, dug into the snow for the knife. Folded the blade back into the handle.

You about ready to head back? Dad asked as he emerged from the trees where he'd gone off to take a piss.

I nodded. My throat too dry to tell him yes. I was ready.

I pocketed the knife. Two knives on me now. Mine, and the one that had started everything.

21

We got home just before dusk, it wasn't hard to busy myself with the dogs then claim I was awful tired and hide myself in my room the rest of the evening. At dinner, Jesse joined Dad and Scott, the three of them barely talking, Helen on their minds. The VSO had called with an update, not that there was much new. Nothing at her house to indicate she'd meant to do something permanent to herself or that she'd only set out to go on a drive. No sign anyone had forced her to leave her house. Jesse, Scott, and Dad chewed and stared at their plates and their thoughts shone up through the floorboards like beams of light. Scott worried he'd left his camera at Helen's, and then cringed, ashamed to be worried over a little thing like that when Helen was missing. Dad's head filled with gruesome pictures, Helen torn apart by wolves, frozen in the forest, murdered by a stranger, smeared on the side of a highway miles and miles from here. Sometimes it wasn't Helen he thought of, but Mom, a painful sort of mirroring, a life full of tragedy, a tugging at the seams that held him together.

I closed my eyes and concentrated.

Seen myself in Jesse's thoughts. The nights we'd spent together, the shadowy parts of me, questions he had about what I knew about him, what I could know. Impressions from his time on the road with Steve Inga, traveling from one checkpoint to the next by snow machine. He'd liked Steve, who had reminded him a little of Tom, his willingness to pitch in with any job, his ease with tools. At the center of Jesse, that same box, locked tight. Things he kept himself from thinking about, things he kept even from himself.

I could feel his thoughts, but I couldn't make him think about the things he didn't want to. It didn't matter. There was other ways to learn what I needed to learn.

I sat with my knees drawn up in the rocking chair that used to belong to Mom, listening to the din that rose up out of the silence downstairs.

Dad poked his head into my room before he turned in, late, long past when he normally might of gone to bed. He was looking more and more like he done right after Mom died, eyes hollow and bloodshot.

Not too late, okay?

I could of reminded him then that I was eighteen and pretty far past needing someone to tell me when bedtime was. But I was comforted more than irritated by him checking in on me. From his perspective, it was his job to look out for me, and always would be.

Love you, Dad, I said.

Would there ever be a time I wasn't waiting to hear the sounds of his sleep from down the hall? I watched the slender moon through my window as it traveled its slow course across the sky. At some point, the house was finally quiet.

Outside, the stars was out. Maybe if I stayed up late enough, I'd get to see the northern lights. I thought of Jesse's handwriting in the Kleinhaus book. *If I do nothing else before I die, I will see the northern lights.* The first time I read that, I'd thought it was Tom Hatch who'd wrote it. Felt like the words made him real to me, but he wasn't never real to me.

The dogs lifted their heads when I got to their houses, then lowered them again when it was clear I didn't have no treats, and I wasn't stopping to say hello.

I knocked on the door of the shed then pushed it open.

Jesse was waiting. He smiled when he seen me, got up from the bed and come put his arms round me. I prodded at him, at the closed-off part of him I couldn't never get to. When he started to pull away, I stopped him. Lingered where I was, him close. The feeling of him comfortable, and the fire in the woodstove crackling and the smell of the shed and the light over everything, same as it always was. It could of been easy to just stay there, ignore all my questions, try to forget Hatch and Helen. Except the gift Helen give me made it impossible.

You okay? His breath grazed my neck.

Fine, I said and flicked the blade of my knife, I moved fast but only with enough pressure to slice through the layers of clothes, to barely pierce his skin.

What—

The word fell out of him and he backed away, his hand plastered over the same spot Hatch had staunched when he stumbled into our yard. Looking for help, I understood now. Not looking for me.

Jesse took his hand away and blinked at the blood, a few drops.

The funny thing about drinking, I told him, is you don't get to pick what it teaches you. You only get bits and pieces of what's on a person's mind, and you almost never get exactly what you're looking for. At least, that's how it is with just a taste.

His mind a whirlwind, never settling on a single thought, howling like the wind had howled the night I killed Helen.

I crossed the room step by step, in no hurry. I was between him and the door. And like I had demonstrated before the race, I was stronger than him. By a lot. He knew it, too.

When you drink enough to kill a critter, I went on, that's a different story. You get everything from that last drink. A whole life. I thought I understood that. How many animals have I killed that way? How many lives have I drunk in? Hundreds?

He backed away, wanting distance from me. Considered rushing me, wondered if he could wrench the knife from my grip. Come up with strategy after strategy, then discarded each one.

How could I of known it would be different with a person? I said.

Silence across the landscape of his head, deafening and brief.

Tom? he asked at last. I thought you said—

I held his shirt with one hand, sliced it open, top to bottom. One layer between us, gone.

I did say, didn't I? I was certain Hatch would come back. I was worried about you. Worried enough that I got you worried, too, huh? Why was you so worried?

Cut open the next shirt. Seen Hatch in Jesse's thoughts, at the window of the shed, begging to be let in.

I thought I was protecting you, I told him. Thought I was protecting everyone. And, I'll be honest, I didn't think I had no choice. If I didn't finish the job I started, I would of got in awful trouble.

Shredded his undershirt, neck to hem, and exposed the skin underneath, the wrap he'd used to flatten his chest. Hatch, angry and red-faced in his thoughts. *You can't leave. No one will want you the way I do.*

Turns out, I didn't have a job to finish, I said and held up the knife so he could see the name on the blade.

Jesse's brain was facile, a word I got from him, he thought it, not about his own wiliness but about Tom, who was also facile, good with a tool, resourceful when he was in a pinch. Fondness there inside Jesse. Surprise at his own ability to fix things. I felt it, the solution falling into place, the first time Jesse run away from somewhere. His own home, stealing away in the night and not leaving a note for his parents, or for Tom, who had showed up a week later at a spot they had talked about, a place they'd planned to go together. Another fight, another night of running. Across the country, all the way to Alaska, and the moment he took the knife in his hand, when he found himself on the edge of the new life he'd chased down, only sort of lost in the woods behind the house. Hatch trailing along behind, and when he got close enough, this one last reminder of Jesse's old life, the knife went in, so easy it might of acted on its own. Jesse looked down at his own hand, round the handle, and wasn't sorry. He wouldn't let himself be. He looked back into Tom's eyes. *Just go home*, he said through clenched teeth.

Now, though, he was telling me he had no choice.

You didn't have to stab him, I said. You could of found another way.

You saw what happened, he said. What Tom did. He was dangerous.

Did I?

The tip of the knife made a dimple in Jesse's skin, the most pressure I could apply without breaking the surface. A flash of red, the barn, Hatch's breath on my cheek, on Jesse's.

Did I see, though? I got pieces. Enough to put together a puzzle. Enough to put it together wrong.

Blood welled, but I didn't need it. I seen Tom through Jesse, felt his rough hands on my body, his lips on mine. I saw him the first day they, we, met, Tom's pretty face already marred by old scars from the car accident that had made him an orphan.

I just want to know the truth, I told Jesse and pressed the knife to his skin.

He winced. You don't need to do that, he said. I'll tell you, I swear.

You're right. I don't need to.

I licked the tip of the knife.

But I want to.

Small cuts. That's what I learned from the times I had dug the knife into my own skin, them times I went weeks without the woods. Small cuts, small tastes. Helen had give me access to him, but his blood was more vivid than his thoughts, tiny bursts of his life, morsels of truth pouring out of him, coursing through me. He'd left Hatch bleeding in the woods. It wasn't regret that brought him back to Hatch but worry, he'd heard the two of us tussling and his concern divided itself, part of him feared Tom might be in trouble. A larger part worried that he might of found help too soon. He dropped his pack and run toward the sound of us struggling.

When he found us, he launched himself at me. Shoved harder than he meant. I passed out, never got to hear him say to Tom, again, *Please, go.* Never got to watch him watching Tom, watching the life drain out of him. That's what Jesse thought, so unsettled he forgot to go back for his pack when he run away again.

Jesse pushed at me, but he was weaker now, his breath come in gasps and his pulse stuttered.

Don't worry, I said as I made another cut. We're almost done.

I never intended to kill him. That's the truth. I never intended to kill no one.

He sat up so fast, I dropped the knife. It clattered to the floor, and then he was up, a sudden surge of strength, he thought he was struggling for his life. He reached for the knife, he was holding it and I was holding him and both of us wearing his blood, we stood together and circled like dancers round the room, my back to the door, my back to the bed, my back to the wall as I gripped his wrist and he pulled my hair. The strength draining slowly out of him. The blood warm between us. I turned him, my back to the door again, then watched his eyes widen, surprise and fear twisted through him, he gripped my shoulders and threw me aside and only narrowly dodged the axe that sliced through the air and sunk its blade into the wall of the shed.

And all the nights interrupted by violence knitted themselves together, and my feet were his feet, my heart his heart slamming in his chest, his whole self one impulse, and when I looked away from Dad, his hands still wrapped round the handle of the axe, Jesse was already gone, already on the run again.

22

Outside, our breath made clouds that evaporated soon as they formed and the stars pierced the sky like holes made by the tip of a knife, and we stood, breathing. Watching the house. The silence between us like the silence after an avalanche.

I moved first. Went back inside the shed and scanned the floor, found the Goodwin knife under the bed where I had kicked it when I'd squeezed Jesse's wrist enough to make him drop it. Then gathered what he would need, a sweater, his coat and hat. His boots. He'd run into the snow with no shoes on, bare chested.

What are you doing?

Dad, stuck in the doorway. Pinned there like a bug on display.

I pulled my own shirt over my head, the front of it wet with blood. Traded it for one of Jesse's.

I didn't mean to— Dad run a hand over his face. I thought he was hurting you.

I know, I told him.

He dropped into the chair at the table. A new day dawning inside him, a truth he'd always suspected, ludicrous as it was, something he'd always hid in his own dark corners and never let fully into the light.

None of this is your blood, he said. It wasn't a question.

What happened? he asked.

So I told him the truth.

I managed all them years to keep the secrets my mother give me. I only ever told them to the one person I thought would understand what it was to stay hid. The one person I thought I was closest to.

I sat on the edge of Jesse's cot and talked. Started with what was easy enough to explain, how I come to appreciate Jesse more and more, till appreciation grew into something else. Then Jesse's secret, something him and me could share. Then Hatch, and what Jesse let me think I had done, and what I had aimed to do about it. I followed the path I had laid myself, explained to Dad how I knew what I knew and why I'd been so keen on hunting all my life. I seen how my words landed, how each one struck him like a fist, but I kept talking, there wasn't no hiding anymore. Hatch hadn't never showed up, I told Dad, I had chased everyone away from the house for no reason.

Including Helen, he said.

She was there, in his head. He carried her with him the way he carried Mom. And I thought of Mom, with all her secrets, things she'd took with her when she went walking along the highway all them years ago. She never told me in plain words to keep what I done from Dad. But she did teach me that some secrets you keep because you don't want to hurt the people you love. He suspected, already. Another thought he wouldn't let himself fully acknowledge. He needed me to say it plain.

So I left that last wall between us. It wouldn't never come down.

Including Helen, I told him.

But tonight, he said. What happened?

It's between me and Jesse, I said.

That's not good enough, he told me but didn't press on when I stayed silent. He slumped in the chair, his head in his hands, not looking at me. I saw him, he finally said.

I blinked. Jesse?

He shook his head. Mr. Hatch. Down in Anchorage. The ceremonial start. Spotted him in the crowd. I caught up with him before my turn in the chute. Asked after him. Said after he got patched up, he traveled around a spell, wanted to stick around long enough to see the race. Told me he'd be on a plane the next day. Dad put his face in his hands, his words was muffled. He shook my hand. Said he appreciated the help I gave him.

Funny, how after days of feeling everything, I couldn't feel nothing right then. My whole self numb. I closed my eyes, and watched Helen fall to the ground. Watched her eyes fill with snow.

I have to go, I said, then cleared my throat. Jesse's already been gone too long. He'll freeze out there if I don't go after him.

Dad stood. I'll do it, he said. He didn't understand that I hadn't aimed to end things with Jesse, only to get at the truth in him.

No, I told him. It's my mess. I'm better at tracking, too. It'll be faster if I go. Anyway, somebody's got to be here in case Scott wakes up.

I could see he was sorting through all his arguments for why I ought to be the one to stay behind.

Dad, I said before he could start in. Please.

He still wanted to argue. He took in the shed, the

blood staining the floor. Me. Finally, he heaved a big sigh, and I took that as my answer.

Inside the house, I drug Jesse's pack out of the closet and gathered what I thought I'd need. I tucked my hair up into my wool hat, put on an extra pair of socks. Then shouldered the bag and headed down the hall. Stopped at Scott's room. Light from the hallway spilling across the foot of his bed. The older he got, the harder he seemed to sleep. He was even snoring lightly when I pushed his door open. I didn't have to worry about waking him as I crossed the room, bent over him, and kissed his head.

Outside, Dad knelt next to my lead dog, he'd put Stella up front and I was glad because she could be trusted not to get distracted by sounds or movement in the trees along the trail, and the other dogs would behave, too, on account of her focus.

I buckled the waist belt of my pack and stepped on the runners. Dad come round and stood next to me. For a long minute, neither of us said nothing.

I didn't know, Dad said.

Know what?

He swallowed. That he wasn't a boy.

He was, though, I said. If you knew him, you knew that.

He—he could've told me. It wouldn't have changed nothing between us.

My throat tight. He thought he had to hide, I said.

I never meant to make him feel that way, Dad told me.

The dogs chuffed, eager to run. No other sound between us.

I should get going, I said.

He moved away, circled the sled, rechecked the dogs' harnesses, even give my pack a little tug.

Dad.

Okay, he said. You be careful. Especially on that lake. It's good and froze over, but that part near the waterfall, the ice is thin there.

My eyes stung and I blinked away the tears that wanted to come. Just another run down the trail, I said. Right?

He didn't step away or pull the snow hook for me. He was so close, I could of reached out and hugged him. He knew more than he let himself admit to, even then he understood, I think.

Right, he said and stepped aside.

I knew he would stand in that spot till I hit the trailhead, till he couldn't see me no more, and still he'd have one hand raised.

It'll be a fast run, I said and he nodded. I'll be back long before morning.

That was the last lie I ever told him.

Only a sliver of moon to light up the snow, and the branches overhead clasped hands and the shadows drew round us, and only my headlamp to light the way, we glided as if through a tunnel, the darkness closing behind us as we went. The farther away we got, the quieter. I could feel Dad fade from me, the last person whose mind I would really know.

Jesse's footprints led down the trail, then vanished into the brush. There was a chance he would only stay away the night. He was just as resourceful as Tom Hatch, he could rub two sticks together for a fire or dig himself a hole to curl up in, keep warm till morning. It wasn't crazy to imagine him returning to the house by daybreak.

But I knew him. He was a runner.

When we come to the lake, I took the trail round the frozen surface, though it slowed us down. I couldn't bear to ride over the frozen water again. There was a cold front coming in, according to what the radio had said that morning, it would bring a few days of hard freeze and then they was predicting precipitation, just a few inches but enough to blanket the woods in a layer of snow. Plenty more snowfalls before May, before breakup come and everything started to melt. The ice on the lake would shrink day by day till all that was left was small floes that finally vanished, and then one day, when the sun was warm overhead and the water almost bearable enough to swim in, Helen would find the surface. Dad's life would change again, then. More loss, another ending. I wished I could tell him I was sorry.

I took the sled as far as Fox Creek, where Dad and I had camped together only hours ago. Took all five dogs off the gangline, then undone their harnesses, too. It wasn't likely they'd get hung up on a felled tree or in some bushes, but I didn't want to take the chance. I stowed the harnesses in the basket, then covered the sled with some branches to protect it from the coming snow.

I knelt in front of the dogs and rubbed and petted and stroked each one in turn. Stella licked my face. When she wasn't focused on the trail she was a real lover, and awfully loyal. When I finally stood up and said, Go on, and shooed them away with a wave, Stella was the only one who paused, waiting for me to follow.

Go on, now, I told her.

Watched her run after the other dogs. It didn't take long for them to be swallowed up by the night.

They would find their way back easy, show up by late morning or maybe that afternoon. Dad would look up from the kitchen sink and see them coming, or else maybe he'd sleep in, exhausted from the night before. Either way, he'd find his dogs back, five of them loose and running round the yard, tired from their journey and ready for something to eat. I hoped he would feed them before he come looking for me. Scott would help with the feeding, maybe, finish it while Dad prepped another sled and got a fresh team on the line then come blazing down the trail. He'd find my sled that first day, of course. I hoped he would understand then. When he didn't find me right away, he would keep looking, I knew. Searching, the way he done before, shouting my name only to have the sound of it absorbed by the new snow and the acres of forest and the miles between us.

When Helen's body was found, someone would come asking about her. Maybe the VSO would remember how reluctantly I had answered his questions, and that thought would rekindle the spark of suspicion he'd felt when he laid eyes on me. Maybe he would come back, ask after me, and find I had gone missing.

Or maybe no one would come. Once the VSO heard I'd vanished, maybe he would understand my dad had been through enough, he oughtn't be bothered with a mystery that didn't have no good answers. It was possible he would even land on a version of the truth and decide it was me who'd killed Helen, but by then it would be too late. Either way, I hoped he would leave my dad and brother alone. That he would learn to live without ever knowing the truth. If I could talk to the VSO one last time, that's what I would tell him: that more often than not, knowing ain't worth it.

The first year, I grew wiry and tough, whatever extra meat I had on my bones I shed. I ate well enough, drunk my fill, but I was relying only on what I could forage and hunt and trap, and sometimes the woods are abundant, and sometimes they are not.

My hair grew long and tangled till I hacked it off with my knife, and then it seemed to stop growing altogether. My nails like claws till they broke off. My skin toughened. My shoes fell apart, so I tied the bottoms to my feet with twine, then finally stopped bothering and went barefoot all that winter and the next, and after a time I couldn't even recall what it felt like to have a sole between the ground and my foot.

The wild was quiet. No chatter from other people's

lives inside my head. Every great once in a while, I would discover a memory inside me that wasn't my own, glance up, and see a hiker on the trail, a hunter hiding himself in the brush. I would climb a tree till the hiker passed, reroute myself round the hunter, feeling for a time her wonder at this wilderness, his patience and focus, till the distance I put between myself and other people diminished their strange lives.

I built shelters and melted snow and climbed trees to gain my bearings. I holed up in caves during bad weather, slept like a hibernating bear. From time to time, I was lucky and stumbled upon a park service cabin. In the winter these places are often unoccupied. I opened the door and dropped my pack and looked round, bewildered by the sight of bunks and tables and benches where people like I used to be sat down to meals they'd eat with forks, out of bowls or off of plates. Once I found a pack of playing cards someone left behind, and I spread them out and spent the better part of a night by the fire just staring at the faces on the cards. Another time it was a glossy magazine that someone left. I turned the pages for hours, taking in the pictures and paragraphs, till finally I tried a sentence. Read aloud words that felt strange on my tongue. Startled myself with the scratchy, unused sound of my own voice.

———————

At the end of the Kleinhaus book, he goes back home. Like a lot of books you read, that's how it ends, with someone coming back to where he started from, but changed. I suppose there's no point in reading a story where the main character don't end up different than how they started.

But just before breakup, when the snow softens and the whole world seems made of water, on the last real day of winter, Kleinhaus scales a tree. His hands and feet scrambling up the branches as a moose charges the place he was standing just a few seconds before. The moose is skinny, he can see its ribs, and its hide hangs off its bones like a too big coat. All the trees nearby stripped of their bark, every plant chewed to nubs. Food is scarce. The moose is surly, in no mood to be startled, which is why it lowers its head and charges him.

So Kleinhaus is up in his tree with an angry moose circling the trunk, and he perches on a branch to wait it out. After a time, he looks up from the moose and out at the land around him. It goes on and on, mountains and rivers and valleys, only a handful of them he's explored. And he thinks, you could roam that land your whole life and never know it the same way this moose knows it. Or the way the bear that nearly killed him early the previous fall knows it. There's a wall between him and the land, and there always will be, because he's a man and not a bear or a moose, or any other kind of animal that lives its whole life in the wild, getting its food from the ground and finding shelter in the trees and drinking from streams and rivers. And right then, he thinks he'll never go back home. He'll stay beyond winter, into the spring, into the next year, and the one after that, he'll learn the land well enough to survive, and if he don't, he'll die out there and decompose and then he'll finally be part of that land.

But of course eventually the moose loses interest in chewing the bark off the trunk of Kleinhaus's tree and wanders away. Eventually Kleinhaus takes his gaze away from the miles of unknowable land and lowers himself from his branch. He pushes his way through brush and the vanishing snow to find the trail that will lead him back home, and he follows it.

I think of them as they must be now. Scott away at college, the way Dad described. Home for the holidays and summers, his camera slung round his neck. Back to help with the dogs. There's fewer of them now, Dad give up racing, he only runs them now when he finds himself missing the back of a sled. Spends his days working in the yard, splitting wood. Alone with his thoughts, no sound but the sighs and chuffs of the few dogs left, dozing in their houses, longing after the trail.

At the end of the day, he sits down to a meal made for him by someone new. Someone he's met, the way he met Helen, someone who laughs easily, who is open and kind and tough and honest. At night, when he wakes up from a dream he barely remembers, he turns over in his bed to find her there, and draws closer to the warmth of her, and goes back to sleep.

Or he steps outside, wanting the frozen night air on his face. He stands in the yard, the dogs stirring, wondering if there will be food. A chill runs down his spine, a shadow moves at the corner of his vision. He scans the trees at the back of his property, the empty trailhead. I freeze, make myself as still as the windless night. A face surfaces in his thoughts. But there's nothing there. He goes back inside the house. The shadow in the trees waits a moment more. Then I step onto the trail, and begin to run.

Acknowledgments

The cool thing about publishing a book for the first time is that after years spent alone in a room, staring at a glowing screen, talking to yourself or your cats (who are fairly reticent with both criticism and advice), suddenly you have a whole army of people working to make your book the best possible version of itself. The first of those people is my agent, Michelle Brower: Thank you for your wisdom and notes and brainstorming sessions and—most of all—your belief in this book. Thank you, too, to the rest of the folks at Aevitas with whom I worked.

Thank you to my editor, Kate Nintzel, who was a dream to work with. And thank you to the rest of the team at William Morrow and HarperCollins.

I'm eternally grateful to the folks who read early

versions of this novel and who gave me insightful advice and kept me from making dumb mistakes. Thank you to Ian Gill, Sara Huff, John Irving, Glenn Lester, Jeff Martin, Craig Nova, and Brooke Taylor. I was able to start this book thanks to the time and space I was afforded during my years working with John and his wife, Janet Turnbull Irving: Thanks to both of you for that experience (and to Craig, who suggested I apply for the job because—in his words—"You know how to drive in the snow").

There were several resources I consulted to get the details of this book as right as I could, including: *Iditarod Fact Book*, 2nd edition, edited by Tricia Brown; "Out in the Great Alone" by Brian Phillips, ESPN/Grantland; the Alaska Department of Fish and Game website; *Winterdance* by Gary Paulsen; *Yukon Alone* by John Balzar; and the blogs from Dew Claw Kennel and SP Kennel.

I've had so many teachers throughout my life who saw that I enjoyed writing and encouraged me to keep it up; others who guided me as I worked to get better. Thank you to Bernita McMichael, Greg Mason, Matt Fitzgerald, Lloyd Kropp, Jo-Ann Mapson, Michael Parker, and Lee Zacharias. And to Vesta Mennemeyer, who was a different kind of teacher.

Thanks to Paw for advice on trapping and hunting.

And thanks, finally, to my parents, Kit and Jim Bradbury, who bought me all the books I wanted and gave me my first word processor; who didn't think it was weird when they heard me through my closed bedroom door, reading aloud to myself (or if they did, they never said anything); who put up with phone calls that started with questions like "How long does it take to bleed to death?" Thanks for always supporting me.

About the Author

B orn in Illinois, Jamey Bradbury has lived in Alaska for fifteen years, leaving only briefly to earn her MFA from the University of North Carolina, Greensboro. Winner of an Estelle Campbell Memorial Award from the National Society of Arts and Letters, she has published fiction in *Black Warrior Review*, *Sou'wester*, and *Zone 3*, and she has written for the *Anchorage Daily News*, TheBillfold.com, and storySouth. Jamey lives in Anchorage, Alaska.